Carrie Cox is a senior journalist, author, mum and timid surfer, usually not in that order. After twenty years of writing and editing for various publications across Australia, Carrie wrote her first novel, *Afternoons with Harvey Beam*, published by Fremantle Press in 2018. It was hailed as a 'brilliant debut' by *The Australian Women's Weekly* and 'sensitive and impressive' by *The Australian*. She was an invited contributor to *Women of a Certain Rage*, published by Fremantle Press in 2021, and an Invited Writer-in-Residence at the Katharine Susannah Prichard Writers' Centre in the same year. Carrie has lived in Perth since 2010.

So Many Beats of the Heart

CARRIE COX

Affirm press

Affirmpress
books that leave an impression

Published by Affirm Press in 2022
Boon Wurrung Country
28 Thistlethwaite Street
South Melbourne VIC 3205
affirmpress.com.au

10 9 8 7 6 5 4 3 2 1

 A catalogue record for this book is available from the National Library of Australia

Title: So Many Beats of the Heart / Carrie Cox, author.
ISBN: 9781922711090 (paperback)

Cover design by Lisa White
Cover illustrations via Creative Market
Typeset in Minion Pro by J&M Typesetting
Proudly printed in Australia by McPherson's Printing Group

To Mum, for the love and the laughs

The world is full of magic things, patiently waiting for
our senses to grow sharper.

W.B. Yeats

1

It's cauliflower that finally undoes Evie Shine. A bed of rough nubs in aisle eleven. Something about its nothingness. A quick silent kick to the chest.

She can't be winded, Evie thinks, and yet the air has shot right out of her and can't get back in. Her hands twist the trolley bar. Does she even need cauliflower today? *Does anyone?*

There are tears splashing softly onto Evie's hands. How long would cauliflower simply sit in the dark vegetable drawer of her fridge before exhibiting signs of oversight? *Try to swallow. Try to breathe.*

She hadn't known her water table was rising. Maybe cauliflower is exactly what she needs. Just a hardy vegetable and a few fresh ideas. Some better shoes. Swifter changing of blown lightbulbs. Deeper lines in the sand. Simple things. *Come on, breathe.*

It used to be that almost everything Evie needed, everything two children and two adults need over the course of two decades, could be found in a supermarket. There she'd made the weekly choices, tiny and vital, that dictated the rhythm of their lives. The factory floor of a family. Now it's all passive-aggressive vegetables and decisions of minimal consequence.

Hand on her pounding chest, Evie at last feels a slip of air find its way back in.

'You okay?'

Evie looks up to see a woman at the head of her trolley. She's young and concerned, dressed as though she'll be going directly from here to a half-marathon.

'Do you need anything?' the woman asks her.

Evie puts a hand to her cheek now, feels its wetness and does her best to smile. 'It's the onions,' she says, pointing loosely at the cauliflower. 'Every time.'

'Okay,' the woman says uncertainly. 'Um …'

They both glance at the rows of vegetables for answers, for a way out.

Keep. Breathing.

'Really, I'm fine,' Evie says now, one hand waving the entire store away, the other wiping the water from her eyes. She makes a better attempt to smile at the kind woman. Sees that her Lycra top says *Run like no one's watching.*

What?

'All good now,' Evie says, loosening her grip on the trolley. 'Sorry about that.'

And she hears herself say it this time. *Sorry*. A fellow tutor at the university had recently remarked that Evie was forever apologising. She'd thought about this for a day or so and waited to catch herself

2

doing it. It was one thing to throw around empty apologies in daily life but another to do so within a school of psychology. Among the cloistered halls of smug dot-joiners.

She knows there are many reasons people become excessive apologisers. Social anxiety. Hardwired trauma. Insecurity. Seldom are those who apologise the people who really need to. Rarely is forgiveness the goal. But now that she's doing it, punctuating her sentences with 'sorry' instead of commas apparently, none of those explanations fly. It's reductive behaviour, and she has no idea how long it will continue.

Evie has become, she realises, here by the stupid cauliflower, the sort of client she'd never enjoyed treating. The case study she now hates teaching: blindsided spouse stuck in a loop of self-pity, anger and leaky moments in the supermarket. A patch-up job at best. *Ugh.*

It's not that good therapy can't do much for a trampled heart, at least in terms of holding it like a broken bird in two hands while time maybe, hopefully, does its thing. But if the trampler isn't part of the process, then it's all just guesswork and brushstrokes. History rewritten for an audience of one.

It should make it easier that Evie's read all the textbooks relevant to her situation, every ironic one, but of course it doesn't. Knowledge can be its own punishment. Insight makes for clean cuts that bleed for hours. You don't want reason and clarity when waking up each day feels like a panicked diver's ascent. You want bad advice and platitudes. Cheap wine and hangovers. Plotless movies set in Tuscany. A welcome loss of appetite.

You definitely don't want moments like this in the supermarket. This is awful. Evie's legs are trembling just when she has to push this two-hundred-ish-dollar trolley of vague meal possibilities and forgettable decisions towards the checkouts.

Just get out of here.

She's not one to abandon a task, no matter how uncertain it's become. She always sees things through, often for no good reason. But Evie also feels an uneasy sense of pointlessness about today and what lies beyond it. She steals a deep breath, parks her trolley behind the potatoes and walks out of the store as though struck by the possibility she's left the oven on.

As though everything isn't already burning down.

2

After enough time you stop reading the pithy magnets on your fridge door. You stop seeing them at all. But today the oldest and grimiest of magnets on Evie's fridge pulls her up short: *No matter where you go, there you are.*

She can't remember who first said that – *Confucius? Seinfeld?* – or even how she got the magnet in the first place, but somehow it's survived every house move (four), every fridge upgrade (three) and every marriage implosion (one) since.

And it stops her mid-thought now as she checks with fresh hope whether there's anything dinner-worthy on hand in the wake of her aborted shopping mission. Anything to cover herself and a carnivorous teenager. It strikes her that this prescient magnet might have known all along how the Shine family would go down: broken and adrift on the wrong side of the country. It knew Evie would end up stranded in an alien city of her husband's choosing, unable to decide whether to stay or go, knowing only that any relocation would be like shuffling a steaming pile from one corner of a room to another.

She looks anew at the other magnets, mostly given by friends from a previous life: *We are all broken – that's how the light gets in*, *Turn your wounds into wisdom* and a dozen or so homages to wine and chocolate and soulmates (mostly wine).

God. Evie leans back on her kitchen bench and wonders how many lives have been ruined by taking far too literally the advice on fridge magnets.

'What's for dinner?'

Angus Shine moves into the doorway of the kitchen like a dalmatian through a cat-flap. His ranginess is almost theatrical, though far from deliberate. It often pains Evie to see the quiet shame her son has about his own physicality. No matter what people say about Angus's six-foot-four frame – and it's always remarked upon – he hears only the white noise of undue attention.

'How about takeaway?' Evie says, waving off the fridge like an old debt. 'Pizza?' *Again.*

Angus shrugs in the affirmative. 'Vegetarian with ham,' he says.

Evie's long stopped questioning the peculiarity of this order. 'How was school today?' she says, knowing the question will be longer than the answer.

'Okay,' her son emits, retreating at pace. 'Boring. I'll keep an ear out for the pizza.'

Angus is in his final year of school. There's no plan beyond this, because plans stopped meaning anything a year ago. Now he's marking time, mostly in his bedroom, and fronting up for meals.

Evie believes he's a good kid and by that she figures he has a kind heart. The weight of unrequested existence elicits from him a quiet acquiescence. He will never be a boat-rocker, unlike his sister. He's never once raised the issue of Hamish's absence with Evie; he's never asked a question or made a protest. Whatever anger and confusion he may feel about his father has no precedent and so cannot be shaped. He seems the least affected out of any of them, seems okay, better than he was, which Evie knows to be a false positive in most cases. Tectonic plates may well be shifting deep within.

She sees a pile of envelopes on the kitchen counter that Angus must have retrieved from the mailbox. A bill from her new skin doctor, a Mater Prize Home lottery brochure addressed to the previous owners, and a Private and Confidential letter for the house two doors down the street. Because Evie doesn't want to open the bill yet, she decides instead to deliver the neighbour's mail.

The street she now lives on, the address hand-picked by her husband via an excitable online search one evening just over two years ago, an evening she now looks back on as one might the feverish booking of a flight for a loved one that ultimately plummets, is typical of Sunshine Coast aspiration. A mixture of young families, blended experiments and seniors not yet going down for the count. In between are people like Evie – caught by circumstance in a place they don't know but can't quite see beyond, perhaps for the glare.

She goes to put the letter in the cream rendered mailbox of number 68 and is intercepted by a girl, maybe sixteen or seventeen, coming up the footpath towards the same house.

'Hi,' she says, lifting the letter out of Evie's hands. 'I can take that. Thanks.'

'It came to the wrong address, sorry,' Evie says. *Again with the sorry.* 'It's the third one.'

'Right,' the girl says.

'But I don't mind dropping them off – it's fine.'

The girl has hair everywhere, wild and pointy like talons, the colour of Pilbara dust. Her face is sunken by furiously smudged brown eyes. 'Thank you,' she says and gestures at the house. 'He doesn't come out to the mailbox much.'

'Probably afraid of all the bills like me,' Evie says and smiles, then frowns, then half smiles. Can't decide the right expression. She heads back in the direction of her house, wondering why she's always felt the need to please ambivalent strangers.

In the fading light Evie looks again at this street they've landed in, a mix of new money and dubious money. High-walled mini compounds alongside porous beach shacks. She knows none of her neighbours and suspects she won't, even though she knew most of the regular faces in her previous habitat. Jill the dog-walker, sad widow Sylvia, Ken the needy conversationalist. And the parents of her children's friends from primary school – those relationships had, apart from one or three, withered from weekly barbecue catch-ups to apologetic summaries in the grocery aisle.

Life hadn't seemed to be winding up in Perth until Hamish announced his golden opportunity: a three-year contract (unheard of in academia these days) as a professorial fellow in politics at Sunshine Coast University. And everything had looked different from that moment, as though viewed from forty thousand feet up – the depth of their friendships, the value of their home, the trajectory of their careers.

We would be mad – *mad*, Hamish had insisted, to pass this up. And Evie had quickly, so very quickly, come to agree. The money, the timing, the vague reminder of a feeling called thrill.

She looks back now on her agreeability as one might regret falling in with the wrong crowd at high school. There just weren't enough obstacles in the way. She'd trampled over red flags. Moved too quickly.

Of course she'd worried about the kids, but, as Hamish pointed out, Sera was just finishing year twelve and her grades would get her into a university on any side of the country. And Angus would be *fine*, Hamish insisted. Hadn't Evie wanted a change for him? Something to ignite his kindling.

The longer Evie took to find opposing arguments, and she didn't, not really, the more rapidly the moving plan progressed. Her own job, as a relationships counsellor at a reputable not-for-profit centre in Cottesloe, had never felt worthy of throwing up as a counter-argument. As much as she felt she was making progress with most of her clients, she knew – and Hamish often reminded her – that their problems were largely universal and her expertise transferable.

What neither of them raised, for many reasons along the spectrum between doubt and fear, was how their own relationship factored into this decision to uproot their midlife. Somehow the conversation didn't happen, either because it wasn't necessary or because it was so necessary as to be impossible.

It had, for a short time anyway, been nice to see Hamish so enthusiastic about the prospect of change. Of *making something happen*. Evie hadn't been tempted to look too squarely at the possibility that Hamish, like so many men she'd counselled over the years, might be trying to run away from his family by taking them with him.

3

Caron and Glen

There came a point in couples counselling, usually during the third or fourth appointment when the set pieces had all been played and the stakes were now abundantly clear, when Evie could see who was lying. Either to themselves or to their partner. Always to Evie.

Perhaps 'lying' isn't fair. It was more the case that one person's agenda suddenly came into clear focus, no longer hidden behind apparent confusion and hurt. It had been there all along: the trick card secreted at the bottom of the deck. It became evident, at least to Evie, just who was captaining this boat and where it would beach.

Caron was clearly a very capable woman, someone who could quickly size up any environment and insert herself at its core. She didn't just win promotions; she expected them. Knew they were coming. She had surpassed Glen's early notions of her capacity and quietly resented him for underestimating her.

But they'd been an attentive couple, neither one wanting to replicate the errors of their parents, both trying to fill childhood voids. They had produced two children, two boys, now in their final years of high school, one easy, one difficult. They couldn't agree on who was the easy one.

Minutes into their first session with Evie, Caron had begun to cry. She consistently wept the minute each session began, six in total, before declaring there was no point continuing at all. It was because of all of the things, she said, *all of them*. It was her exhaustion, his ambivalence, her long hours, his long hours, the relentless march of it all, on and on and on into too-familiar territory. It was, Caron said, the meaningless conversations that felt like scraping mould off cheese. It was libidos that no longer signalled themselves. It was old resentment (the sheer engorgement of early motherhood) and new resentments too: his lack of fresh ideas, his acceptance of *this* … whatever this was. This *place* in the supposed middle of their lives that felt very much like the end, at least to Caron.

That Glen couldn't *see* it, that she alone was left to identify the decomposing body of their marriage – this was what had upset Caron the most. This was what had brought her to Evie's small office in Cottesloe one rainy August.

Caron needed to make Glen see how bad things had got, she said, or else they'd never be able to fix any of it. But that, Evie had begun to feel, wasn't the truth.

It wasn't Caron's desire to fix her marriage, not anymore. Caron had done the building inspection some time ago, had deemed the structure unworthy. Her gaze was now elsewhere – quite possibly an exit affair, Evie had suspected – and she wanted out. But it's not easy to call time on a well-established marriage without a bomb, especially if you're a woman.

In the absence of exposed infidelity, abuse, financial ruin, chronic illness or insurmountable grief, first-time marriages in middle age can't easily be detonated. They're like murder trials without a smoking gun, entirely reliant on the weight of circumstantial evidence. One needed to mount a substantial case.

Because really, Evie often thought in spite of herself and in spite of her job, what was any married couple of a certain duration expecting at this point? She had heard it too many times: years and years of listening to couples collapsing in upon themselves, looking for answers, for validation, for a way out. So often the qualities they first saw in each other had become the focus of their respective disappointments. This was both cruel, Evie knew, and partly inevitable. Sometimes fixable if that was the shared goal – if therapy wasn't simply an expensive ruse to please the jury.

She used to be more hopeful, of course. She used to be better at this. Once Evie had been painstakingly methodical about helping couples identify the hurts they were projecting on each other – most often the scars of childhood rearing up like fully grown vipers. She had been proudly successful in helping them at least reach a point of mutual understanding (the highest form of love, she would tell them) and to recalibrate their expectations about sex and romance post kids, career and calamity. Her talent, she knew, or at least assumed, helped insulate her own marriage.

But Evie had begun to see that most people simply come to counselling too late. And that at least one party is telling lies.

She would see Caron again, about six months after their last session. She spotted her at a weekend market throng, her head thrown back in joy at the taste of a tangerine. She was with a man, not Glen, and Evie had watched them both from behind a rack of clothes. All tanned limbs and sun hats. Side smiles and reinvention.

Evie had wondered what Glen was doing right now. She'd hoped he was okay.

4

There was a window after Hamish left through which Evie could have quietly crawled back, back to what came before, but somehow didn't. There was a clear return route to her former life, the setting of it anyway, so recently abandoned that Evie imagines the fairy lights she'd strung up in branches for their leaving party are still flickering their tiny shards of joy. No one would have questioned it. She'd have returned an object of pity, but that would have been the worst of it. Like the dolt who throws in their job to travel around the world for a year, only to return a month later, sheepish and broke. *It happens. Nothing to see here.*

But Evie hadn't moved – hadn't even teetered like the last bowling pin. She is caught somehow. Drawn to disorientation. Stuck in Bono's moment. Sometimes she recognises the signs of emotional inertia wrought by trauma – the resistance to courting any more unwelcome change. *Stay still. Just wait.*

But it's more than that. More than not knowing what picture Hamish has apparently drawn for them.

In the last three years of her life in Perth, Evie witnessed a steady degradation of the partnerships in her friendship circle. One by one, as though each had somehow infected the next, her friends' marriages ended. There were spectacular combustions and predictable dissolutions. There were third parties, no parties. There were tacky divorce parties. There were exceptions.

An ethnographer might have reported a quiet pandemic of pain in the city's suburbs. A steady fracturing of street-front houses into nondescript little units at the rear of battle-axe blocks. Kids biting skin off thumbs. The packing and unpacking of sports bags. Teachers wanting quiet words. Bottle-shop boom times.

They might have noted the few commonalities – the certain vintage of most partnerships, kids not quite finished high school (but close enough), the absence of the sort of economic or societal pressures that might excite a documentary maker. Problems of privilege.

These were the marriages that had already made it through the early chicanes. Made it out of the dark forest of weariness, the tedium of toddlerhood, the contest for careers, the tandem tilts at joy and temptation. Evie had counselled many couples over the years who'd never made it this far, who'd tripped at much earlier hurdles, but these are not the cases she now looks back on in unbidden moments, the ones landing on her windscreen like bright yellow flyers. Now she remembers the couples who almost made it out of the wild, almost to the clear air.

At each denouement of her friends' marriages, Evie felt worse about her professional place in it all. A firefighter standing in a charred field, cheeks blackened, eyes white. The front-page picture of valiant failure. But these hadn't been her clients – they were her friends. She never provided professional counsel to any of them, yet their marriage break-ups had left her feeling guilty and exposed, as though her skills were no more valuable than those of a self-help evangelist collecting cash for hopes and dreams.

Within her group Evie had started to play down the intactness of her own marriage. She would echo complaints about estranged husbands with observations of her own: Hamish's blind obsession with his work, with politics, his intolerance of polite conversation, a failure to top up old friendships, and other such middling criticisms that only bore weight when run in quick succession. 'We've just been lucky so far,' she would also sometimes say, and that had been true. They'd not lost their life savings to a charlatan stockbroker, hadn't buried a child, nor even a parent yet. They hadn't watched every last box of possessions turn to ash. Nothing perversely unfair had ever caused them to turn on each other. But while Evie had freely acknowledged this good fortune to her friends, especially when they chided her during wine-addled dinner deconstructions, she'd no longer given any suggestion of the contentedness – and relief – that came with such random blessings.

Evie no longer said out loud that she was still happy to share a life with her husband. She rarely even said it to Hamish.

It was all too easy to leave that behind, that little cluster of dysfunction in Perth, and it's not something she is keen to return to, not yet, not while her own rupture presents such rich conversation fodder. This is cowardly, she knows, and also unfair because her friends would be compassionate and kind, if a little too salivating in their delivery. She simply isn't ready for them. For any of it. For questions she has no answers for.

And there is more at stake besides. There is Angus.

In their last year in Perth, Angus had begun pulling out his hair. Weeding it out of his scalp with red bony fingers, hiding it beneath his pillow, under his bed, unable to hide the holes in the wake of his pulls and tears.

Angus's turmoil had consumed her. She'd wanted to hold his hands in hers until he promised to stop, to at least explain it to her. But she also knew that the cause of his searing anxiety was school, was the hapless posse of grunting fools he'd somehow landed in, was six or seven circling dogs, and from all that she was powerless to save him. To simply reach in and pull him out.

Evie had pushed Hamish to let their son change schools for his senior years. But Hamish was adamant that the school wasn't the problem, that to move him might even make things worse. Society was the problem, Hamish said. There wasn't enough for kids to be hopeful about anymore. The quicksand of social media.

Hamish liked to make sense, liked to craft it out of reason and evidence like art from stone. He made sense feel like love to Evie. He told their son to take *positive action*, to change his social group, as though that was possible for a giant boy with fresh welts on his head and terror in his marrow. As though a private boys' school playground wasn't the Gaza Strip.

When Hamish found Evie sobbing at the dining room table one evening, he offered to speak to the school principal. Angus roared in pain at the suggestion.

Evie took him to see one of her colleagues, a specialist in adolescent anxiety and depression. Angus had walked out of the counselling room within fifteen minutes. 'An idiot,' he told her on the drive home. 'Wanted to know if I was cutting myself,' he said. And Evie thought, *Are you?*

It doesn't help, Evie knows, that Angus's sister is so self-assured. So present. Sera navigated her final year of school like a pentathlete. Like she had life's CliffsNotes in her schoolbag: not quite cocky about the future but absolutely *ready*.

Sera is of Hamish, and Angus is of Evie. Some families are painfully obvious.

Now, at least, here in this still unfamiliar neighbourhood, Angus's hands don't fly up to his head at the slightest sound. His scalp is covered, albeit unevenly and with no hint of style, by brown downy fuzz that Evie can't help but touch sometimes with gratitude. She no longer finds clumps of despair in his room or at the bottom of the shower. And while she doesn't know precisely when Angus's self-torture stopped, she knows it was soon after the move east. He'd just needed to be airlifted out of the killing fields. That Hamish was wrong about this is now a moot point.

So it has not happened, the inelegant tiptoe back west. Back to before. 'Not yet,' she sometimes says to Sera, who has regardless taken to college life at Perth's sandstone university and who carefully never mentions her father to Evie.

A little more time please. A little less. More and also less. Just look away for now.

Evie sometimes imagines sitting opposite herself, in a chair in

19

one of her old consulting rooms. She looks down upon her body, on time's sneaky victory over effort. *The thickening*, her mother once called a woman's midlife. She looks at the empty chair beside her. She wants to wring her own neck. She wants to slap her face hard.

She passes herself a tissue and lets the silence find its space.

5

Ali and Tom

They were the first couple Evie saw in the Cottesloe rooms, instantly filling the pretty little space with gales and fissures, with words that ripped like hot wax.

An affair. His. A turbulent flight from all he had known, from Ali, from himself. Six months in foreign hotel rooms. So easy. So unlike him. So unthinkable. Brought undone by a receipt for flowers. *Flowers*. This, of all the details, of all the imaginings, drove Ali to the precipice again and again.

'He won't even tell me what type of flowers they were,' Ali wept at Evie. Then to her husband: 'Why won't you fucking tell me? Just *tell me.*'

And Tom would say each time, 'I don't remember,' and 'It doesn't matter,' and 'I'm so sorry.'

And Ali would look at her hands in her lap, rolling over each other, tearing at history. And Evie would gently bring her back from the flowers.

Evie had once watched a snake-catcher in Africa wrestle a large feisty serpent into a bag. It was an impressive act, humble for its quiet deftness. Like the other frozen onlookers, Evie was instantly relieved by the sight of the full bag, by the containment of the snake and all the danger it had promised just moments earlier. A hostel room full of terror had been stuffed in a bag.

'Isolate, identify,' the catcher had said to the grateful crowd of backpackers. 'It doesn't matter in what order.'

Evie had spent years honing the same approach when counselling affairs: get the snake in the bag. Contain the danger. Calm the room. Identify.

Flowers.

Few people in established relationships set out to have an affair. The exceptions, in Evie's professional experience, are those people who want to make a statement, those with a form of sex addiction, and those who want to leave. She didn't think Tom fitted into any of these categories.

Instead she'd quickly surmised that Tom's affair was of the 'split self' kind, a reductive description for perhaps the most complicated and destructive brand of infidelity. A person who has this sort of affair is often startled, at least initially, by their own response to a situation that clearly threatens their relationship, that winks murderously at everything they've spent years defending and propping up and trimming into photo frames. Suddenly, in a moment that enkindles a dozen more, in a room alight with tiny explosions, they are not what they knew themselves to be. They are *seen*. They are vulnerable. They are the truest version of themselves – a child embraced at last.

These are the people who sit in Evie's room and say, 'I didn't mean for it to happen.' They say – even with every detail, every unknotted scarf, every glistening sternum and fleeting recoil, cast inside their skulls like precious cave paintings – that it's all a blur. It's in the distant past, irretrievable by memory, a giant mistake, an unrepeatable travesty. These are the things they say if they want to reverse the damage.

It's what Tom said to Ali over and over as the weeks passed in Evie's room. *I'm sorry. I can't remember. It doesn't matter. She doesn't matter.* No detail. Detail would crush her like flowers.

Tom knew what Ali needed to hear because he alone knew her. They'd been together since high school, married since their early twenties, co-travellers through parenthood and multiple overseas postings, through ambition and disappointment and the terror of empty weekends. In this sense, they were not unlike Evie and Hamish: together for more than half their lives, two people shaped by the movements of the other.

At the start of every session Tom was complicit in helping Evie put the snake in the bag. Sometimes they were successful. Sometimes Ali stopped crying long enough to hear Tom reason through the maze of his motives and mistakes. (If there was one word that Evie heard most often in her counselling room, it was 'mistake'.) Tom would talk about his mother, about growing up in the narrow tributary of her depression. Ali heard him trying to make sense of his own behaviour, his unforgivable detour. She heard him answering Evie's questions, following her purposeful lead to the past, to the holes dug in the sand before the tide had rushed in.

It was only in these moments that Ali even looked at Tom in this room of smashed secrets. Evie saw flashes of guarded tenderness in Ali's eyes when her husband talked about himself as a boy, before he was a man who formed offshore subsidiaries and hosted corporate boxes and crushed human hearts in his hand. He spoke of being shy, of being short, of being not enough. And it was there, in the past, that Evie had made progress with the couple, gently shifting Ali from the bastion of blame to something resembling hope.

It's no trick of Evie's craft but sometimes it works: this connecting of dots across decades to engineer new ways of understanding a person. Sometimes it even lasts. Sometimes men like Tom don't go ahead and do the very same thing a few years later.

6

There's a coffee place at the end of Evie's new street that is a half-formed thought: a traditional Italian-styled cafe not quite able to overcome the building's origins as a bait-and-tackle shop. Rich bean-coloured panelling barely hides rusted old deep-freeze boxes. Settees of red velvet and wobbly chairs flank formica tables. Elegant pastries in glass boxes look hopelessly misunderstood. It is always busy, always loud, and Evie has come to appreciate hiding out in its haphazard alchemy.

This is where, soon after Hamish left, Evie took herself each morning to check if she was sound – if she could drive herself to the university, teach Therapeutic Practice to a theatre full of earnest ambition, smile at her colleagues in long hallways, drive home again and not once implode into tiny matter. She would grasp her hands around the warm mug, grateful for its curve, for its limited expectations, and she would wonder again at the best way out of this, about all the things that would have to be done. Now she needed Glen's advice, Ali's advice, the help of every former client who'd been left to make sense of an altered future.

Evie had drawn comfort from her invisibility in this boisterous cafe setting, yet she had been seen.

Ronni Vella, the sister of cafe owner Rita, flies into Le Cose Semplici most mornings, arms full of muffins and tarts and constellations of flour. She is a human weather front, every facet of her overt Italian-ness instantly charging the room. Ronni's eyes throw to all corners as she kisses the staff and swears above the cacophony. 'Fanculo, it is hot out there!'

Not long after Evie had found her little corner sanctuary in the cafe, Ronni had launched to her side one morning, pushed a warm cannoli on a plate beside Evie's mug and said, 'What has happened to you? Let's make it better now – let's do this.'

And Evie had laughed, at the gentle urgency of her concern, at her apparent desire to ensure no one in that cafe at that moment was nursing despair while drinking the good coffee.

'If it is a man,' Ronni said, 'then we can take him out. Next Thursday. My cousin leaves Thursdays free for quick jobs.'

Evie laughed again, fairly certain Ronni was joking.

'It doesn't have to be the full death. Injuries are quick, easy jobs. A limb. His pene! Troppo facile!'

There were other coffee shops Evie could have switched to – at least eight more between her street and the beach – but if it was truly anonymity that she craved, her resolve was unconvincing even to herself. She continued to return to Le Cose Semplici most mornings, for the often too-hot coffee, for the quick crush of unfamiliarity in a still foreign place. She allowed Ronni to descend upon her life, to blast away at her edges with utterly mad stories that either couldn't be true or must be.

Even before Evie had shared a single detail about Hamish, about all she'd not seen coming and still didn't understand, Ronni brought her tales of infedelta. She did this with some authority, Ronni insisted, because Italians stray more than any other nationality. 'It's true,' she once said, shrugging. 'The men they cannot help themselves, especially in the summer. The women are worse. There is too much of everything in Italy – too much beauty, too much dreaming, too much of the skinny ankles under lovely skirts. Too much forgiveness from *Him*.' At any mention of God, Ronni would make a sign of the cross over her chest and then appear to toss it on the floor.

Most days Ronni speaks like someone who just moments ago stepped off a plane from Rome and has less than thirty minutes to expel all the latest news to the world.

'Calabria. Just this month!' she'd reported to Evie one morning. 'Good-looking couple. You know, gym types. Bodies are a *temple*. I hate these people. What would they even do with a struffoli? The woman, she has one of those fitty bits, those things you wear on your wrist? I don't really get what they are. Why do you need to know you've walked sixteen hundred steps? Weren't you there? Who's keeping score? I hate these people.

'And then one day she is walking, walking, walking, okay? And her fitty bit tells her that she has just weighed in at fifty-six kilos. And she thinks, *No I haven't*. I'm not on my scales. I haven't weighed myself since this morning. And I was sixty-four point five. Evie! The scales are connected to the fitty bit thing, *do you see?*'

Evie had nodded, as always amused by Ronni's lively delivery. She was both grateful and ready to flee in equal measure. She thought of Ali and the flowers.

Ronni continued: 'So this woman thinks, who is standing on my bathroom scales right now, at two in the afternoon? It's not me. Because I'm right here. I'm just here walking really fast.

'And so she turns around, Evie. She circles back along the Corso and she goes home, back to her bathroom scales, and what do you think she finds there? *What?* She finds her dick-on-the-head husband with Little Miss Fifty-six Kilos in their bedroom!'

Evie had looked squarely at the table, tried to maintain a smile.

'I mean, who *does* that, Evie?' Ronni demanded of her.

And Evie had thought: *Too many people.*

'Who gets on the scales before sex?'

'Oh,' Evie replied. 'That is weird.'

'And who weighs fifty-six kilos? That's like having sex with a parcel.'

'And does she kill him?' Evie had asked then, because Ronni's face looked like the best part of the story was still to come.

'I don't know!' Ronni exclaimed and then threw her hands to the sky. 'Maybe. Let us hope so! I mean, who are these people? How hard is it to just love someone until one of you dies?'

Ronni's main issue with the world is over-complication. In her reasoning, delivered at a constant frequency like the hum of a fridge, most people simply miss the key points of existence. Love, family, food, repeat.

One morning Evie had watched Ronni all but accost a man in a suit ordering takeaway coffee in the cafe. 'What do you *do*?' she had said to him, as though the size of his lapels naturally demanded an explanation.

'Well, I, I mean I …' he'd started to flub a little before clearing his throat. 'I … there are a number of companies and boards that I consult to on … it's primarily in the area of benefits realisation management and some products-based planning … there's a move towards—'

'Ah!' said Ronni. 'You got one of those jobs. See, I do *hair*. My Vince does *cars*. You got one of those jobs where you don't really know what you do but you get paid a lot of money – I want one of those jobs!'

Somehow Ronni had made this sound like a compliment rather than a stick shoved in a spinning wheel. The businessman had looked a little smitten.

Of course Ronni does not want one of those jobs at all. Evie knows that Ronni views much of corporate culture (apart from its denizens' capacity to pay top dollar for home haircuts and new head gaskets) as an unfathomable waste of human endeavour. There are just too many people in the world actively missing the point of *everything*. Thank God they're still ordering coffee, Ronni often says with a measure of hope.

If Evie was back in Perth now, if she'd given in to the buckling of her legs in those first few weeks and months of uncertainty, she knows that her friends would be clambering over each other to fix her. There would be vouchers for indulgent facials, movie nights, weekends down south and a never-ending stream of memes to her phone about the restorative power of wine, the vagaries of love and the inherent flaws in all men. All of this would be earnest and kind and Evie would appreciate these things that women do for each other to make disaster look like something else.

But she would also have wanted to silently shut it down, to make it stop, for the price of all this cauterisation would be endless analysis of the wound. Secrets would be expected, pried open like mussels. Long lunches of detective work would be disguised as empathy. And all their marriages, every single relationship, would be turned over and over above the lightbox of Evie's. Her own cataclysm would be everyone's learning opportunity, as theirs should have been for her – their watershed or Waterloo.

It's not selfishness that would stop Evie wanting to provide this receipt for service. It's more that after dedicating hundreds and hundreds of hours to engineering these discussions for *other* couples, to navigating bombsites and heartache and to finding clues amid the ruins, she is simply tired of looking too closely at anything.

Ronni has never once asked her about Hamish. Of course the topic comes up from time to time but never at Ronni's beckoning. She acts as though the events that landed a broken Evie in a corner of a coffee shop constitute a conversation too obvious to be necessary.

Instead of vouchers and movie nights, Ronni gives Evie irreverence and inappropriateness. She gives her wild theories framed as incontrovertible truths. She gives her frank assessments of Evie's hair – 'There's, like, an old rotting bit at the back – I can probably work around it' – and acne creams for Angus and recipes for mushroom sauce. Once she had given her, apropos of nothing, a new mop that she simply described as 'a deeply, deeply satisfying clean'.

Once Evie had shared an anecdote about Ronni with her son and found that she faltered when explaining how she knew this eccentric Italian. Was Ronni a friend? How would Ronni describe Evie to others? For a moment she was back in high school, standing on the edges of groups and wondering if this counted as being in them.

Ronni has quickly become such an unexpected and persistent force in Evie's recast life that she's come to think of her as she does certain books that had thrust themselves in her path with unquestionable prescience, as though they were meant to be found. Yet it seemed entirely possible that Ronni had no such description for Evie, that Ronni had never recounted one of their discussions to another person and that Evie was simply one of dozens of people who punctuated the woman's daily hurtle through the atmosphere.

And then one day Ronni arrives at the cafe with a man in tow. 'This is Vince,' she says to Evie. 'He does cars. And sometimes he does me!'

Evie suppresses a laugh, a hopeless rival to Ronni's cackle in this moment.

'And this is my friend Evie,' Ronni says to Vince, 'who I tell you about when you're never listening.'

'Hi, Evie,' Vince says with a self-conscious little shrug. He is handsome and worn and wearing something akin to racing stripes. 'Veronica's told me a lot about you.'

'I *tell* him,' Ronni says then, ostensibly to Evie but equally to the next few tables, 'that you're like that beautiful rose bush he accidentally killed last year because the idiota tipped out engine oil too close to the garden. You're just starting to grow back.'

7

Felicity and Sarah

It's true that grief and tragedy can bring a couple closer together, can even create something entirely new and unrecognisable, a clay masterpiece fired in volcanic temperatures. But these were seldom the splintered, beaten couples who arrived in Evie's rooms to be fixed.

It's also true that some couples are expected to stumble through much more of life's darkness than others are. That these weary souls even found her, that they somehow managed to assemble and direct all their shattered cells into chairs opposite her had never ceased to astonish Evie. It was also terrifying – the possibility that her work might cause them to feel more pain.

These couples looked to Evie less for advice than for absolution. They wanted to be released from their torment and possibly from each other – they didn't quite know. What could be trusted anymore? What was left, what could be rebuilt, and at what cost?

Love was clearly an inadequate instrument. So what now?

Felicity and Sarah had been together for eighteen years

since university. Sarah had known she was gay since late primary school; Felicity had known only since she'd met Sarah (her parents still quietly regarded it as a phase). They were compatible in the classic manner of counterparts and over the years had leant into their differences with project-management-style efficiency. Sarah was driven to make money a little faster than most, having been influenced by a father who applauded affluence via short cuts, while Felicity was a highly content and compliant attendee to the screw-turning of other people's dreams. Together they'd bought and sold investment properties across Western Australia, neatly skipping around mining cycles and the increasingly unwilling movements of two adopted children. Sarah watched the market and Felicity watched the kids. They loved each other enough not to have to say it anymore.

'It's always important to say it,' Evie had gently said during an early session, 'even if it's just to check that you still feel it.' She would make a point of saying it to Hamish again soon.

Three years earlier, Felicity had had a cycling accident that led to a small bleed on her brain. Subsequent testing had showed the bleed was probably not a consequence of the accident but more likely the cause – she had stage 4 brain cancer. She had eleven months to live.

Eleven months. The specificity was wicked.

Grief had engulfed Felicity only briefly before she roared out of its gates ready to fight – chemo, radio, high-risk surgery, a thousand pills from hopeful websites. And she ran. She ran hundreds of kilometres, day and night, each footfall a flight from danger, every step a violent protest against death.

Sarah had admitted to Evie in one of the couple's appointments, during a Perth winter storm that threw dark branches against the windows of the Cottesloe room, that she had watched Felicity's reaction to her diagnosis in a state of quiet horror. It had seemed such a waste of their precious time. The running. The pills. The expensive surgery. Such selfish delusion when there was so much to do to get their affairs in order, to ensure their adored children would be okay when Felicity was gone.

But Felicity did not go. She didn't vaporise at eleven months. She survived – most likely due to the surgery, her oncologist had surmised, because the cancer had been blessedly close to the exterior of her skull, not deep in its core. At two years post diagnosis, a scan showed the beast had been completely vanquished – for now. The oncologist said Felicity should have T-shirts printed: *Ms One Per Cent.*

But Felicity wasn't finished with the business of surviving. And Sarah wasn't finished being angry.

Survival had taken on a perverse form for the couple, looking very much like death. For Felicity, only eternal vigilance would keep it at bay – endless running through streets lined with panic. For Sarah, death had already arrived. It had moved into their home two years earlier and wouldn't leave until someone else did.

Evie couldn't help but recall a comment Hamish had once made, as throwaway as it was morbid at the time, that should he be struck down with a terminal illness, he would quietly disappear over the horizon rather than put his family through such worry.

The cruel stasis wrought by Felicity's diagnosis, during which time there had been no physical intimacy, none at all, as though to touch each other would surely bring down the sky, had left the couple completely unprepared for what came next: the sudden death of Sarah's father, found hanging in his garage.

Yet again the couple's coping strategies had fiercely diverged. Sarah became obsessed with the details of her father's death, convinced it had been some sort of misadventure involving the maintenance of an old car. There had been no note, no warning, no reason – certainly nothing to frame Sarah's grief. She would almost violently reject Felicity's attempts to comfort her when clearly there was a mystery to solve in her father's honour.

Felicity meanwhile let her body do what it now automatically did whenever death came within close range – she ran and ran and ran.

Evie had felt acutely for this broken union. They were both clearly intelligent people – smart enough to seek help before the house burnt down – but equally unable to find their way back to each other. Sitting opposite her, arms perilously close to touching, Sarah and Felicity looked tired beyond their years. Grief, Evie had reassured them, could not be intellectualised, nor even outrun. 'Especially those couples who grieve in very different ways can be profoundly tested, even wiped out, by tragedy,' she'd said.

In that moment Evie had thought of herself and Hamish, of the series of miscarriages they'd experienced before Angus finally arrived, intact and laden with expectation. Evie had crept into her grief like a hidden room; she would not come out until it was all over. Like the carpenter who won't fix his own house, Evie had refused to talk about it with anyone, professional or otherwise. She didn't want advice or reassurance or solemn rubs of the upper arm.

And she could remember hearing Hamish on the other side of that hidden room, his bellicose retorts to evening news presenters, songs sung happily to Sera in the bath, phone calls with his mother about house prices and foreign trade agreements, and she remembered thinking: *You awful man. You have no idea.*

But that had been a long time ago.

8

Angus's urgent need for a doggie door has brought Evie to one of the experiences she enjoys least about being newly alone: Saturdays at Bunnings.

In their version of the largely unspoken delineation of domestic tasks within a marriage, Bunnings excursions had always fallen to Hamish. Even if every other aspect of the project at hand, everything before and after the requisite trip to Bunnings, rested with Evie, she had always left this part to her husband – this soulless trek through the cold concrete badlands of disparate parts and par-boiled plans.

These empires of towering shelves labelled with tiny hieroglyphics – a place where only giant tradies with exquisite eyesight can feel at home – always make Evie feel small and lost, overwhelmed yet again by just how many things in the world need fixing and how small are the bits holding everything together. Especially since Hamish left, the concept of DIY had seemed an almost cruel joke. *Like I have a choice.*

More than a few couples in Evie's professional experience had cited Bunnings in the litany of complaints about their partners. 'He can be gone for *hours*,' one woman had said of her stockbroker husband, 'and come back with nothing but onion on his chin.' It was a place to hide away from families, to slough off bad sleeps and escape difficult young children on the premise of needing a drill bit. Bunnings was either saving or killing marriages, Evie couldn't be sure. She only knows she hates the place.

'Can I help you with anything?' says a male voice behind her.

Evie turns and finds herself standing over a man in a wheelchair. He has on a Bunnings shirt and a badge that reads *James*.

'Hi,' she says. 'Ah, thanks. I'm looking for a door for a doggie. I mean, a dog. A puppy. One of those, you know … flap, flap.' Evie does a strange thing with her hands.

James looks at the shelf alongside them, brimming with paintbrushes and drop sheets. 'Well, we're a long way from that area,' he says. 'You happy to follow me?'

The question seems to be rhetorical as James swiftly spins around and moves off. Evie obediently trails the wheelchair, which moves arrestingly fast and smoothly in and around the mid-morning crowd. By the time they reach the aisle promising *Pet Enclosures and Structures*, Evie's almost out of breath.

James pulls up quickly and startles a young shaggy man deeply lost in his phone, someone Evie instantly decides has no pets but most likely a toddler, a baby and a pregnant wife with undiagnosed post-natal depression. He has bought himself an hour.

'What size dog do you have?' James says to Evie now as she wills her panting chest to subside. He's looking at her with an almost

39

familiar grin, as though they've just shared a joke together rather than an epic trek across time zones.

Evie checks herself. She thinks James must be about forty-five, but he has one of those tanned complexions that can swallow decades. *Handsome*, she thinks, and can't remember the last time the word occurred to her.

'Shit,' she says suddenly, 'I forgot to measure him.' Evie realises she will now have to go all the way home again and check the length of the dog. *Fucking Bunnings*.

'That's okay,' James says. 'What breed is he?'

'It's a … it's my son's dog,' says Evie, wiping the sheen from her forehead and attempting to tuck her hair behind her ear before remembering that Ronni last week gave her, of all things in the quagmire of her late forties, a *fringe*. 'He wanted a rescue dog but there weren't any available that weren't enormous. I know, I know,' she continues, 'everyone should get a rescue dog – I do feel bad. I probably made the decision too quickly. You know when someone's sad and you just want to make them happy? My son was … he was … anyway, I looked up local breeders and quickly ended up with a little ball of black fur. He's very cute. Tiny little brain. He's a' – *it'll come, it'll come* – 'a Maltese Shih Tzu crossed with a toy poodle.'

Evie says 'toy poodle' in the same embarrassed way she sometimes orders 'soy chai latte', as though modern life is giving us only ridiculous options.

'So it's a shitpoo?' James says and waits a long beat before smiling hard at Evie.

She splutters forth a laugh, then gives in to it generously. 'It is definitely the shittiest of poos,' Evie says. 'And I guarantee you it won't know how to get through whatever door I buy.'

James edges his chair slightly forwards. 'That's a small breed. He won't get very big even when he's finished growing.'

'Oh he's tiny,' Evie says. 'I'm terrified I'll step on him. I'm forever looking down.'

'And I'm forever looking up,' James says with a wink and a forgiving grin. He points to a shelf just above Evie's head. 'That's a decent brand, easy to install. I wouldn't think you'd need anything bigger than the Small-to-Medium.'

'Okay,' she says, 'perfect. Thanks.'

Evie reaches above her shoulder with a quick pang of guilt and lifts a box off the shelf. She glances again at James's name badge. 'Well, I can't thank you enough, James. Where are you during all my Bunnings trips?'

'Pleasure,' James says. 'And what's his name?'

Evie falters. 'The dog?'

'Yes.'

And Evie cannot in this moment remember the dog's name. *Shit.*

Shit shit shit.

This is happening more often these days: momentary lapses of recall – usually a name – that cause Evie to briefly panic before reminding herself *it'll come, it'll come.* And it does. Recollection will come with a euphoric rush and a quick flush of apology. She understands this might be a symptom of impending menopause (because almost everything is, according to her recent internet searches) but isn't sure where the sisterhood currently stands on blaming anything as non-political as oestrogen. For a long time it's felt safer to remain silent about the wild alchemy of hormones, to stoically sweat and forget and fatten up like a cow while re-reading *The Handmaid's Tale*. Lately, though, Evie's noticed a shift in the discussion, a momentary swing perhaps, to talk of a 'feminist menopause', one that empowers women to defiantly acknowledge the fact they're sweating and forgetting and fattening up like a cow. Anyway, Evie hopes her sporadic forgetfulness isn't a sign of something more nursing home-ish.

'Well, nice to meet you,' James says, looking slightly abashed and beginning to turn his chair around.

'Polo!' Evie almost yells. 'The dog is called Polo. I think it's after some foul-mouthed rapper.'

James laughs. 'Great name,' he says, 'rapper notwithstanding.'

And this, Evie thinks as she starts to make her way to the checkouts somewhere just short of Alice Springs, is easily the least soul-destroying trip she has ever made to Bunnings.

~

She drives the long way home, along the coast, a vista that still feels borrowed, not one she should get used to. It gives her time to call Sera in Perth. This one thing Evie appreciates most about the digital age, being able to have long phone conversations while driving, even if it means she often arrives at her destination with no idea how she got there.

Her daughter sounds buoyant and assured today, as she does most days: Hamish's confidence in a different vessel. She's keen to relay her latest assignment results, an executive summary of ongoing success, and various pieces of news from the grubby trough of student politics. Amid a disturbing anti-China sentiment that's been wafting about the campus since the pandemic began, Sera's part of a group organising care packs for international students stuck overseas.

To most onlookers, including Evie, Sera's life appears to be a series of expertly timed set moves, which in fact it is. But this worries Evie sometimes in the same way it impresses others. It's all so very careful, so calculated in its balancing of risk and reward. Sera never does anything she doesn't already know she is good at, having practised and mastered it well out of view. She's her own life hack, fastidiously finding work-arounds and keeping her risk of failure as low as possible, taking on nothing and no one that might stop her short. Evie has never been entirely sure whether this approach should count as conquering life or side-stepping it.

And she often wonders what Sera must really think about the current state of her parents' union. For if Evie herself didn't see it coming, whatever 'it' really is, surely Sera didn't. And what should this tell Sera about the unpredictability of life, about the risk inherent within all relationships, even those of two decades' vintage? *Perhaps especially those.* She wants her daughter to know and accept that sometimes life can take out your legs, but that doesn't necessarily mean you shouldn't have been in there to start with, making mistakes and taking chances.

But Evie strongly doubts she presently looks like someone Sera would trust for life lessons. She certainly won't be sending her any pictures of the new fringe.

After Sera quickly winds up the call, having realised she's running late for a club meeting, Evie pulls the car over to find a podcast episode to play. The one thing she can't listen to these days is silence. Since Hamish left she's filled every moment of her waking hours with strident noise – with the busy coffee shop, with Ronni's ravings, with raucous lecture theatres, podcasts and playlists. Even having Angus's rap music pouring through the cracks around his bedroom door like poisoned gas is better than hearing only the dark hollow drone of self-awareness.

Hamish was loud in every sense. Evie imagines he still is. Striding through every room like it's a hospital corridor and he's the chief physician. Singing, badly on purpose, at the top of his voice to win a cheap laugh. Yelling at thunder storms, at radio hosts, at the heads of university departments. He is the wildest clapper in any audience, the most aroused of any football fan. His appreciative laughter could crack plaster.

When you were near Hamish, Evie finds herself thinking now as her car drifts closer to the big headland, to the best view along this domesticated coastline, you couldn't help feeling noticed. Captured by something bigger. And somehow you felt safer in those moments, as though all her husband's noise and movement made a buffer against life's dangers.

She turns up the volume and drives home.

~

Evie hears it just seconds after she walks in the front door, her bra already soaring from the cuff of her blouse to the couch like an albatross: *laughter*. From Angus's room. Exuberant and female.

She stands rigid. The air feels disrupted. Has there been anyone besides Evie and Angus in this house since Hamish left? How did the outside world get in here?

She hears Angus's door open, the sound rushing out with a pungent scent. Evie sniffs the air. *Marijuana?*

And then he is standing there in the living room, her towering boy, looking alarmingly happy and not alone. The girl beside him smiles at Evie. She is shoeless, glowing.

Polo races to their side, slip-sliding on the cold tiles with elation.

'Hi,' the girl says, shifting slightly behind Angus and reaching down to scruff Polo's woolly ears. 'Sorry if we were too loud.'

'No, that's absolutely fine,' Evie says, and even she can hear the squeak of too much enthusiasm in her voice. 'It's so nice to meet one of Angus's friends.'

'This is Cobie,' says Angus. 'She's from school and … down the road.'

'I live two doors down,' Cobie says. 'You've dropped our mail over a few times.'

'Yes!' Evie says, suddenly recognising the girl's storybook hair, its tremendous flaxen redness like a flame tree. 'And what year are you in at school, Cobie?'

45

But Angus stops his mother there, says: 'I'll walk Cobie home now.'

'I can drive you,' says Evie, instantly realising how silly the suggestion is. 'I mean, of course, off you go. I'm just … okay then … good. I'll … dinner something.' *What?*

And as Angus shuts the front door behind him, it's all Evie can do not to run after them with the fresh bananas she'd yesterday pulled off the tree outside: anything to help Angus secure a friendship.

Polo leaps at the glass panel beside the front door, forlorn and ecstatic in similar measures. Evie picks him up and rubs her fingers under his chin until the pup's little heart steadies. She wanders into the kitchen and leans against the island bench, wonders if it's too early to pour a glass of wine.

Recovery from pain, Evie had often told her clients, happens faster when you notice the tiny victories along the way. They may be hard to see, crushed underfoot, pushing quietly through the divots, as small and hushed as symbols are entitled to be. A morning without tears, a sleep without terrors, a compliment from a colleague. They may look like a human lifeline at Bunnings on a Saturday. Or the first smile from your son in twelve months.

'Keep your eyes open,' Evie has said to those bleeding hope. Squint if you have to.

9

Ronni wants Evie to try online dating and this, Evie assures her, is not going to happen.

'But your vagina!' Ronni says with theatrical volume. She is now standing beside their table in the cafe, waving her hand in large circles between her legs as though indicating where a cyclone might make landfall.

'Your vagina will slam shut. Chiusa! We will hear it for blocks.'

Evie smiles apologetically at the people at the next few tables, all of whom she imagines are now picturing her vagina or trying very hard not to.

'It'll be fine, Ronni,' she says, her eyes flicking back and forth to the chair she'd like Ronni to return to. 'I am absolutely fine.'

'Vince could take care of it but then I'd have to kill him.'

'I am *fine*.'

'So, what then? You just die now?'

'What do you mean?' Evie carefully tries her coffee, which is finally as she likes it: tepid. 'I have plenty to live for.'

At last Ronni sits down. She looks to the ceiling for understanding. 'Of course you do,' she says. 'But what is life without love? What is the point of even getting dressed? Of doing your hair?'

'To keep going,' Evie says, and she hears how inadequate that sounds, especially to someone as wired as Ronni. 'Honestly, I am not missing love. Or sex. Or romance. I don't want to replace anything.'

And this is true, Evie thinks. She has not, wittingly or otherwise, sought to fill the space left by Hamish with anything shaped like intimacy. She simply hasn't wanted to, though it could have gone the other way. Grief, Evie knows from clients past, can ignite an urgent need for sexual arousal – a compulsion to throw one's whole body over the pain like a fire blanket. But it's a reaction usually produced by death and Hamish is not dead. Not in the literal sense. Not that she knows of. He's alive, though altered. He is, she's lately come to imagine, walking streets in a city on the other side of the world. He is drawing breath from the same atmospheric layer as Evie.

Ronni's in a furious tussle with her phone now, tapping and pressing hard in the manner of a generation still dubious about touch-screen technology. 'Evie, you need to trust me on this,' she says. 'It's time to get back on the horse.'

Evie glances down at her own phone. Zero activity. 'I'm sure the horse is patient,' she says.

Ronni continues undeterred. 'I did some research for you,' she says, now looking like someone about to roll out a map of the seabed. 'So, everyone is using the apps these days, even the smart people. I think it's all crazy, but sadly I'm still not in charge.'

'It's only a matter of time.'

'Let's hope so,' Ronni says. 'In the meantime, phones are in charge. On charge and in charge! See what I did there?'

'I certainly did.'

'Most people use an app called "Tender". It's basically—'

'Do you mean Tinder?'

Ronni engages in a furious round of scrolling. 'Yes, Tinder!' she says, then looks up agog. 'What a stupid name.'

'I think it's meant to reflect, you know, starting a spark.'

'But *Tender* would have made more sense,' Ronni says, shaking her head at the world and all its resident idiots. 'All any of us wants is tenderness.'

Evie smiles at her friend, at the spark and crackle of the way she sees life.

'Anyway, Tinder isn't for you,' Ronni says. 'It's mainly for people who want a quick, handy pa-pow.'

'Okay then.'

'Which is still, you know … good to remember.' And at this Ronni looks pointedly over her turquoise glasses at Evie as if to say *Write it down.*

She goes on to explain 'Bumble' ('It's like Tinder but only women can choose') and 'Zoosk' and 'Happn' and 'Badoo' and half a dozen other apps that sound more like tricky Scrabble hands than portals to destiny.

Evie imagines that midlife dating apps are much like middle age itself – poorly defined. The vast horizon-less chasm between youth and old age. No sharp edges, no dedicated helpline, no discount card, no recognised celebrity ambassador. Midlife is like

49

the house that realtors struggle to market. Not a knockdown, not a fixer-upper, not new, not old. Not *anything*.

'I think they're having a midlife crisis,' Evie has heard from too many clients in tearful earnest – so often she's begun to suspect that the real crisis may be midlife itself.

Though she's playing at naivety this morning to service Ronni's enthusiasm, Evie has some knowledge of the online dating world, albeit from a step removed. Several of her newly single friends in Perth had either waded or leapt into the scene, convinced the statistics were true: that almost no two people met conventionally anymore. Eyes can't meet across a crowded train carriage if they don't lift above a phone screen. Now Harry swipes Sally.

There had been successes. One of Evie's friends had met a book-loving paramedic online who quickly ignited their social circle with lust and hope and envy (mostly envy). In Evie's last check of social media – something she too often reserved for a Friday night after three glasses of wine – Monique had gushingly announced the couple's engagement and Evie had felt an instant flash of guilt about all she'd left behind.

But there had been misfires too. One woman in her book club had elected to use a 'premium' online dating service that pledged to find a person's true soulmate, someone who both identified the same Rorschach images and who had also paid a sizeable fee to be on the service's database. The woman had filled out a forensic questionnaire, so detailed she told the book club the process had 'uncovered parts of myself I didn't even know', and then sat back to wait for the sorcery.

One week later she was given two prospects, one of whom was her ex-husband, a man she sometimes referred to as 'the pothole', so keen was she to avoid running into him. The second soulmate turned out to be divorced in a way that was far more aspirational than actual.

Online dating, Evie had observed from the cover of her marriage in recent years, seemed to have become something unintended. Technology had swallowed purpose: the means to an end had become the end itself. Meeting someone in person was seldom the goal anymore. Loneliness, it transpires, is less physical than virtual and can easily be sated with a phone full of witty pen pals lobbing little heart bombs and naked selfies into the ether.

She sometimes looks over lecture theatres full of students and sees not a single head raised in her direction. They're lost in their phones, updating profiles and responding to messages as though stamping out constant fires. How risky to settle for one person when there are clearly so many. Both safety and terror in numbers.

'Can we at least write you up a profile?' Ronni says now with an almost childish whine. 'We don't have to post it. We can just have it ready to go like passata in the freezer.'

'God,' Evie says, tacitly grateful for her new friend's zeal. 'I can't even think of a single interesting thing I could put in a profile.'

And she really can't. Evie had stopped looking at herself as others might. She no longer trusted what she couldn't see: which part of her Hamish had stopped seeing. She'd stopped moving purposefully through time, stopped checking calendars and mirrors.

Doggie door aside, Evie hadn't started a single new project in twelve months.

And she knows it will shift, this smog of indecision. She even feels it loosening sometimes. But for now, while she waits for sense to somehow make itself, Evie's not ready to meet anyone she won't bore or scare or disappoint. Hamish took away a part of her that hasn't found its way back.

Evie smiles at Ronni across the table marbled with coffee rings. 'How short can a profile be?' she asks.

Ronni looks up with delight. 'As short as you like!' she says. 'One word. A sentence. It doesn't matter. Are we doing this?'

Evie glances out the cafe window, at the steady rush of people getting on with things. She pictures her son glaring impatiently at a TV screen, his heavy heel rapping on the floor of his room, the wifi failing to keep up with his game.

'We could just write,' she says finally, '*Evie Shine. Forty-nine. Still buffering.*'

10

Margaret

She was one of Evie's last appointments before they'd left Perth. But that wasn't the only reason Margaret hadn't readily left her mind. There'd been something so earnest about her presentation to Evie, the way she'd held up her pain and confusion like things she'd just found at the bottom of a drawer and was desperate to have identified. Like she'd just woken up in a strange bed.

'Can you start from the beginning?' Evie had said to her. And it was the last question she'd had to ask.

'I don't know where that is,' Margaret said. 'I don't know how I got here. I feel like I've spent twenty years in the back of a car. It's always moving; I'm always moving. The car doesn't stop. And you know when you're little and you can't see properly out the window of your parents' car? It's like that.

'You get this glimpse every now and then of places and scenes and dreams ... you see car wrecks, missed opportunities ... they all fly by ... moments you should have made the car stop somehow ... but it doesn't stop.

'And then one day it does. And you get out of the car and you have absolutely no idea where you are or who you are.

'It all happens too quickly and all at the wrong time. Does that make sense, Evie?'

Evie nodded.

'It's like one day you're this young angry woman who wants to kick down all the big doors – the patriarchy, capitalism, inequality … all of it. And you don't. You barely make a dent.

'But you try anyway because there's a whole life just blazing away inside you. Every inch of you is on fire. Do you remember that?'

Evie did.

'And you don't feel it slide away because it happens so very slowly … and also so quickly that you can't see it and you don't grab it. How is that possible?

'I got lost in motherhood, Evie. It hollowed me out. The weight of all that love. The work of it all. The worries, every day, every night, eating through your skin.

'But mostly the love – it rewires you from the inside. No one can see it. Stephen didn't see it. Did you feel that too?'

Evie had.

'That's the trick of it all. The unfairness of it, the shitty division of labour – you're too addled, too recalibrated by devotion, to do anything meaningful about any of it. What sisterhood? You're engulfed.

'Running. Always running. Leaping in and out of train doors to not be the last mother picking up at childcare again. Running to make the school assembly when they win a prize. Or don't win a prize. Running down the street to make the noise stop.

'How are we meant to keep careers going between kids' sick days and the house and the husband and the non-stop roar of it all? How did you do it, Evie? What am I missing?

'Because here I am now … a middle-aged woman. And the car has stopped. I don't know how that happened and I'm not ready for it. I don't want it.

'The smallness of it. Don't you think we deserve more?

'I want to be angry again. I want doors to kick down. I want to run and I want somewhere to run to.

'But I'm exhausted. I'm so tired, Evie. And this body – this is what I'm meant to work with now? After everything? After all the running and leaping and holding children back from the road?

'How can it be that I feel terrified and fearless at the same time? I want to jump on a plane and fly anywhere to see if I'm there. I want to fall in love. I want to smash plates. I want to burn it all down. But I also want to stay in bed and wait for it all to slip away, every last disappointment.

'Who am I now? Am I what I started with or only what is left?

'What does Stephen see? I honestly don't know. I'm too scared to ask and too angry that I might have to.

'Because he won't understand – how could he? – and I will hate him for that.

'Stephen is the same person I married. The exact same person. I am not.

'I have been a hundred Margarets and now I am this. I need to work out what this is.

'Evie, I am so lost.'

11

Stephen

Margaret had been adamant her husband wouldn't attend counselling of any description, that he didn't believe in it, but a week after Margaret's appointment Evie saw that he'd booked a session with her. It wasn't her practice to see couples separately from the outset but there was no way to reset things.

'She won't let me touch her,' Stephen had said just seconds after he'd sat down in Evie's room. She watched as he placed a fist squarely on each knee and pulled back his shoulders as though ready for a team photo.

'Is that where you want to start, Stephen?'

'No,' he'd replied. Then, 'Maybe. What did she tell you?'

Evie explained she couldn't share that information with him, that this session was just for him to share his feelings. Stephen seemed to shake off the word with his shoulders.

'It's menopause,' he'd fired at Evie then. 'The change. Whatever you call it these days if you can call it anything.'

Evie had shifted in her chair, buying herself a few moments

to consider her response. Margaret hadn't said anything about menopause.

'She knows that's what it is,' Stephen continued, now lurching forwards from his chair. 'I've seen the search history on our computer. The prescriptions. I've heard her talking to her sister about it. I've Googled it myself. The not wanting sex. Crying all the time. Always angry. It's made her batshit crazy for about eighteen months. It's not about me.'

He looked victorious. Proud. In that moment Evie couldn't remember the last time she'd instinctively disliked a man as much as she did Stephen.

'Have you discussed this with her?'

'Yes. Couple of times.'

'And how did that go?'

'How do you think it went?' Stephen had laughed.

Evie cleared her throat.

'Sorry,' he said then. 'I know that sounded bad. But it's just … I've put up with this for so long now. I'm tired of it. I can't fix it. It's like torture.'

'It sounds like it's been very difficult for Margaret too.'

Evie knew the statistics, malleable though they are. There's a discernible peak in divorce rates for couples in their late forties and early fifties – the menopause years, certainly, but equally the time when nests may be emptied and lacklustre marriages laid bare. She didn't believe (at least she didn't want to) that menopausal women were detonating relationships on the basis of hormones alone, their minds no longer their own. What pronounced menopause could

58

do, Evie preferred to think, was amplify the very things that few relationships can withstand too much of: clarity and introspection. Menopause could obliterate distraction.

'You'll need to be patient,' she'd told Stephen. *Patient and gentle and kind.*

'But she won't even let me touch her,' Stephen said, returning to his opening statement. 'How can I make things better if I can't show her how I feel? If we can't have sex? What's a marriage without sex?'

Evie had heard this last question too many times. It wasn't the primitiveness of it that bothered her as much as the inadequacy of most answers.

'Sex,' she'd told Stephen, 'might be the last thing to return. It might be the thing Margaret will want again *after* she's worked through these other feelings and doubts she's experiencing.'

'But how long?' he'd said, looking pleadingly at Evie as though she were a doctor delivering terrible news.

'I don't know,' Evie said. 'How long are you prepared to be patient?'

Bizarrely, Stephen had chosen that moment to look at his watch.

'Well,' he'd said after a silence that even Evie found uncomfortably long. 'I guess I'm here, aren't I?'

12

Angus has to make a prosthetic limb out of household items, presumably because his science teacher has it in for parents. The assignment, which her son has just handed Evie via a piece of paper that looks like it's been through a war, includes a detailed marking rubric designed to crush any young soul. She laments an education that wasn't strangled by life-defining assessment.

But it's been a long time since Angus has presented any evidence that he's still attending school and Evie is keen to meet the gesture with an enthusiasm that's sufficiently measured not to frighten him back to his room. 'Okay,' she says, 'we can do this. When is it due?'

'Monday,' Angus says, mouthing an 'eek' expression. Polo is doing frantic circle work at his feet.

'Right,' Evie responds, mindful not to ask exactly how long the assignment has been sitting in the Chernobyl exclusion zone at the bottom of his schoolbag.

For a minute or ten, the pair glance around the kitchen and living room, hopeful a household item might suddenly present itself as having untapped potential as an arm or leg. The options appear limited.

'I thought, like, maybe we could use a broom handle as the leg,' Angus suggests, surprising Evie with this forethought, 'and, like, use the wheel of an office chair as a ball joint and, I don't know, stick an old shoe on the bottom or something.'

Evie's impressed. 'Well, that sounds better than anything I would have thought of,' she says with an air of triumph. 'Let's do that.'

This had always been Hamish's territory: school projects with a practical element. He would dive in from the high tower, spray the entire house with fervour, enlist all willing (Angus) and unwilling (Sera and Evie) participants to the task and ultimately create something just short of marvellous. Bongo drums out of Milo tins and old chair leather. Spinning solar systems. Exploding volcanoes.

Angus would look upon his father in his mid-project madness as any boy might gaze upon a demigod. And Evie would in these moments be grateful she'd married someone who had become a decent father, because no one knows this for sure: what kind of parent a partner will turn out to be. She'd counselled many couples for whom the cherished goal of having children had proved a pyrrhic victory, the sins of other fathers and mothers ricocheting across generations.

Hamish may well have been absent too often, choosing to work long hours and turning down too few indulgent conferences but when he was present, he was at least very much so. A good father, interrupted.

'You know, I don't think we even own a broom,' Evie says, briefly recalling a pre-Dyson time. 'I think we'd have to buy one.'

'It's okay – don't worry about it,' Angus says, making a swift move for his bedroom.

'No, no,' Evie almost yelps. 'Let's go and buy a broom. We'll need other things anyway – stuff to hold it all together.'

Oh God, Evie thinks. *Bunnings*.

~

The Sunshine Coast sky is ablaze today, calling time on the final days of winter in almost cocky fashion. Evie drives a route that prolongs the car's closeness to the ocean before heading inland, a habit from Perth where 'the coast' is more crudely defined: you have to be able to either see or smell the Indian Ocean or you're kidding yourself. Here, the very name of the region – apparently a controversial eight-year decision in its day that ultimately became a masterstroke – means you can feel as coastal as you like all the way to Maleny.

Evie glances at Angus in the passenger seat, his head lilting out the open window like a briefly satisfied Labrador. She can't remember the last time they were in the car together like this, Angus having mastered the local bus system the minute they moved here. She lets him play his Spotify tunes through the Bluetooth and tries to bob her head along to something about grave-diggin' mofos.

Testing the bandwidth of the scene, Evie decides to ask Angus if he's heard from his father lately. She knows there was a rally of text messages in the first month or two after Hamish left but the exchange had left Angus so clearly wounded that she hadn't felt confident about broaching the topic again. Every instinct to comfort him was tempered by the fear she could too easily make things worse. In her worst moments, Evie felt as shamefully unable to fix her son as she did to fix herself, even though she suspected that the former couldn't occur without the latter. Thinking about it now makes her freshly angry. *What have you done here, Hamish?*

'I just wondered,' Evie says, very gently turning down the volume on the stereo, 'if you'd heard anything from Dad lately? You don't have to tell me but I also thought you might want to talk about it. If it helps.'

Suburbs pass by and governments collapse. Finally Angus pivots his gaze from the window to the windscreen, still a right angle short of Evie's face. 'He still sends messages sometimes,' he says, 'but not as often. I just ignore them.'

'Why?' Evie asks, knowing she's now pushing things much closer to the edge of comfort than either of them might be able to handle. 'Why do you ignore them?'

Impossibly, she hears Angus shrug. 'I don't know where he's texting from,' he says. 'I don't know who he's with – anyone could read what I write. I just can't picture him. I can't see him standing there holding his phone. It doesn't seem real.'

'No, it doesn't seem real.'

'It feels easier to hate him.'

'Yes it does.'

'I mean, he's not coming back, is he?'

Evie pulls in behind the long convoy heading slowly into the carpark as though awaiting rations for the apocalypse. She looks at her son, his dark hair flattened against the car's ceiling. 'I don't know, Angus,' she answers. 'I haven't heard from him. I don't know what his plans are.'

'Well,' Angus says with a shrug, as though about to share a concluding thought that might end all of this. But the word doesn't find any others.

Evie feels the quick sting of guilt. Asking him about this now, a captive in her car, wasn't just a matter of checking in on Angus. It was equally, if Evie's honest with herself, borne of her own curiosity, the desire to know, at least sometimes, how Hamish is framing the situation to others. Too often she finds herself thinking back to past clients, to people like Margaret and Stephen, who when asked the same questions about the state of their relationship provide such vastly different answers that truth seems obliterated by perspective. Even a trained professional isn't sure where to land.

What Evie does know for certain is that Hamish's last deposit into their joint bank account happened a month ago. She's no way of knowing if there'll be another at this point. For now she can cover the mortgage payments and bills on her teaching income and their savings but not for long and certainly not forever. Money issues might smoke out Hamish well before any emotional ones.

Evie turns to look squarely at her son now. 'Look,' she says, inexplicably conjuring the manner of Hamish, who always liked to wrap up meetings with an action point. 'I think it would be good for you to write a letter to your father. You wouldn't have to send it to him, not unless you want to. You could decide about that after you've written it. But I just think … Angus, we need to get this stuff out. It's not healthy to keep it inside. It doesn't disappear in there; it just gets thicker. Writing a letter is a good way to get things out.'

Angus doesn't answer her, not that Evie expected him to. 'There's a park,' he says at last, and Evie dutifully pulls into the tiny space.

~

She's about to tell Angus about her last trip to Bunnings, the one that didn't feel like dental work thanks to a helpful man in a wheelchair, when she sees him, James, moving towards them. He looks focused, as though fixed on a task just beyond them, but then pulls up smoothly when he sees her.

'Hi, Angus,' he says, smiling in that way that some people do, with every part of their face.

Evie looks confusedly at her son, who is smiling back at James.

'Hi, James,' Angus says. 'How are you?'

'I'm good, mate,' James says. 'It's one of those crazy busy days here but that's okay. What are you up to? Need a hand with anything? Is this your sister?'

Evie laughs, almost a theatrical guffaw. She's certain he can't possibly remember her. 'I'm his mum,' she says and instinctively pulls at her fringe to make it longer. 'You actually helped me last time I was here.'

'I remember,' James says, flicking his upwards gaze between mother and son. She sees that his eyes are that rare shade of grey. 'How did the doggie door go – was it the right size?'

'Well,' Evie says, 'the door is perfect. Unfortunately the dog has zero interest in it and is happy to keep peeing inside indefinitely.'

James grins generously, says: 'He might need more training, Angus. You might need to show him how it's done.'

Angus's response is an odd combination of shudder and grunt, the tortured dance of self-conscious adolescence.

Evie rescues him. 'So how do you know Angus?'

'He's Cobie's dad,' Angus says quickly, evidently keen to frame the situation. 'You know my friend Cobie? They live on our street.'

My friend. 'Of course!' Evie says brightly. 'Cobie with the beautiful hair. She seems like a lovely girl.'

'Yes, we think we'll keep her,' James says. 'It was touch and go there for a while.'

And while she knows James is joking, Evie is briefly reminded of her own daughter's mid-teen years: the firestorm of rage and pain and obstinacy Sera had unleashed to test the foundations of their household. It had bruised her marriage, that period of smashed mirrors and landmines, and Evie knows Hamish expected her of all people to have many more solutions than she did.

James appears keen to stay and help them, even as a constant mass of people shuffle by the trio in collective confusion. Angus explains to him what the science project entails.

'Ah yes, Cobie has the same assignment,' James says. 'I think we're making an arm out of an old vacuum cleaner and roller-skate wheels. What are you thinking?'

Angus looks to Evie with an expression that suggests he's no longer confident in his idea.

'We're keeping it pretty simple,' Evie says. 'The main thing we need is a broom.'

James pivots his chair to let a large pallet of potting mix be pushed by. 'What kind of broom?'

'Just a really cheap broom that will never get to enjoy its reason for being,' Evie says with an uncertain laugh. 'Because we're going to cut it into pieces. So actually, maybe a saw too. A cheap saw we'll never use again.'

Intrigued, James extracts the full plan from Angus, who would have been embarrassed about its few rudimentary parts if James weren't so careful to react with measured admiration. 'That's genius,' he tells Angus. 'And the good news is I have an old broom in the shed you can use and an office chair that was due for my next trip to the tip and plenty of tools, so you actually don't need to buy anything. Just come over tomorrow morning and grab them if you like.'

Evie now takes a closer look at this man who has twice given her contentment at Bunnings. His hair, like Cobie's, is curly – a frothy brown wave that would likely grow up instead of down if left untended. The grey eyes are serious and deeply set, almost retreating from view in spite of their dominance. He looks purposeful and tanned and perceptive – all of these things Evie registers in an instant, as though she might later be quizzed on them – and she wonders how and when it happened for him: the wheelchair. What that does to a life.

In staccato fashion, Angus arranges a ballpark time to pick up the items from James's house the following day. Evie notes her son's struggle, this adult-like effort to line up intent and availability.

Normally he doesn't breach until well after midday on a Sunday.

She thanks James effusively and watches him move swiftly away from them, disappearing around a corner to a fresh round of problem-solving. Curious that she has never seen him in the neighbourhood since they moved here – you'd notice an attractive man in a wheelchair, Evie thinks.

On the way out of the shop, Angus stops at the sausage sizzle marquee with a suddenness that appears almost involuntary. His rangy frame needs urgent sustenance; that smell cannot be ignored. And Evie feels it too now, though she's barely mustered a normal appetite since Hamish left, the pressing desire for this national dish.

'Two with,' Angus asks of the gaggle of young netball players playing shop today. 'Extra onions under the sausages please. No sauce.'

And it is, Evie thinks in spite of herself, exactly what Hamish would have ordered.

13

You can't say no to Ronni in the same way you can't say no to kids selling lemonade at the end of their driveway. It's the enthusiasm, the earnestness, the enterprise. Resistance isn't just futile; it threatens to invite misfortune.

How else to explain this: Evie is sat in the corner of a Mexican restaurant awaiting the arrival of a man called Ryan. A man she doesn't know. A man with whom she must now share a meal and conversation because Ronni has deemed it so.

'One date,' she'd pleaded with Evie. 'One date to get you out of this solco.'

(Evie had assumed solco was an Italian derivation of 'sulk', which she roundly rejected – she has not been brooding, not in a wilful way – but subsequently learnt it means 'rut', and Evie supposed that wasn't entirely unfair. Separation *is* a rut, much like war is an inconvenience.)

Ryan, Ronni had explained to Evie, was the divorced father of one of her son's friends from school. An architect. Cyclist. Keen chef.

Surf club volunteer. Hands-on dad. Travel enthusiast. 'That sounds like seven people,' Evie had said. *Like someone trying too hard.*

That she was here in the restaurant first is not from Ronni's playbook, the long list of instructions she'd provided to Evie covering everything from which handbag to bring to how to best describe her career ('Maybe talk about the teaching more than the couples counselling,' Ronni had insisted, 'because, you know, scary.') But Evie had miscalculated the length of the drive here – it took seven minutes rather than twenty – and she also, if honest, just wanted to get this over with.

Ronni had showed Evie several photos of Ryan from his Facebook profile – Ryan on a bike, Ryan on a surf boat, Ryan holding aloft some sort of novelty trophy – so Evie recognises him when he walks into the restaurant, albeit bereft of sporting accessories.

And this is happening now. This is awful, she thinks, attempting to keep both eye contact and a smile that's starting to shake at the corners as Ryan walks the Camino-esque distance from the entrance to Evie's table. *Why on earth do people do this to themselves?*

Evie has never dated, not really. Before she met Hamish, she'd slept with a handful of men in the various share houses that had given unwieldy form to her university years. There'd never been a restaurant, not unless you counted half a dozen students gobbling handfuls of the goodbye mints at Sizzler. No candles or cards or first kisses, and no expectation of them. Just young lonely people occasionally flinging themselves at each other.

She'd met Hamish on an aeroplane. He'd offered her both the window seat and chewing gum for the ascent – excuses, he later admitted, to initiate a conversation that might mitigate his dread of flying. 'It's just the take-off and the landings that terrify me,' he'd confided, 'and that big bit in between.'

They'd both been on their way to visit grandparents in Melbourne, each out of obligation more than desire. Hamish told her of his political aspirations, of his Whitlam-inspired ambition to restore socialist ideology to the bedrock of modern leadership. Something lofty like that. Evie told him she'd just landed her first counselling job and was finding the experience far more challenging than expected. 'You can put a teacup back together if the pieces are big enough,' she'd explained to him over their complimentary wine, 'but how do you even begin to fix something that's shattered?'

Hamish had been caught from the start, as smitten by the way Evie talked about people as by the way she organised her tray table like a game of Tetris. When they were back in Perth, he investigated which counselling centre she worked at and booked a session. There he told Evie that he hadn't stopped thinking about her, that he thought they might be meant for each other, and that together they could fix any broken teacup. *Good God*, Evie had thought. But also, *yes*.

She looks now at Ryan, awkwardly arranging his jacket on the back of the chair. Random seat allocation on a plane certainly makes for a better wedding speech than forced matchmaking by well-intentioned friends, she thinks, and then stops herself. Ronni's effort deserves better from her than this.

It quickly transpires that Ryan is an accomplished conversationalist, seemingly well practised in the art. He shares and requests information almost rhythmically, gathering details to inform the next question, punctuating anything remotely boastful about himself with a quick stab of self-deprecation. He's articulate too, using impressive words without sounding pretentious or rehearsed. By the second margarita, Evie finds she's actually enjoying herself, enjoying whatever this is.

And he's pleasing to look at, she now decides over soggy nachos, because it's taken this long to properly take in Ryan's appearance. Sandy-coloured hair, neat eyebrows, even teeth. Nothing she couldn't bear to look at on a regular basis. *What?*

But she is failing, Evie now suspects, to keep Ryan's genuine interest. Because while he talks of cycling tours in Italy and tennis tournaments and shark scares at surf club practice, she finds she can only talk of her children, of their interests and hobbies. She hasn't, she finally admits to Ryan, done much in the way of getting a life since becoming separated. *Since my husband left with no clear explanation.*

'That's okay,' Ryan reassures her. 'We all go through these things at our own pace.'

And it's a kind response on his part, Evie thinks, but also she *really* needs to do something about this test pattern of an existence.

'To be completely honest,' Ryan says now, taking a sip of his drink that leaves a little salt on his top lip. 'The only reason I've thrown myself into so much activity is because I was actually obese.'

He looks at her hard now, as though she's a pile about to topple. Evie doesn't move.

'I weighed twice as much as I do now. My wife didn't say that's why she ended our marriage but I know it was a factor. I was hideous and I hated myself. That's pretty hard to love.'

She hadn't expected this, not at all. It's a raw admission and one Evie suspects Ryan hadn't planned to share – his voice had faltered midway through and now he's looking at the empty plate of nachos in front of him like it's a hung jury.

Sympathy floods her, the familiar surge of tenderness she always felt when a client held aloft their pain for her to see, to understand.

'You know,' she says, 'the easiest thing is to give in to the way the world sees us. The hardest thing is to change ourselves for the better. Losing all that weight – you should be really proud of yourself.'

And she is counselling now. *Stop.*

'Thanks,' Ryan says, but his voice sounds diminished, his practised momentum gone. 'It wasn't enough to win her back, as it turns out. Now she's with one of the partners at her firm. Younger guy. Fit, with tatts.'

The dessert menu arrives with horrid timing.

'Anyway,' he continues, 'that was a bit of a conversation-killer, sorry. I won't say anything more about that.'

Evie glances momentarily at Ryan's watch and sees it has just gone eight-thirty. The sight of numbers makes her tired. Two-and-a-half hours seems an adequate amount of time to call this outing something other than a bust. It should hopefully satisfy Ronni.

'No need to apologise at all,' she says to Ryan, just as a large group takes up a table alongside them. *They'll be eating their mains when I'm already in bed.* She briefly wonders if 'reading in bed until

I pass out' would suffice as a hobby on a dating profile. 'This has been really lovely.'

'Yes, it's been great to meet you, Evie,' Ryan says. 'Ronni was right – you're really easy to talk to. A good listener.'

'Thanks,' she says. 'I've had a lot of practice.'

He smiles at her, detects the salt on his lip and licks it away.

What now?

Can we go now?

'I guess I should get going anyway,' Ryan says at last. 'I've got a big ride on early in the morning.'

And Evie thinks she should probably ask him how far and where to and who with but instinctively doesn't. She pictures him now as one of those shiny cyclists taking up half the road when there's a bike path right beside him, a peeve she's inherited from Hamish.

He insists, in a manner that Evie can't quite identify as either assertive or resigned, on paying the bill. A younger woman might have made a bigger show of splitting it, she thinks, and briefly wonders why, of all the inequalities heaped on women, this is one they think is worth fighting for. Let men pay for dinner, Evie reasons, if they can't breastfeed or give birth. *Cheap at half the price.*

Together they walk outside to the dark restaurant carpark, where Evie realises with abrupt panic that the worst part of the night is still to come. The goodbye.

Please don't kiss me.

Oh God.

I can't do this.

But Ryan doesn't. He doesn't kiss her. There's no awkward lean in, no hopeful positioning of feet. Instead he picks up one of her hands and holds it in both of his. The gesture is swift and assured and Evie's surprised to realise she is being touched by another person, a man, by large soft hands in a carpark. How can this be her life now?

'Thank you for a lovely evening, Evie,' Ryan says. 'I'm really glad I met you.'

'Me too,' Evie says, leaving her hand there to still be held, willing it not to sweat.

'And I meant to say at the start of the night,' he continues, 'but forgot to because I was so nervous, that you look incredibly beautiful. You really do.'

And Evie finds no words to answer this, no way of expressing a feeling that sits between suspicion and elation.

Incredibly beautiful.

Surely not.

~

The drive home is long, much longer than it should be. Evie sees that she's taken several wrong turns, possibly on purpose. She's not yet ready for home, and she hadn't been ready for this: for tonight's unwelcome testing of nerve endings, tiny rubber hammers on her reflexes. A stocktake of broken parts. Her cheeks are catching tears.

What happened to you, Hamish? What did I miss?

She stops at a featureless cafe, open unusually late, and orders a coffee she doesn't want. Evie knows she's about to do what she promised herself she wouldn't, the thing she's advised countless clients not to do, yet somehow the act feels less transgressive in here, a little safer.

She opens her phone, clicks on Facebook, and looks up the name of a woman.

Hamish had said he was moving out of their home to 'work on some things about myself, just for a while'. He'd promised, in the face of all Evie's subsequent protestations and allegations, all her desperate questions, that there was no one else. He was not that person. He still loved her. He loved what they'd made together, loved the children. He just needed some time to work on himself 'away from everything'. He didn't know exactly how much time. 'But not too much,' he'd said.

This was, Evie knew too well, the unceremonious way in which so many marriages ultimately end, not with orchestral roars but a series of bagatelles. Requests for time, requests for understanding. A cruel game of inches. She knew it even as he said it.

'It's like,' one client had said to her, his wife having moved into a spare room several months earlier, 'I have to wait for her to keep tossing rocks into the water, guessing at the depth.'

It's also, Evie had levelled at Hamish, the way many people squeeze infidelity into every tiny corner of a suitcase, hiding it even from themselves.

Hamish had bellowed at this suggestion. 'I am not a client in your chair, Evie!' he'd said. 'I'm not ending our marriage with paper cuts. There's no one else. I just *need some time*.'

The next day Hamish had left the house before she'd woken up. His time had evidently begun.

Evie learnt some weeks later, after several text messages to Hamish went unanswered, that another academic at their uni had also taken unplanned leave at the same time as him – a history lecturer called Jo McBride. She'd gone back to Scotland to tend to a sick mother. Scotland, the ancestral home of Hamish's flock, the place he'd always pledged to take Evie but hadn't, not yet.

And she'd stopped sending him messages after that, unsure where they were landing and who was seeing them. She stopped asking awkward questions of his parents, of the few friends he had. She wasn't yet ready for the sort of neat heading that would sum up one of her client's cases: Addiction. Boredom. Abuse. Grief. Affair.

Instead Evie took back the time Hamish had asked for and sat in it herself.

She types the woman's name into Facebook now. There are multiple results, the first few being from the local area. Evie keeps patting at her phone – she's painfully slow at this, it infuriates Angus – until at last it's there: a woman's face fills her screen. *Jo McBride, academic, Glasgow. Single.*

She's looking directly at Evie, splintering time with large eyes and a smile that already knows the answer. Beautiful of course, Evie sees that. *Incredibly beautiful.*

And there is nothing, Evie thinks as she drives home on near-empty roads, nothing more robust than hope to inoculate a marriage. Time is not enough. Not children. Not love. Just hope. And yes, luck too. An absence of gross misfortune and shiny arcs across the night sky. That is all.

Finally, as she crawls into her bed just after midnight, so tired that sleep won't be enough, Evie also thinks: *Why didn't Ryan kiss me?*

14

Sanaya and Arjun

'Never underestimate this thing.'

It's what Gerard Keane, an early counselling mentor to Evie, had said about their profession. 'Never underestimate how much you can help people,' he'd added, 'and how much you can harm them.'

It was good enough advice but redundant in Evie's case. If anything, and especially in her first few years of practice, she'd earnestly overestimated what counselling could actually achieve. She'd believed every problem could be fixed, every underlying issue exposed like gold in a pan, if only enough patience, urging, empathy and practical advice were applied in the right amounts and at the right moments. She had placed considerable pressure on herself to rescue every case, even the most hopeless, putting in far more hours than her billable time to research, reflect and analyse. Hamish had often ribbed her for 'staring into the void again', when really Evie had been rolling a client's situation over and over in her mind like baoding balls.

As her career progressed, Evie had begun to realise that the only thing not to be underestimated about relationship counselling was the real role it was playing in the drama. Sometimes it was an excuse, a foil, a distraction. Sometimes it was just an emotional boxing ring away from little prying eyes and ears.

And sometimes it was everything, a couple's only hope, the last chance saloon. This is what it was for Sanaya, though less so for her husband of twenty-one years. Arjun had come along to counselling willingly enough but equally he might have agreed to cooking classes. He didn't, Evie could see from the outset, believe that his relationship and family were truly at stake. He didn't share Sanaya's view that they were at a crossroads, that difficult decisions were forming themselves if certain things (and even Sanaya didn't know exactly what those things were) didn't change.

When Arjun surveyed the landscape of his life now he saw what any man might expect: a loosening of expectation, of waistbands, a shifting down through the heavy gears. He saw their children claiming adulthood, shaping themselves into people he might not immediately recognise at a busy intersection. He saw the world circling back on the same old problems, the nightly news a turnstile of accidents and avarice. The men around him, old friends and colleagues, seemed no more surprised or enlightened than he. Arjun wasn't missing anything. This was it, the thing you land in. A life.

When Arjun looked at Sanaya these days, he didn't so much see the passing of time as time itself. Immovable. You could do nothing bar chalk it up. Sanaya, in increasingly stark contrast, saw time as entirely malleable, something they could now reshape if they wanted to, if they *both* wanted to. She saw other couples making a much better fist of this, of redefining their relationships beyond children, of travelling together, grinding off the rust.

Sanaya saw that Arjun had become stuck somehow. Withdrawn and increasingly silent. As though he'd already expressed every emotion he was ever going to have. He'd stopped looking at life as something mostly unwritten and, Sanaya had said, her voice catching on this point, Arjun had stopped looking at *her*.

Once, Sanaya said in perhaps the couple's very first session, the family had holidayed in Esperance, back when the kids were very young. There'd been a day when she and Arjun had stood on the sand watching their children weave boogie boards through choppy waves, a magic morning of sun and squeals. Suddenly and without any warning or clear cause, the tide had begun to recede at speed, drawing further and further back like a cloth ripped from a table. Sanaya had watched with rising terror, feet jammed in the sand, uncertain where to move and knowing there was no time, knowing she was about to witness some form of annihilation.

When the tide came thundering back in, Sanaya saw her children flying towards her on their boards, hysterically joyous, their trust in random danger as innocent and misplaced as any person riding the rollercoaster at a carnival. They flew right by her, landing at the edge of the beach's carpark, upturned eskies and umbrellas in their wake.

'That feeling,' Sanaya had said, looking at Evie out of sad eyes, 'when the tide began to disappear, imagining the very worst and not being able to do anything about it … that's how I've been feeling about us.'

Sanaya had come to counselling not just for answers but for safety and hope. She didn't want her marriage to end if it didn't have to. She cared about her husband enough to think she probably still loved him. But she also couldn't stay like this, feet in the sand, unable to move.

Evie had found these cases the most challenging. Unlike many of her colleagues who believed that those relationships riven by adultery, addiction or abuse were the hardest to salvage, Evie found time itself to be an often insidious rival to work with – elusive by nature and duplicitousness in the context of a marriage. The hero and the villain.

Most of the couples she counselled at this point in their relationships were really arguing about time. About the value they each placed on it, what was spent and what was left. Such arbitrary decisions, entirely unique to every person and shaped by thousands of factors outside them, made Evie's role almost benign and reductive. She was in these cases simply a listener, albeit the most attentive kind, waiting for a breakthrough.

Sanaya's breakthrough was to realise, two years into the couple's time working with Evie, that Arjun was not going to change, not in any way that might make a post-children future together something to look forward to. Her imminent fiftieth birthday had become a deadline of sorts, a violent bell sounding their final lap. It was possible, Sanaya had decided with a measure of relief, to still love someone and not want to be married to them any longer. The switch had been flipped.

As disappointed as Evie had been about Sanaya's decision, having come to know and like the couple very much, she didn't necessarily think separation would be a mistake, nor did she suspect it would be permanent. Space could be as illuminating as time was suffocating.

It's far more probable than not, Evie has said to many clients, that a couple might reach their fifties, maybe even their forties, in completely different shapes and wanting entirely different things. None of us, even those who've shared a bed, a home, the raising of the same children, move through space and time at the same rate. For many people too, midlife brings with it a rude awakening of long-buried pain. The easiest thing is to either look away or run away.

Arjun had asked Evie if he could continue to see her on his own. He wanted to work through some things he couldn't understand, things about himself that had stopped him responding to Sanaya in the ways she'd wanted.

And it took Evie some time to get there, to the source of Arjun's inertia. He didn't want to revisit the fifteen-year-old boy looking after a cancer-stricken mother, staying home from school day after day because the words and the numbers didn't make sense anyway, not anymore. He didn't want to meet that friendless, stunted boy again, not until Evie gently showed him that he had to, that only Arjun could reach him.

Sanaya too returned to Evie for counselling on her own. She conceded that she'd found the idea of leaving her marriage much easier than the reality of it. That the loneliness had proved vast and confronting. That furniture assembly made her weep for days. That *Eat, Pray, Love* was a crock of shit and should be banned. Evie had laughed at this and thought that Sanaya would have proved a wonderful friend if she hadn't been a client.

And she had looked them up some time later, a casual search of social media in a moment of reflection between clients. Both Sanaya's and Arjun's profiles had their status as 'Married', their recent posts scattered with sun-bleached photos of a holiday together.

Evie was pleased but in no way proud. This hadn't been a triumph of counselling, she knew, but more of the good fortune that two people might still, after time has played all its tricks, want enough of the same things to stay together for still more time.

The only thing you could never underestimate in this thing was luck.

15

In less than six months' time, Sera will turn twenty-one. It pulls Evie up short when she thinks about the looming date, disbelief and unease jostling for position. Her little girl. *Our little girl.*

Evie's been through a string of altered milestones since Hamish left, but this, Sera's twenty-first, is disrupting her every thought, pulling her under again. She wants to make it something special for Sera, better than that, but to do so will mean she can no longer avoid what she has for so long: communicating with, or even about, Hamish.

Even if Evie understands nothing about her husband anymore, and it seems clear she doesn't, and even if she never really did, she's certain he will want to mark Sera's twenty-first in a definitive, if not grand, way. Hamish was always one for big occasions: not in an ostentatious sense – he was far too proud a socialist for that – but in ways that showed considered attention.

For her own fortieth birthday, an event Evie now thinks she might have wholly imagined, Hamish had orchestrated a surprise party in reverse – a lunch event with friends that he'd organised with Evie's knowledge only to reveal on the day that no one was coming, that the two of them were actually flying to Alice Springs that afternoon for a sunset flight over Uluru.

And it was everything Evie had long suspected the sacred rock would deliver – a heady and undeniably spiritual experience, colours that sear the retinas, a largeness to seize the heart. It was her favourite memory up until Hamish left, up until it became like all the other big moments they'd shared: questionable and tainted.

Evie no longer trusts the purity of joy.

She wonders if Hamish still thinks about the day of Sera's birth. The many hours they'd spent walking the corridors and carpark of the hospital together, assured by an assortment of well-meaning nurses and midwives that to do so would accelerate this process about which they knew so little. Hamish had held her arm, made her laugh, watched her cry with exhaustion and then cried too.

For all the talk about hospitals being too surgery-happy these days, this one had clearly run out of scalpels. Time expanded until it seemed to stop altogether. The couple had been left alone to labour for the best part of a day, yet Evie's contractions were still short and manageable long after conversation had run out. 'Do you think we're maybe just not good at this?' Hamish had said with a laugh, though Evie could see he was only half joking.

Finally a doctor had walked in and broken Evie's waters with a finger that might as well have been stabbing a broken button on a vending machine. 'You're off and running now,' he said, ripping off his glove and flicking it in a bin.

'Surgeons and pilots,' Hamish had said as the doctor flounced out of the room like a rock star. 'Fucking God complexes.'

And things had moved quickly then and Evie remembers only parts of it – the desperate sucking on the gas, Hamish furiously rubbing her lower back with his knuckles, a nurse inexplicably changing the sheets in the middle of it all. The pain, white-hot and savage like bullets of lava – it's a fallacy that you don't remember it.

When Sera finally moved out of Evie and into the world, Hamish had looked so surprised, so utterly frozen in astonishment, that Evie thought he must have briefly forgotten this is what they had come to deliver: a tiny person, alive and expectant.

He'd thanked her over and over, cradling Evie's head in his arms as Sera was weighed and washed. And when later he held Sera, it was with the purpose of someone who would never, ever be handing over this rare and precious discovery.

Do you ever think about this, Hamish?

Evie was never so naive as to assume such seminal events as a first child being born provided any kind of immunity for a marriage – too often she has seen quite the opposite – but she has lately succumbed to sentimental moments of remembering Sera's birth, Angus's too, as evidence of the love she and Hamish had once shared. It had been real.

Sera's been trying to make it easy for Evie. Whenever her mother has brought up the topic of the upcoming milestone in recent months, she has batted it away. 'I had a fantastic eighteenth, Mum,' she would say. 'I don't need a twenty-first. No one does twenty-firsts anymore. They're so lame.'

But the tone of their more recent conversations has shifted. Evie senses a hint of impatience, even annoyance, on Sera's part that her mother has not been back to Perth since the separation, not once. And Evie has no defence on this front except the usual: work, money, Angus's schooling – the trio of reasons she bundles together to mask the weakness of each on its own.

Perhaps Sera has now worked it out: that Evie's aversion to leaving this place that is not her home, a place she might well have come to on false pretences and still barely knows, has everything to do with her inability to make a move, to call time, to call a lawyer, to call *him*. She'd allowed herself to become willingly stranded, stuck until pushed or pulled. Now Sera was pulling.

'It's harder,' she wants to say to her daughter sometimes, 'so much harder to swim when you can't see the shore.'

Evie's almost always thinking about Sera in the moments before her daughter calls. It's less maternal intuition than Evie's crowded mind, unfinished thoughts left lingering for days like smoke. She's in the car now, having just dropped Angus at the local sailing club, a new interest fostered by Cobie that Evie's actively championing with ready lifts and too many keen questions. Sera's talking quickly and a little loudly today, a sure sign she's about to pitch an idea that will not be up for debate.

'Mum, I know you've always said you'd like to give me money for a big trip for my twenty-first,' she rapid-fires, 'but COVID has kind of crapped all over that.'

'It has,' Evie says and wishes it weren't true, wishes young people could put hopeful pins in the world map and find themselves anywhere the way that she once had. 'For now anyway, but maybe next year …'

'Well, regardless,' Sera continues, sounding unconvinced, 'I've been thinking that all I really want right now is to have all my friends and family together in the same place at the same time. Before the world ends.'

'Oh, Sera,' Evie says and manages to produce a laugh. 'It's not ending.'

'I know that Mum. I was kidding. Or am I? Anyway, I think I've made the decision that I *would* like to have a birthday party this year.'

Evie pulls the car to the side of the road. The motorway is ahead and she realises she's not ready for it.

'Not a huge one or anything,' Sera adds. 'Just my friends and you and Angus and any grown-ups you think should be there. And Dad.'

Evie stares at her dirty windscreen. Can never remember to fill the water thing.

'Of course,' she hears herself say.

'And I'd love it if you could help me organise it. I'm so busy with uni.'

'I'd love to,' Evie says when the words find her.

A still life fills her vision now: a large room of people looking upon a small, fractured group – Sera flanked by Evie and Hamish, and perhaps a fourth person she can't bear to look at. Balloons hugging the roof, threatening to pop.

After a long time Evie moves off, unsure for a minute where she's headed.

16

Evie's trying hard not to look like a person hiding behind a large ice-cream sign but here she is.

On a whim, she'd decided to stay back and see what her son and Cobie actually get up to at the sailing club, where she's dropped them off several Sundays in a row. There's no way Angus would appreciate her being here. He's long been a child who wants no audience and Evie spent many primary school sport carnivals perched behind a tree. But there are no trees close enough to the water here at the marina, so Evie had opted to stand behind the ice-cream sign, a giant fibreglass cone. She knows it probably looks suspicious but also figures that pretty much everything does these days.

That Angus has found an interest outside of his bedroom is cause enough for Evie to be hopeful. That it's something so removed from her own world is frankly exciting. Unlike Hamish, who took great delight in Sera's inherited love of politics, Evie's always wished for her children to see beyond the limits of what any one household exposes a person to. Too many parents want their kids to become quote-unquote better versions of themselves, immortality projects. Evie would be very happy to see them develop into people who might open *her* mind to new things.

Sailing is a long way outside the comfort zone of Evie's own experience. Though she grew up near the water, her parents were not outdoorsy people, nor did they seem to attract them. A trip to the beach was a rare, almost obligatory outing, and she imagines her family must have looked among the most confused and frightened of all those scattered on the sand, which they likely were.

When Evie had once returned from an island camping holiday with a school friend's family, her parents had greeted her at the door as though she might have news from the moon. In fact, as Evie recalls it now here by the ice-cream sign, that camping holiday had also been when she'd first set foot on a catamaran, skippered by her friend. It had capsized on a sharp turn, pitching them both into the ocean, and Evie can't remember now if it was hilarious or terrifying.

Regardless, she's not a ready water-goer. Nor does she have any grasp of the mechanics or physics involved in boat operation. Evie would often look at the hulking iron vessels on the horizon between Fremantle and Rottnest Island and concede to herself that she was far too stupid to understand why they didn't simply sink.

So this. This toe-dip into sailing by Angus is both curious and a little thrilling.

'Mum.' Evie leaps at the voice behind her and spins gracelessly to see Angus. Cobie is beside him. They have orange life jackets on and *God this is embarrassing.*

'Mum, what are you doing,' Angus says, 'besides spying on me?'

'Nothing,' Evie says, leaning casually on the ice-cream sign, which lurches violently towards the ground before righting itself. 'Just spying.'

'Right,' Angus says, stretching the word across several seconds. 'What did you think we'd be doing here ... besides sailing?'

'Nothing,' she says, smiling now at Cobie, who looks generously amused, a much safer option than her son. 'I was just interested to see how it all works, you know, with the water and the boats and everything.'

'You should give it a go, Evie,' Cobie says and then her gaze darts to a spot over Evie's shoulder. 'There's Dad!'

Evie turns around, endeavours to see what Cobie's now pointing to. But there are boats everywhere and the sun off the water is an explosive assault on the eyes.

'There,' Cobie says now, standing at Evie's shoulder and directing her gaze to a sailing boat with a single occupant, James. He is looking skywards, pulling hard at things, wrestling choices. Evie sees a man in a moment of purpose, a long way from everything else. She checks herself for an instant and recognises, of all emotions, envy.

'Your dad sails too?' she says.

Cobie steps forwards a little, as if to see her father more closely. Her face is alight. 'He's the one who got me into it,' she says. 'It's his thing but now I've made it my thing too.'

They watch James for several minutes as his boat draws closer to the long and busy dock. It's a traffic jam down there, vessels of every size and description weaving past each other as though tracing an invisible grid. The dreamy sight of billowy sail tips stroking the sky belies the muscled frenzy fuelling it down below.

Evie's learnt a little about James from Cobie during their recent trips to and from the club, though she's careful not to miff Angus by being too chatty, by being *that* mum. She knows he is a paraplegic with minimal feeling from the waist down, that his injury happened in a car accident seven years ago, that he's a schoolteacher (Bunnings is just a weekend gig, a recent thing), and that his wife, Cobie's mother, now lives in Darwin.

Cobie often calls her dad 'the ninja' because he appears only when he wants to apparently, hiding all the secret movements in between – the transfer from his wheelchair to his car, for example, and the way he gets out of bed each morning. 'He's always up before me,' Cobie says with clear affection, 'even when I set my alarm to beat him.' It's become like a game, she says, in which she's always trying to catch him out – *gotcha!* She thinks it's less about James not wanting her to see him in a particular way and more about how he wants to see himself, which Evie quietly regards as a very clever observation on Cobie's behalf.

Now James sees the girl on the dock and gives her a vigorous wave as the boat slows alongside a pylon. Evie, before she can catch herself, waves back too. Angus looks at his mother as though she's just sprouted leaves of weirdness. 'He was waving at Cobie, Mum,' he says. And Evie knew this, but still. Embarrassment has a much shorter spin cycle than it used to, she's noticed with some relief.

Mindful of Cobie's ninja observation, Evie decides to leave the marina before James has to get out of the boat. She admires this approach of his, if Cobie's interpretation is correct: the manipulation of outwards perceptions to improve our own inner ones. Why not beat the mind at its own games?

She takes one last look at the scene before her – the coastal revelry, the good fortune, a sky shot with every colour. It's possible, Evie has thought of late, to feel a little happy and completely lost at precisely the same time.

17

'Fuck me drunk, Vince, this cream is off. Smell it!'

Ronni pushes a spoon hard at the nose of her husband, who ducks and pivots with expert precision. In the same swift movement, Vince reaches for keys on top of the fridge and heads for the front door of their home, presumably to go and buy cream.

Evie watches the scene, the opera of Ronni's kitchen at mealtime, from a table adjacent to the kitchen. Theatre in the round. The table is piled high with swatches of fabric – Ronni's eldest daughter is making her own dress for the senior formal – and it's making Evie nervous just how close the expensive-looking material is to a large, blackened car part on the same table.

Ronni has three children, two girls and a boy, all of whom Evie has spotted on various hurried missions in the past hour. Francesca, the dressmaker, running out the back door with a towel dripping something wet and purple. Lucia, timing herself to sprint down the hallway with a makeshift baton. Robbie, hurtling out of the kitchen after swiping a bread roll from a basket on the bench dangerously close to his mother's elbow. Ronni had given chase in explosive fashion.

And it's a privilege, Evie thinks now, to witness this as an observer, the lawless whirlwind of a functioning family in motion. The rhythm, or lack of it, that gets every last member through this thing once again – the taunts, the cries, the demands, the accusations. Love in all its forms.

Ronni's family in particular, direct from central casting, makes domesticity look like life itself, not the bits in between. Every exchange seems vital and amplified, kinetic energy on constant display. Colourful but not contrived. Evie may well be a spectator, but none of this seems like a performance. There's simply no self-consciousness on display and no need to feel it herself.

And it's just a small part of the joy she's experienced on several occasions at Ronni's house for dinner now: how little she's required to contribute to simply marvel at its beautiful madness.

Evie's certain her own little family, if still intact, would not have been the same in any onlooker's presence. They would have felt watched. Judged. As though they needed to be funnier, smarter, more irreverent somehow. Just being themselves wouldn't have seemed enough. Hamish especially would have wanted to put on a show of sorts, not necessarily for more attention but to somehow warrant it.

Certainly Evie would never have wished to be watched in her kitchen, a place she's only ever felt comfortable in when all evidence of food preparation is gone, every bench gleaming with relief it's all over. Yet here's Ronni, a whirling dervish of culinary purpose in her engine room, swapping out oven trays and throwing oily tea towels over her shoulder as though she couldn't help it even if she tried.

Evie looks on with wonder, and with gratitude too for this friendship that requires her only to be a depleted version of herself. *Still buffering.*

Vince returns to centre stage with cream. He shows it apprehensively to Ronni, his facial expression indicating he will absolutely go back to the shop again if it's not the right kind. Ronni looks on approvingly then grabs Vince's face in one hand, the hand not holding a large pot, and pulls him to her and her to him at the same time, kissing him hard. He looks to Evie like a man who's always ready for Ronni's kiss.

Many years ago, a whole lifetime, Evie had attended the fiftieth wedding anniversary celebration of Hamish's grandparents. It was an overtly Scottish affair in that most of the men wore kilts (Hamish had to buy one for the occasion) and the accents were laid on thicker than usual. Evie couldn't understand much of what she heard, especially as the well-watered afternoon wore on. A tartan-ribboned cake was finally cut and Hamish's grandfather, ignoring the directions of his wife to 'just sit down for God's sake', shared with the assembled party his secret to long-lasting love.

'It's no' hard,' the old man had said, conspicuously rearranging himself through the front of his kilt as though working on a puzzle. 'You pick one person and you make it work.'

A too-long pause had ensued before the room dutifully applauded. But Hamish's grandfather was not done.

'Because,' he continued, 'you're gonna meet other people, aye?

Better lookin' people. Funnier people. Smarter people. People who can cook better.'

At this point Evie had looked at Hamish's grandmother but she was many miles away, her gaze fixed on something outside the window of the community centre at which they'd gathered.

'People who can drive themselves to the shops, aye?' the advice continued. 'People who can keep a tune. People who don' ruin the ending of the movie. Thinner people ...'

Hamish had wildly gestured for his grandfather to wind it up.

'The point is,' he went on, 'that you've already picked your person. You don't get to pick another person. That's your person. You just have to make it work.'

It was a speech they'd often return to, Evie and Hamish, in those welcome moments of levity that vitally punctuate parenting, in movies that got too mawkish. Hamish would always add a fresh reason in exaggerated Scottish tones, sometimes clearly about Evie ('People who don't snore after drinking too many wines') and often about himself ('People who fart with secret joy') and they would laugh loudly and fall into each other, ever grateful for the clueless honesty of Hamish's grandfather.

But what had seemed so funny, so wildly unromantic, for such a long time had washed up on a different tide. Evie had thought more generously of the curmudgeonly old man in recent years. Perhaps there was something to be said for his idea of enduring resolve, of making the same decision over and over again. Maybe that's all love was, nothing bigger or smaller than that, the only caveat being that all parties remain subscribed to the deal.

Evie looks upon Ronni and Vince in high definition. She would, if prone to gambling, put all her chips on this couple staying the course, not because they had to – though Ronni would likely not give Vince any option – but because it seemed likely they'd both always want to. There was something about the scaffolding they'd erected around themselves that seemed strong enough to outlast the children within it. A whiff of hardened devotion about them.

There won't, Evie imagines, be an awkwardly long period of silence and second-guessing between children and grandchildren trampling these floorboards. No panicked assessment of convenient alternatives and shiny young things as the window hinges slowly stiffen. Just more food and wine and patience and 'Fuck me drunk, Vince!'

She's idealising their relationship, of course, and knows this is fraught. No one really sees what goes on inside a marriage, not even experienced counsellors sifting through the evidence and looking for clues. There is only, Evie knows, what any couple chooses to show people, what they tell people, and what they tell themselves. Rarely do any of these line up.

18

Evie drives home from Ronni's with four plastic containers of leftovers for Angus. If home-cooked food is an expression of love, Ronni loves with her entire pantry. She's never content until everyone at the dinner table is groaning with visible discomfort and begging to be excused. That's amore.

Polo races to meet her at the door, leaping with frantic affection and pretending it isn't about the food. That he isn't in Angus's room suggests to Evie her son is likely at Cobie's again, hopefully not overstaying his welcome or … she doesn't let herself finish the thought.

They've an unspoken agreement, she and Angus, that Evie doesn't go into his bedroom when he's not at home. For her part, it's as much about the smell of too much teen spirit as it is about respecting his privacy. But tonight, for no reason she'd be able to articulate, Evie decides to go in there.

And there are no rude surprises – for example, that it might be tidy and navigable – not at first. But when Evie lifts up a pink jumper (Cobie's?) on Angus's side table, she sees two things that stop her short: the first is a bong and the second is a page full of her son's handwriting, as jumpy and angular as a cardiogram. At the top it reads *To Dad*.

Evie has minimal experience of drug use – the three or four times she was passed a joint during her university years there'd been no discernible effects bar the ones she falsely enacted for onlookers – but she does at least know what a makeshift bong looks like. And it would be a more alarming sight at this moment if not for that page of frenzied writing beneath it.

She should be pleased. Shocked, too, that Angus has clearly taken her advice to write a letter to his father, to get some of what's inside him, if not all of it, *out*. She'd suspected that writing a letter might too closely resemble a school assignment to win Angus's acquiescence. But here it is.

And it should be enough for her to see that he's written it. That he's undertaken this difficult task, either for himself or for Evie. It shouldn't matter to her what the letter contains, what questions or demands Angus is silently working through. These are private labours, much like her own.

But as she stands here now in his room, it all seems to matter. Evie's desperate to know what's going on inside her too-quiet boy, what injuries he might be carrying, how she might tend to them. For she might be doing all of it wrong right now, missing all the signs and hitting all the wrong targets. She might be killing him with her paralysis, this suspended sentence she's put upon them both.

The letter may well be her map out of this.

Read it.

Don't you dare.

Evie's sister had once read her diary, the secret missive she'd started in early high school when everything about life had started to feel big and consequential, strewn with false positives. Her sister, two years younger than Evie, must have found her secret spot. Must have thought there was more going on inside this quiet paper cut-out of a sibling than was being transmitted. She was right.

Young Evie was hiding a boulder in her heart called Jeremy Faulkner. The tall boy in her geography class had set alight an almost painful constellation of new feelings inside her. If not for her diary, where Evie would nightly detail every tiny encounter, real and imagined, she had with Jeremy each day for well over a year, she would surely have imploded under the precious weight of it all.

Her sister had never admitted to the crime, not even as an adult. But when Jeremy came up to Evie one day after class, when he actually *approached her and knew her name*, when he told her that sorry, he didn't like her back and could she please stop riding past his house in the afternoons, then she knew what had happened. And it crushed her even more than his rejection.

It was an unforgivable act, Evie had decided, and fortunately, perhaps predictably, they'd never become close enough to test that conclusion. Evie has long kept her sister well out of striking distance. She's heard from her just once since Hamish left.

Evie looks more closely at Angus's letter now but wills the words to swirl and scramble before her eyes, delaying any sin. She knows the letter is just as private as her diary. As private as any of her counselling sessions. She understands that the only way she could justify reading it would be if she knew for certain it might somehow save her son from doing something dangerous. Something unthinkable.

But do I know that?

What she does know is that boys who are left by their fathers are likely to feel abandoned, overnight unworthy. More likely to linger longer on the sides of bridges, play with metaphorical fires, keep drugs in their room.

It's possible, of course, that Angus doesn't actually feel abandoned at all. Maybe Hamish has been able to assure his son that he took a break only from the marriage, not from his children, that he's forever Angus's father, that he's sorry, that he's coming back fully mended. That there's a really clear explanation for all of this.

How would I know?

Evie tells herself now, looking down at those loaded words *To Dad*, forcing herself not to let even one more word come into focus, that she's been right to give Angus space to work this out for himself. That doing so has saved her son from feeling he has to take a side.

But what would I know? I don't actually know anything at this point.

One line, she decides. She will only read one line.

Evie sees Polo by her feet. A potential witness. She has no idea how long he's been sitting there, how long she's been standing here.

One line.

She hears a noise behind her, from the front of the house.

Angus?

She sees only this before replacing the pink jumper and moving quickly out of Angus's room: *Mum told me I should write to you, so yeah, this is me writing to you.*

19

Hamish had left less than twelve months after they'd landed here, just enough time to hang old pictures on the wall, but not enough to unpack twenty years of boxed miscellany in the garage. Evie looks upon it now: at least a dozen boxes piled to the ceiling, many with multiple removal company stickers on the sides. Domestic detritus or hidden treasure – she's no idea.

Though not a hoarder or even particularly nostalgic, she was loath to throw anything away after Hamish left. And then, after enough time had passed, she'd stopped seeing the boxes at all. Until today.

This morning, a full-wattage spring Saturday empty of plans, she'd woken with a feeling that was something like the resolve to tackle a fresh task. It could just as easily have been procrastination about the teetering pile of unmarked uni assignments on her kitchen table. The garage had beckoned.

And so she's here now on her knees, one of which is threatening to give out any minute, full of arthritis apparently, wearing an old shirt that belonged to Hamish and trackpants that belong to Angus and a bandanna around her hair that shouldn't belong to anyone. It's uncomfortably hot and she would open the garage if the sight of her wasn't likely to offend people walking by.

The first box contains a dinner set wrapped in newspaper. Evie recognises it as the one Hamish's parents had given them as an engagement present. She pushes it to one side: *charity*.

The second, third and fourth boxes are full of papers and books Evie vaguely recognises as having to do with Hamish's PhD thesis, completed soon after they were married. A provocative position on Gough Whitlam's dismissal that had landed him a book deal and his first academic position – the death knell, it transpired, for a political career of his own. Evie had proofread every word.

And what would you like me to do with these now, *Hamish? What's still of value to you?*

She tapes the boxes back up, sets them aside and moves on. A memory lands without warning: Hamish in his mortar board crossing the stage of a vast hall, Evie looking on with his parents, each smoothing away tears. And she's at risk now of crying herself, just fifteen minutes into this bad idea.

Keep going.

Evie quickly opens another box. It's full of loose photographs escaped from albums, sliding in and around each other, jumbling time like a badly plotted movie. Babies and toddlers and dogs and sandcastles and birthday cakes and *no*, she won't be dealing with these today.

Evie hears a doorbell ring close by and realises it's her own.

She'd forgotten the house even had one. She hopes in vain that Angus might climb out of bed to answer it, but finally does so herself, knee locking up as she stands to go.

And it's James in front of her when she opens the door, not the raffle ticket seller or Mormons she'd expected, and this is awful. *I look a mess.*

She says it before he can say anything: 'I look like a mess, James.'

He smiles at her, laughs considerately. Says: 'Not at all. You look like … Saturday morning. What's the BP?'

Evie glances down at shoeless feet, her toenails a cry for help. 'BP?'

'Big Project.'

She pulls the bandanna off her head, instantly realising that might have been a mistake. She didn't look at her hair when she got out of bed and has no idea what's going on up there.

'Sorry, I wasn't expecting … I just. There are all these boxes in the garage.'

'And how's it going so far?' James asks, still smiling.

'Not great.'

'Well, hopefully these will give you a lift,' he says, handing Evie a small box she hadn't noticed sitting on his lap. 'They're chocolates to say thanks for all the mail delivery. I finally got on to the post office. I think the issue should be fixed now.'

Evie looks at the box, neatly wrapped in navy blue paper. She would feel fresh embarrassment if any more of it was possible at this point.

'You shouldn't have done that, James,' she says, 'but thank you.'

'No problem,' he says. 'I hope you like them.'

Evie wonders if he's waiting for her to open the box.

'Do you want to come in for a coffee?' she asks him. Thinks, *But the wheelchair.*

'Sure,' James says, 'that'd be great.'

And he lifts his elbows as if to wheel forwards and Evie isn't sure what to do except open the door wider and step back. James moves easily past her.

Evie steps quickly around him to lead the way to the kitchen. 'I'm sorry, James,' she says, 'I've no idea how wheelchair-proof this house is. I haven't really, um …' And she realises 'proof' was totally the wrong word to use.

'No problem at all,' he says, stopping the chair at the edge of her kitchen bench, which Evie glimpses is probably a little high for him to drink anything with ease. 'These newer homes are all pretty accessible.'

She walks into the kitchen, instantly having no recollection of where or how she makes coffee.

'So I'll make us a coffee and then we can have it at the dining table,' Evie says, hearing now the flutter in her voice. 'Or would you prefer tea? I like coffee but some people prefer tea.'

Ridiculous thing to say.

'Apparently tea is hip again among the cool crowd,' Evie continues, 'although the cool crowd probably don't say "hip".'

Stop. Talking.

'Coffee would be great, thanks,' James says. 'And don't let the wheelchair make you nervous.'

Shit.

'Sorry.'

'Completely fine and normal,' he says, managing not to sound dismissive. 'But honestly, it's just a chair with wheels, entirely overrated as a mode of transport. You stop seeing it after a while, or so Cobie tells me.'

Evie opens the fridge to hopefully find milk – Angus chugs it down faster than she can replace it. She wonders how often James has to make people like her feel better about not having a disability.

'She seems like a lovely girl, Cobie,' Evie says, 'and mature for her age. I'm just so happy Angus has found a friend.'

'You don't think they're having sex?' James asks, and Evie drops the milk onto the floor.

'What?' she says, jumping back from the spillage and reaching for a tea-towel.

James laughs. 'I'm so sorry,' he says. 'It's my worst habit. People get nervous around me and I try to shock them out of it. It's just quicker. I'm sorry – terrible trick. Here, let me clean that up.'

He starts to move the chair into the kitchen, but Evie assures him it's fine. And it is. *It is.* The weird air of Evie's creation has been effectively dispersed. She barely mops up the milk with the towel, leans back against the bench and lets out a breathy laugh.

'That's a neat trick,' she says. 'You could run workshops on that.'

Not so long ago this wasn't an unusual event for Evie: opening the door to a neighbour for a cuppa and a chat. Her Perth neighbourhood was proudly kettle-ready. Even as modish coffee shops and holes-in-the-wall bloomed on every third corner like

109

wildflowers in September, there would be knocks on the door and opening lines like 'So Kristine got those test results back.'

But this sight – James at her dining table, drinking her coffee and awaiting conversation – is unexpected. Jarring, not unwelcome. Evie feels the moment nudging her on the shoulder, willing her to catch up.

This house has been too easy to hide in. The street has looked right past her. Evie must appear, she imagines, like what she is: a person on pause. Unworthy of further inspection. She's as out of practice in the art of neighbourly conversation as she is at jogging. But this should be easier. *I can do this.*

'So why aren't you working today?' Evie asks James, just as he notices in front of him a student's assignment that has loosened itself from the marking pile.

He picks it up and reads aloud: '*The Use of Action Methods to Help Explore and Resolve Personal Blocks to the Counsellor Role.* Well, that sounds intriguing.'

'Less intriguing than you'd think,' Evie says a second or two before she realises he's probably being sarcastic. 'Sorry, it's a first-year unit and it's all very dry. There's a high drop-out rate in the first year because you need to get rid of those kids who think they're modern Dr Phils or who only want to be psychologists because they actually need one.'

'Well, that makes sense,' he says. 'But don't we all need a psychologist? Asking for a friend.'

Evie laughs again and then tastes her coffee for the first time. It is *cold*. Did the kettle even boil? Has she just given this man a cup of undrinkable brown fluid?

'It's lovely,' James says, reading the facial expression that must have just escaped her. 'I hate hot coffee. Honestly. I've never understood why people need to burn the insides of their mouths.'

And he's being very nice, Evie thinks, *because this coffee is well short of tepid.*

'I only work every second Saturday,' James says, returning to her original question. 'They like to give the young ones most of the weekend hours, which is completely fine with me.'

At that moment Polo flies into the room, frantic paws slipping on the tiles in his haste to get to Evie's side.

'Ahh,' says James, 'that looks like a dog who's happy with his own door.'

Polo starts leaping up on the wheel of James's chair. Evie's certain he will shortly wee with excitement.

'Sorry,' she says – and there it is again, the apologising – 'he's quite mad. Still very much in the puppy phase.'

'No problem at all.' James laughs. 'Most receptive audience I've had in a while.'

Much like Ryan, James is a natural at chatting, someone who acts as though every person is a vessel of infinite interest. Evie wishes she had more to offer. She also wonders if all those years of counselling have permanently ruined her conversation game, that she's far more comfortable asking questions than answering them.

And there's also the fact that she's sitting here looking like a pile of laundry while James appears ready for a Country Road shoot. That's not helping either.

But an hour slips by unnoticed, during which time Evie makes a better fist of the coffee-making and Polo does in fact wee with excitement. At one point Angus appears from his bedroom, does a messy double-take and hastily retreats in a cloud of pungent air.

Evie learns that James still teaches at the local high school part-time – politics, history and English. The Bunnings gig is just to supplement his income until a full-time position becomes available but they're rare in his department and he'd prefer not to change schools.

He tells her about his injury, though not because Evie asks. It's a quick summary that seems well practised, designed for the listener's curiosity and comfort, devoid of any implicit emotional trauma.

'I was in a car that hit a kerb and left the road,' he says. 'The seatbelt failed and the only thing I remember about the accident is looking up at a tree, hearing my back break, and thinking, Shit. Paralympics.'

Evie laughs politely because it's clear James wants her to. She can only imagine what he's really been through to reach this point of apparent equanimity, the many deals he's had to make with himself, the dark rooms he's sat in.

She wants to share something significant, something honest, in return, but what? What is there? Evie doesn't tell him about Hamish, about the reason she's stranded here in this street, in this chapter of suspended time. (But neither does James say anything about his wife, so maybe these are the rules of engagement.)

She does share with him that she used to be a relationships counsellor, that she's now teaching psychology units at the university, that lately she's developed a habit of kneejerk apologising. And she tells him about Sera, the fact she's about to turn twenty-one and how this more than anything – more than arthritic knees and insomnia and the inability to find any new music she can bear listening to – has made Evie realise that more than half her life has vanished.

'Age is just a number, Evie,' James says with a smile. 'An enormous number.'

Evie laughs. But she's also keen to pursue this point – it's been on her mind.

'I actually think I just wasn't ready for this stage of life,' she admits, for the first time to someone other than herself. 'I feel like it arrived before I could prepare for it and now I'm scrambling. Like I missed a whole big section of time when I was technically young.'

James gently lifts Polo off his lap and onto the floor. Evie hadn't even noticed that the dog had at some point taken this liberty.

'You know what?' he says. 'You should come sailing sometime. It's impossible to feel old on a boat. There's something age-defying about it.'

'Does it come in a jar too?' Evie smiles.

She suddenly remembers to retrieve James's gift-wrapped box from the kitchen and insists he stay to share at least a few of the artisan chocolates inside. And she realises that she's got through this somehow, this unexpected morning with a near stranger in her home. It's been so enjoyable, so much easier than she might have imagined, that Evie knows she won't be going back into the garage today; nor will that pile of marking be getting any love from her. It's a day for the beach.

At her front door, Evie thanks James again for the chocolates and for kindly ignoring her unkempt appearance.

'Oh I didn't ignore it,' he says and winks at her. 'It was impossible to ignore.'

A wink.

'And I'm serious about coming sailing,' James says over his shoulder as he wheels down the front path leading to the driveway.

20

Gideon and Lelia

Shame was an unfamiliar emotion to Gideon. He was a man wilfully prone to confidence, viewing it as an inevitable consequence of success, an aspirational state of being. The men he most admired were arrogant, and so they should be. You didn't get to this floor of the high-rise unless you were breathing different air.

So this unwelcome condition, *shame*, was one he hadn't yet got his head around. He hadn't even landed on the word itself in his many attempts to explain to Evie what he had done. The closest he'd come was in their fourth counselling session when he said, 'I guess I must have been much drunker than I thought.'

Lelia, Gideon's wife of twenty-seven years and mother to their four children, was able to be much more specific: 'He had sex with a prostitute and gave me genital warts.'

What Gideon *was* adept at articulating to Evie was his love for Lelia. It was, he said – and Evie had believed him – honest and absolute. He adored his wife, always had. It was a love that had only grown and deepened with time, the envy of his friends. They still made love (or had until recently), still holidayed together, still surprised each other in large and small ways. Lelia still looked to Gideon like the most arresting woman in any room.

So this. This thing that had happened … it made no sense. And now he was scared, a feeling as equally foreign to him as shame.

One of the many misconceptions about infidelity is that there has to be something fundamentally wrong in a relationship for it to occur. Sometimes – long-term emotional affairs notwithstanding – there may be just opportunity and weakness. Uncharacteristic idiocy. A large, significant fuck-up.

When Evie suggested this to the couple, she hit two walls. The first was that Gideon couldn't conceive of himself as someone who would make a large, significant fuck-up. The second was that Lelia didn't know if she was someone who could forgive one.

It was a position in which neither of them had expected to find themselves. This was not *them*. A thirty-year relationship pushed cliffwards by a drunken night of corporate wheeling that had ended in the backroom of a karaoke bar in Singapore. A night Gideon insisted he couldn't remember.

If not for the smoking gun, the one that required an expensive cream and regular check-ups, would Gideon have admitted anything? Would he have had no cause to rifle back through memories so unclear as to be entirely unreliable, inadmissible in any court of law? Was it the only time he'd been unfaithful? How could Lelia know? How would she ever *know*? The dark jungle of Gideon's work life could hide anything.

Each question for the couple carried new ones – spider sacks full of fresh danger. They were stuck in a holding pattern, running out of fuel.

Evie tried to help Lelia arrive at her line in the sand: what was she prepared to accept as truth? Only from there could the much bigger question be turned over for inspection: could she forgive Gideon with enough purpose to move on?

Most people think they know what they're prepared to accept and forgive within a relationship. Most have their own firm ideas about what constitutes infidelity – that point along the spectrum between watching porn and an intense emotional affair complete with secret children. But as Evie had seen many times, these suppositions can blow up in the face of real transgression.

Of herself, she'd long suspected she wouldn't tolerate either a physical or emotional betrayal on Hamish's part, but equally she couldn't imagine the situation ever occurring. Evie was, by her own admission (and in spite of all her professional wisdom), quietly confident about the fortitude of her marriage. She figured any other approach might invite an entirely different problem.

Gideon was not only purposefully arrogant; he was transparently impatient. He demanded assurances from Evie that this painful tempest the couple had thrown themselves into in the form of counselling would ultimately yield positive results. 'Because obviously,' he'd said to her quite emphatically, 'this can't go on forever.' The man stopped just short of asking for a money-back guarantee.

Evie was measured in her response. Many relationships, she told Gideon, emerge from infidelity in a stronger position than they were before the event, often with deeper levels of intimacy and renewed commitment. Many do not. Counselling could prove the difference, shaping the difficult conversations that needed to happen so they were constructive rather than destructive, but there were simply no guarantees.

Gideon had looked out the window as though doing a few quick mental calculations on a pale Perth sky.

Evie had known another couple, old friends, not clients, who broke up because of an indiscretion that had happened fifteen years earlier. Holly had been pregnant at the time. Kent had been selfish and scared and stupid, as had the woman he'd slept with for six months. They'd buried the entire agonising episode under metres of promise, under an entire paddock of regret and remorse, under two more children. But it transpired they'd simply buried a time capsule that would one day have to be opened.

'It's best to do the work,' Evie had said to Gideon, 'even if it only shows that you care enough to do it.'

21

Evie has visited Angus's school twice since they moved here – once to buy uniforms at the very start, before Hamish left, and today. There's been no need to come here at any other time, nor would Evie have felt particularly welcome either by Angus or the staff. Unless your kids are winning awards or performing to captive assemblies, high schools are no place for parents. With the same fervour she'd thrown up her hand for canteen duty and reading time at the kids' primary schools, Evie has respected the ring fence around senior education.

But today she's here at the request of the year twelve coordinator, a woman called Ms Keenan. Angus doesn't know about the meeting, which Ms Keenan discreetly organised out of school hours. She'd simply said, in a quick phone call to Evie that had robbed her of decent sleep for the next two days, that she'd like to have a chat about Angus.

Even though Evie had left work early to get here, she finds she's now cutting it fine. Prior knowledge of the school's layout is clearly assumed – there's little signage to speak of and Evie is quickly lost in a sprawling tangle of walkways and buildings spanning several eras of origin. Angus must have found this overwhelming, she thinks now, as the school is maybe twice as big as the one he attended in Perth, but at least it had been his choice. Hamish hadn't pushed his own school preference upon Angus this time, perhaps quietly recognising his limitations as a school-chooser.

And Angus had seemed to like it, in so much as he didn't say it sucked. He didn't protest about going each morning like he had in Perth. He wasn't pulling his hair out to lance the pain. His only complaint was that it was boring, but Evie expected and even endorsed this view, having long felt the traditional school system hopelessly misunderstands most kids, especially boys.

Finally she locates Ms Keenan's office, an afterthought of a room at the back of the library. Evie apologises for being both late and out of breath but Ms Keenan happily ushers her in and offers her a seat at the corner of her desk, a tiny city of paper towers.

Ms Keenan – *call me Kate* – is a small-boned woman with bright hopeful eyes and a streak of blue in her cropped hair. She could be older or younger than Evie – it's not something she can readily pick these days, having no real sense of how old she looks herself. There's a framed photograph on the windowsill of a family – three children arranged in size like Russian dolls, a very tall man in a Hawaiian shirt and Kate looking far less burdened than she does right now. Beside the photo is a trophy shaped like a tennis racquet and an ornamental Buddha. Evie feels that jolt of surprise, apparently timeless, that teachers are people too.

'I hope my call didn't alarm you,' Kate begins, reaching up to remove a pair of reading glasses hiding in her hair, 'because there's nothing to be immediately concerned about. I just thought I'd touch base with you about how Angus is going.'

Evie adjusts the handbag in her lap, suddenly aware she might not have all the answers to any questions Kate puts to her today. The space she'd been giving Angus to heal, to simply be, could have made room for all sorts of new problems about which she has no idea. She thinks of the bong, whole days spent in his bedroom, tips of possible icebergs. Maybe she's doing no better at parenting than even Hamish is at this point.

'Angus is in my English class,' the teacher continues, 'and he's a good student – quiet and attentive. Always polite. You've done a good job there.'

Evie swallows a pop of air that wants to come straight back up. *Here it comes.*

'Recently we had a class assessment where the students had to write a letter of complaint to get some sort of fair result – a refund for faulty goods, for example,' Kate says.

Oh God, the letter.

'Angus wrote a letter to his father and it was very … Well, I felt particularly moved when I read it because it was clearly from Angus's own experience, from his heart. He's evidently feeling a lot of anger and confusion about his father leaving.'

'Yes,' says Evie, noticing her throat thicken, her eyes starting to cloud. 'I did encourage him to write that letter but I didn't know he'd submit it at school. I just thought it would be a way for him to get out some of his feelings. He hasn't really made those clear to me.'

Kate deftly hands Evie a tissue and the very act of kindness makes her start to cry. *God, again?* Last week she'd wept in a thirty-second TV ad for pet insurance.

'I think it was a wonderful idea,' Kate reassures her, 'and like I said, there's nothing to be alarmed about with Angus. He's a terrific kid and he's working things out. I just thought ... can I be really frank with you?'

Evie nods.

'We've had two senior students attempt to take their lives this year and that's ... unprecedented,' Kate says, pausing a moment to take in a slow and deliberate breath. 'And the conversations I'm having with my contemporaries at other schools ... there's something going on. Like a wildfire of despair. And my job ... I should be seeing it better than I have been. It's right under my nose. It's in everything these kids say or don't say, in what they write. I'm trying to look harder.'

Now Kate reaches for another tissue and Evie sees a single tear suspended in the woman's eyelash. She dabs it away and smiles at Evie, then shrugs at her kindly as if to say *Life, right?*

'I'm trying to be more observant with our students,' she continues. 'I'm trying to see warning signs and then head things off at the pass. Sometimes that means having these difficult conversations with parents.'

'But that's a lot of pressure to put on yourself,' Evie says. 'Often the warning signs aren't there – they don't want us to see them.'

And she's thinking now about a couple she saw maybe four

years ago in Perth, their lives razed by a child's suicide. A bright child, roundly liked and self-motivated. Anger had kept the couple together at first, united them in causes of fury and public advocacy, but when that fire had burnt out, their grief lost its centre. They were left only with hollow questions. Unspeakable blame. What did we miss? What did *you* miss?

Evie suddenly wonders if Angus's letter might be here somewhere on Kate's desk, one innocuous sheaf swimming in the paper ocean. She pictures herself grabbing it and sprinting from the room.

'That's true,' Kate says, 'and I'm not suggesting Angus has given off any warning signs anyway, only that he seems sad. Troubled. Sometimes when I raise a concern with a parent, it's the first they've heard about it. But I can see that's not the case here, so that's good.'

Kate pauses here, rubbing a coffee stain on the desk with an inky thumb that only adds to its prominence. Her shoulders, Evie now notices, are perched high and possibly locked that way after years of teaching with a chest full of hope and concern.

'We're on the same page then,' the teacher continues and then starts nodding determinedly as though she's just now decided to back herself, 'and we can let each other know if anything else comes up. It's easier now that we've met.'

'I very much appreciate it,' Evie says, thinking that it's not schools that are good or bad or progressive or otherwise. It's the people within them.

She leaves Ms Keenan's overstuffed envelope of an office and somehow finds her way back to the carpark with none of the disorientation she'd experienced in reverse. It's been completely displaced with fresh worry over Angus.

Sad. Troubled.

Of every thought she's had about Hamish since he left, every feeling that's had nowhere to go, this one is the hardest to make sense of, for Evie's never felt angrier with her husband than she does right now and she's also never missed him more in her life.

~

She takes the long way home. Evie has four preferred 'thinking drives' now, but this is her favourite – a zig-zag sweep of the coast, in and out, in and out between the ocean and the bush, as back and forth between landscapes as any addled mind can absorb.

The initial panic she'd felt after leaving Ms Keenan's office has started to dissipate. If anything, Evie is grateful that someone else is looking out for her boy too. And the teacher hadn't told her anything she didn't already know about Angus: that Hamish's leaving has clearly unsettled him. What Evie hadn't closely considered until now is how important it might be for Angus's wellbeing to physically see Hamish again.

Where are you?

She's thinking about how to broach a fresh conversation with Angus about his father when Sera calls. Her daughter is loud and animated, careening across small talk to get straight to her key messages.

'So, Mum, I've been thinking lots about the party – dates and themes and venues and everything,' she says, each word riding roughshod over the next. 'I'm actually getting quite excited about it now. It's been a tough year so, yeah, this is something good to look forward to … for all of us.'

'It is,' Evie says and winces a little with guilt. She hasn't really had a sense of how difficult things have been for Sera, not just because of the many filters her daughter places over life, but also because Evie has been five thousand kilometres away tending her own wounds.

'I think the final weekend in November might be good,' Sera says, 'provided we're not locked down or anything. Angus will be finished school and you'll be finished teaching and it's close enough to my actual birthday, so what do you think?'

It's one of Sera's most admirable traits that, for all her self-purpose, she seldom neglects to factor the rest of the family's needs into her plans. Evie replies quickly to avoid sounding hesitant: 'I'll check flights but yes, that should be fine, love.'

'And I'm thinking we could have it at that restaurant where we had Dad's fortieth, because you can hire out the whole place and shift the tables for dancing later in the night – what do you think?'

'Sounds perfect,' Evie responds. And she pictures Hamish cutting his birthday cake now, a homemade croquembouche that had threatened to topple over at any moment.

'And so,' Sera goes on, 'here's the really cool thing – the theme.' *Please, no theme.* 'I'm thinking the year 2000, so people can come as pretty much anything attached to that year. Cool?'

'Yes,' Evie agrees, 'that might be fun.' She's bracing herself for what she suspects is coming next.

Sera doesn't make her wait. 'Also,' she says, 'Dad says he's coming to the party. So, yeah. Okay then.'

Evie looks hard at her hands on the steering wheel. Old hands. The hands of someone who gave birth in 2000.

Say something. Find words.

'Okay,' Evie manages and swallows hard, trying to flatten the sudden inflection in her voice. 'I'll start to think about costumes.'

22

James had been very specific about the details for this morning – where to park, what to bring and, most importantly, what time to arrive. 'There's a small window,' he'd said to her, 'between the fishermen leaving and the clubbies arriving – it's your only chance of getting a park.' Evie preferred to be early for most things in life, but she'd compliantly followed his advice.

She finds a park easily enough, her small car diminished further by the herd-like SUVs in every direction. The air outside is dense with fish scent, tempered by salt and engine oil, and it must be just the right combination because Evie finds it weirdly pleasant.

She's wearing knee-length white shorts (barely a paint swatch paler than her post-winter legs), a long-sleeved cotton shirt and the only hat she could find, headwear being an accessory she's never been able to pull off. 'You look like a person trying to wear a hat,' Hamish had once said when Evie had paraded a floppy woven thing bought at a market.

Following James's directions, Evie heads to the jetty directly adjacent to the marina office. There's a touch panel at the side of a tall metal gate and Evie enters the code he gave her, trying not to look like a person clearly in possession of someone else's code, as foreign to this habitat as a fish in a forest.

The gate obliges and Evie assumes the walk of a person on a jetty, deciding this should probably be a mix of confident and casual, of someone not-quite-but-almost walking on water. She heads all the way to the end, past vessels of every shape and description, Meccano sets of steel and canvas. Even the smallest ones have names, Evie notices, and she slows a little to read them, each a clue about whatever hole is being filled in someone's life. Most are women's names – wives, daughters, mistresses – but there is also *I Told You So* and *Lucky Escape* and *This Time With Feeling*. Every boat a story.

She arrives at *Sans Serif*, the boat James told her to look for, and she sees him on board, his back to her inside a console area. A wheelchair sits discarded on the dock. Evie wonders now if James's explicit instructions about her arrival time were less about parking availability and more about her not seeing him get onto the boat. *The ninja.*

She's about to yell hi when James turns around and sees her. He beams at Evie, a smile as big as the day. His curls have been displaced by a white sailor's cap. He has on a navy blue polo shirt and dark wraparound sunglasses and all of it, the deep tan included, might look contrived if it didn't look so effortless.

'You made it,' James says. 'How beautiful is it?' He waves his arm in an arc across the sky, the sun, the water, all of it.

'It's amazing,' Evie says, and it really is. The sun has spilled all its shiny innards on the water today, a sheet of silver beneath a vast blue dome. 'It's a perfect day to fall overboard.'

James laughs but Evie quickly realises she may have just offended him.

'And it won't be because of you,' she adds. 'It'll be my lack of sea legs, whatever they are.'

Legs! Stop.

'You'll be absolutely fine,' James says and issues a wink as though to reassure her either that she hasn't offended him or that she's not going to die today. 'Now let's get you on board.'

James talks Evie through a quick series of manoeuvres to best spirit her from dock to boat – a hand here, a step there, a mind-your-head – and it sounds like a list he's committed to memory and it works perfectly. She takes a seat on the padded square just behind and to the side of him, tucking her feet under her as there's really no other place to put them. It doesn't seem like a boat meant for a human throw-rug of admiring guests – more a self-against-world style of vessel.

'Welcome aboard,' James says, handing Evie a life jacket. 'She's nothing fancy but she's got a big heart.'

'And what about the boat?' Evie says, wending her arms into the jacket. James laughs and does something that appears to start an engine. The wood panelling beneath them begins to loudly hum and shake and Evie finds herself momentarily startled, as though it's happening too quickly. Shouldn't there be a safety demonstration? *Where are the exits?*

'She's called a folkboat,' James tells her as the vessel starts to move away from the jetty, presumably at his behest. Evie watches the narrow strip of water beside them start to expand, dissipating her second thoughts. She has no idea how any of this works and realises there's a measure of delight in that abandon.

Folkboats, he tells her, are of the Nordic imagination. The Scandinavian Yacht Racing Union ran a competition in 1942, in the midst of World War II, to come up with a boat design that was low cost, easy to sail and 'for the people', the very antithesis of any war vessel. There was no clear winner – instead, six or seven promising entries were ultimately combined to create the single-mast folkboat.

'It was classic Swede neutrality,' James says, 'and one of the few examples of good design via committee. Isn't she beautiful?'

'She is,' Evie says, unsure what an ugly boat might look like.

The boat isn't his, not entirely. James co-owns it with another man, Lenny, also with paraplegia, who completely modified the vessel to take it on long solo voyages throughout the Pacific. 'I'd read about him in the local paper soon after my accident,' James says. 'You read all the rousing stories about people overcoming disability. People are practically throwing them under your nose the minute you're in a spinal ward. But this one really caught my attention.'

Evie removes her hat now, wanting to feel the sun on her skull. 'Why this story?' she asks.

James leans back a little and his shoulders briefly settle for a moment. He appears to consider her question carefully.

'Lenny just sounded so single-minded about his purpose,' he says, 'which was simply to get back on the sea, back to what he loved. He didn't talk about walking again or miracle cures or spiritual journeys. None of that stuff. He's inspirational because he doesn't care about being inspirational. He's just making the best of a shitty deal. That kind of spoke to me at the time.'

Evie nods understandingly and shuts her eyes, her vision already seduced by the bright water. 'I've often wondered,' she admits, 'if people with disabilities are offended when others call them inspirational. There must be so many things that people like me do and say that piss them off. Piss *you* off.'

James laughs. 'You'd have to get up very early to offend me, Evie,' he says and turns his head to smile directly at her. 'But seriously, I think it's like everything in life – it comes down to the person. Some disabled people *are* inspirational, they really are. They *want* to be. They do incredible things and devote all their time to busting myths and breaking down barriers. They're bloody awesome humans. But even many of them, especially those who weren't born with *this* –' James directs his gaze accusingly at his knees '– would trade being inspirational for being able to walk or talk or see again.'

'Of course,' Evie says, feeling now like her counsellor self rather than a friend, yet she doesn't want to. 'I can see that.'

A too-long pause follows, in which time Evie wonders whether she should change the subject completely or double down. 'So,' she says finally, 'how did you end up meeting Lenny?'

'It was about a year after I got out of hospital,' James says, the strengthening breeze now whipping his curls around his neck. 'I woke up one morning feeling marginally less suicidal than I had every other morning, and it was a stunning day just like this one, the sort of day when you think *surely* only good things can happen today. I came down here to the marina and a helpful woman at the office led me down to Lenny's berth. And he and I sat on the boat like this and talked for hours. It was like he'd been waiting for me.'

'Maybe he had,' Evie says. 'Who knows how life works?'

James smiles generously at Evie. 'Exactly,' he says, 'who knows? At any rate, Lenny and I became good friends and when he ran into some money issues a couple of years ago, I offered to pay him a monthly co-owner fee so he wouldn't have to sell the boat. That's part of the reason I got the extra Bunnings work. These things aren't cheap to keep.'

'But worth it, I imagine.'

'Absolutely,' James says. 'I never feel less than myself out here. The sea doesn't judge, not even when I say wanky things like the sea doesn't judge.'

Evie laughs. She's been watching him closely as they talk. There's a tranquil rhythm to his constant movement at the helm, a practised vigilance. His gaze moves in successive glances from the front of the boat to the horizon, sidewards to Evie, then back again to the front of the boat. James clearly wants her to enjoy this and Evie realises that she is and also that she hadn't expected to. As soon as the lapping water coats her face in mist, the hot sun drinks it up. Sounds of fading engines and gulls and the sea work hard to push away thoughts. The rushing air now reminds her of a forgotten sensation: yelling joyously into a pedestal fan as a child. It's a welcome assault of elements and sensations, messy and disruptive and intoxicating.

Place, Evie thinks. We underestimate it, how much we are different people in every place. Context isn't just a backdrop or a photo filter. It enters our pores. It changes how we see things. Here on the water, relieved of any responsibility but to simply soak it all in, she finds she's feeling her most benevolent self, scrubbed clean of worry and keen to make it so for others. She is – however fleeting and false the feeling may prove to be – a woman moving forwards today, face to the sun and heart to the sky. She would do anything for anyone, even herself.

And maybe, Evie thinks, pulling herself back now and casting her eyes to the shore, it was this power of place that had somehow changed Hamish upon moving here. Maybe he'd felt instantly different – untethered and untested. Maybe he wasn't himself when he'd left her, just a product of too much bright light and newness. Maybe he was the happiest he'd ever been and she simply wasn't keeping up. Maybe he'd felt lost. She wishes right now she could ask him, just to know, just to understand. She wishes she didn't need answers when there might be none.

Maybe I don't.

'You okay?'

James's voice reaches Evie. She looks to him just as a rogue spray of water launches into the boat and wets both of them, making her laugh. 'Never better,' she says.

23

Tony and Farida

The skin specialist who would regularly check Evie for errant moles probably knew the landscape of her body better than anyone, better than Hamish. Yet he always seemed unnerved by the intimacy of the exercise, self-conscious enough for both of them, and while it bemused Evie at times, watching him cast twitching eyes to the wall when she rolled over, she didn't and couldn't judge.

As a counsellor given licence to sift through her clients' lives, she nevertheless felt cautiously uneasy about discussing their sexual interactions. It wasn't that Evie was prudish (though prudish people, she knows, seldom think they are), but more that she was acutely aware of just how personal it can and should be, this most raw and biological way people communicate with each other. The best and worst things in life are the hardest to talk about.

At the same time, sex is seldom isolated from a couple's issues, even for those who insist it's 'still good' even while everything else about their relationship is burning down. It's the same for those who claim to be very much in love with each other and are yet unhappily sexless. There's something there, tucked inside the unmarked box in the attic, that must at some point be removed and inspected. For damage. For clues.

Evie's approach was always to wait for a couple to raise any sexual intimacy issues rather than unsettle them with a question that might abruptly shut a door. She didn't have to wait long with Tony and Farida.

Farida had first seen Evie on her own. She'd balanced precariously on a corner of the cushioned chair in the Cottesloe room, her legs in a race position as though ready to bolt for the door. Farida admitted she'd never seen a counsellor before and wasn't sure if it was for her but she'd also run out of whatever it took to sustain denial and distraction.

'He doesn't want to have sex with me,' Farida had said, her shoulders collapsing as though the declaration had landed on her from above. 'It's been three years now.'

She was not quite forty years old – a real estate agent and weekend triathlete. She appeared, Evie thought, like an old-world Egyptian beauty scooped into a trouser suit, a neatly cultivated look that may well have been more armour than aesthetic.

She'd first discovered Tony's pornography habit by accident when working from home after having their second child. The house computer had started to falter and Farida called a local techie to call by and pick it up for repair. When he returned a couple of days later, the techie had apologised that in rebuilding the hard drive, he'd had to remove a lot of big files, 'especially the videos'. Confused, Farida pressed him on this until he finally said, looking warily at his shoes as he did so, 'You might want to ask your husband.'

Farida did, and Tony's reply had been that, sure, he sometimes downloaded the odd adult movie when he couldn't sleep or needed a stress release. 'Like pretty much every guy in the Western world,' he'd said dismissively.

And Farida had let it go then, but not completely. When Tony had started finding constant excuses – all of them connected to sleep and stress – not to have sex with her, not to even respond to a suggestive touch, not to notice when she'd gone to the 'frankly embarrassing' effort of parading lingerie that she'd felt quite mortified buying and had no adequate facial expression to accompany, Farida pushed the issue again.

This time Tony was indignant, defensive of behaviour that he said was 'perfectly normal', not something he should have to feel dirty about. He loved her, he said, as anyone with eyes could tell. He would never be unfaithful to her – watching porn was a habit, not a betrayal. Most couples were lying about how much sex they had, he said.

This flight to anger rather than admission of any sort had so bruised Farida (and plunged Tony into weeks of obstinate sulking) that she hadn't dared go there again. Instead, she'd gone within herself, she told Evie. She'd tried to better occupy the other parts of her life, the ones that didn't make her feel unwanted – family, friends, work, exercise – until the lie needed rebooting again. Until three whole years had gone by. Until she'd needed to tell someone, a professional, who could test her pain for validation.

Tony had run the same furious lines with Evie when he joined the next counselling session. Arms folded in seething consternation, he didn't even try to conceal his unhappiness about having to sit in a room and talk about his actual sex life, or the lack of it, with a prying stranger. Evie assured him there would be no judgement, only discussion that might help each of them better understand the other's position.

In her first decade of counselling, Evie had never worked with a couple whose central issue was an apparent porn addiction. In the past five years they'd walked through her door with alarming regularity. Either social recognition of the term itself was setting off lightbulbs in quiet bedrooms or the online evolution of pornography had turned occasional habits into brain-altering problems as effectively as putting cocaine into toothpaste.

It took several sessions, each of them as strained as the next, before Tony stopped pushing back against the term 'problem' (though he still rankled at 'addiction'). When he was finally prepared to spell out the scope and shape of his porn viewing activity to Farida, even Evie had found it difficult to hide her shock. That any person could maintain a normal physical relationship while at the same time consuming such vast amounts of graphic, emotion-less, often violent sexual material seemed patently impossible. The disruption of reality was too profound.

It helped Farida to hear Tony walk back through the origins of his obsession, if at least to see that the man she'd married had indeed been who she thought he was. He hadn't been a porn-obsessed young man, merely curious and a little relieved that even when he felt his most alone and unloved, there'd been an outlet of satisfaction

– a sated woman who seemed to be looking right at him. As with any pleasant experience, he'd started to want more. He'd started to want better. Dependence eats itself.

And he hadn't lied about any of it to Farida, Tony assured Evie, only the scale. He'd never been unfaithful with another real person. He'd never viewed his habit as a betrayal. He still loved his wife intensely and the thought of losing her was unimaginable. But yes, the sex between them had become ... a problem for him. And he was sorry, so very sorry it had come to this.

At this point, at Farida's breakthrough and Tony's end of the line, Evie had referred the couple to a quietly reputable service in Perth that specialised in treating porn and sex addictions. There was work to be done now, she told them, more than just talk. Especially for Tony. Sex could be harder to disempower than heroin. She'd felt like an anxious parent waving off the bus for school camp.

Cases like this had always given Evie cause to look upon her own marriage with fresh scrutiny. Did she and Hamish have the sex life she thought they had? Was it enough for him? Enough for her? And if it wasn't, how would they know? What was the midlife sweet spot between passionate and perfunctory?

Being able to talk about these things with other couples didn't necessarily make it any easier for Evie to have the difficult conversations within her own marriage. If anything, being a counsellor made it less likely. Eyes that look too hard can burn holes.

24

'Sailing?'

'Yes.'

'On a *boat*?'

'Yes.'

'But ... *why*?'

Ronni is looking at Evie now as though she might have gone quite mad since they last caught up, as though she'd just told her she was becoming a professional roller-skater or getting a perm.

'Because it's something different,' Evie says, 'and, you know, relaxing.'

'*Relaxing*?' Ronni almost yelps. 'How can putting your life in danger be relaxing?'

'How is it dangerous?'

'Evie, swimming is one thing,' she says, '*also* dumb but a thing, but if humans were meant to move *over the top of* water, then—'

'We'd have used our brains to invent boats?'

Ronni's hands are now flying in every direction. 'Just because something is *invented* doesn't make it a good idea,' she says. 'Waxing! The internet! What about cricket, all those good-for-nothing uomini standing around all day, too lazy to even get their own drinks?'

'Women play cricket too now.'

'What? *Why?*'

'Anyway, I was in very good hands,' Evie reasons. 'James is an experienced sailor and I didn't feel unsafe even for a second.'

Ronni's facial features appear to cease moving all at once. Finally she speaks with uncharacteristically careful deliberation: 'James. With no legs?'

'Ronni, he has legs.'

'But they don't *work*,' she says. 'How can he do … boat things?'

'His boat is modified so he only needs to use his upper body. It's actually very impressive to watch – he's very skilled.'

And now Ronni does the thing she normally does when in danger of being nudged beyond a view she's already carved out of rock. She side leaps to a tangential topic and drowns all previous logic in an amusing anecdote.

'Cruising,' she says. 'So stupido. My older brother, the one I told you about with the back hair shaped like a crucifix? His wife got him into cruises. That's what happens when you marry an American. They want big everything. Big hair, big bums, big cars. So she says to him, "Matteo, we need to go on a really *big* boat, too big to even float, okay? With big bars and big pools and big people who eat all day."'

'That's what she said?'

'Of course. And my brother? Evie, he came home from their first cruise like a man who had been *brainwashed*. Entire brain, *washed.* It could have been one of those Scientology cruises – I've only just thought of that. He's like "Ronni, it's so amazing! You can play poker all night, you can swim, you can dance, you can watch the sun set!" And I said, "Matteo, name one of those things that you can't do on land. Where you won't *drown.*" He couldn't name *one.* Not one. Are you getting a thing for James?'

'*What?*'

'James with no legs.'

'He has legs.'

'Are you attracted to him?'

'I don't know. I admire him.'

'*Well.*'

'*Well.*'

'Plus it just takes one person to get sick on a cruise ship and then it's vomit island. That's how the whole pandemic started! Bats on a boat.'

What?

Ronni's question was not so different from the one Evie had asked herself driving home from the marina that day. Was it admiration or attraction she'd felt for James out on the water? They were symbiotic states and hard to separate, plus she no longer trusted herself to identify any strong emotion in a line-up.

At any rate, she's pleased to be here today, at her favourite corner table in Le Cose Semplici. It's the mid-semester break at uni and it couldn't have come soon enough. The past eight weeks at work have been rough, with Evie's teaching load crowded out by an unprecedented number of personal health issues among her students. One by one they've come to her, if not in person then via long desperate emails (the last lines of these usually reading *Can I please have an extension?*), about broken hearts and abusive partners and panic attacks and suicidal thoughts. Though she's obligated to refer them to the university's counselling service, Evie also feels compelled to respond personally and thoughtfully, to show them the compassion and understanding that underpins all that she teaches and is, regardless, who she is. It requires an enormous amount of time, all of it as vital as it is finite.

She's not alone in this contested space of both teaching counselling and essentially providing it for the same audience. It's a daily topic of discussion in her department's lunchroom. As one colleague said last week, when the world had finally opened its doors to talking openly about mental health issues, the world wildly underestimated the queue that would form. That counselling has become one of the nation's biggest growth industries is hardly cause for celebration even among those whose jobs rely on growing student numbers. And even with more counsellors hitting the ground and more public money being spent on advocacy, there remains this inconvenient truth: all the bad numbers are going up. Depression. Anxiety. Self-harm. Suicide. The conversations are happening but Evie worries they're the wrong ones.

Ironically, her decision to switch from counselling to teaching when they'd left Perth had been driven by a desire for less after-hours stress in her work. But lately Evie has started to miss her little Cottesloe room and its safe containment of mangled hearts and promises torn asunder.

None of this is the right material for a Ronni conversation, at least not today, which is welcome relief. Evie's enjoying her second coffee this morning as her friend finishes her fourth or fifth. The coffee shop is a fuss of chatter and movement, a confluence of two large and mismatched tribes – a senior cycling group and a young mothers' group. If forced at gunpoint to join either, Evie would probably have picked the former, her memories of mothers' groups being less than fond. The women themselves hadn't been unkind, but Evie's propensity to compare herself unfavourably to everyone, so overwhelmed was she by the emotional demands of the baby years, had tainted her view of tribal activity forever.

'You look tired,' Ronni says, holding up her thumbs to the edges of Evie's eyes, the creases on each side, as though to rub them out.

'Thanks.'

'Owl's legs.'

'Crow's feet.'

'That's it. So what's up?'

Evie now holds her fingers at her temples like tiny flower presses. 'It's been a hard couple of weeks at work,' she tells Ronni. 'And I think I'm starting to get more worried about Sera's party. It's been keeping me up at night.'

Ronni rips a chocolate muffin in two and shoves one half in front of Evie. 'What is there to worry about besides seeing your bastardo husband for the first time since he left you like a flat tyre on the side of the road?' She points at the shredded muffin. 'Eat.'

'Yeah I guess that's mainly it,' Evie says. 'And there's also the issue of what to wear. Sera's theme is trickier than it sounds. The year 2000 is really just a blur of bleeding nipples and crying to me.'

'Why do people even *have* party themes?' Ronni asks with a mouthful of muffin. 'I just want to look hot at a party, not like a stupid Wiggle or a sheep or something.'

'I actually think,' Evie says, now articulating what she'd been mulling over for the past few sleepless nights, 'that having a theme is Sera's way of taking some of the pressure off the night. It's a distraction. She must be as nervous as I am about her father and me being in the same room.'

'Well,' Ronni says, abruptly taking back the muffin half she'd given Evie, 'you can still do a theme *and* look smoking hot. We will show that stupid Hamish what he's missing.'

Ronni now takes a concentrated dive into her phone for costume ideas, something to which Evie has already devoted far too many empty hours. For a year that sounded so momentous and historic, 2000 was actually (Olympics notwithstanding) fairly anti-climactic. Sandwiched between a year that had prophesied planes falling from the sky and a year in which planes actually did fall from the sky, 2000's big news events were relatively benign and, at least in terms of party planning, uninspiring. George W Bush was elected, the Concorde crashed, Mad Cow Disease had people briefly concerned.

'Of course Brad and Jen were married in 2000,' Ronni says with grave earnestness, looking up from her phone and over the frame of bright green reading glasses. This is possibly her favourite conversation topic, Ronni having come to believe that virtually every single thing humankind needs to understand about relationships is contained within the arc of the truncated union between Brad Pitt and Jennifer Aniston. She will not rest until either they're back together or Angelina Jolie makes a public apology.

'But that might be too close to the bone,' Ronni concedes somewhat reluctantly. 'Although I *could* give you the perfect Jen hairdo for the night.'

Evie shakes her head, no thanks, and continues surveying the cafe as Ronni wills her phone to offer up the just-right costume solution. The cycling mob is leaving early, apparently rattled by the screaming babies. The mothers' group takes up their vacated chairs without hesitation. Evie briefly notices the string of social distancing stickers on the floor around them, now scuffed and torn and lifting at the edges.

'Can you leave this with me?' Ronni asks. 'I will find the right costume. Perfetta! You will blow Hamish away.'

'That's not actually my goal.'

'It's *my* goal.'

'Okay, but you do know,' Evie says, 'that Hamish might not be alone at the party? He may be with another woman. I don't know. That's what I keep picturing in my mind. Sera's standing there, and Hamish and I are on either side of her, putting on our best twenty-first-birthday parent faces, but there's this other person there too. And she's probably feeling awkward, maybe even more out of place than me, but Hamish would have said all the right things to make her feel better about the situation – that's what he does, he's so good at it – and she'll smile bravely and get through it, while I'll be wanting to slide through the floor cracks and disappear forever. And everyone in the room will be silently making comparisons.'

Ronni absorbs this like the trailer for a dramatic movie. '*God*,' she says.

'I know.'

A car loudly backfires at the front of the cafe and everyone's shoulders jerk like pistons. Ronni doesn't move. After a minute that feels like many, she looks hard at Evie and says: 'You know I have not left my children for one night since they were born? Not one.'

Evie blinks with uncertainty. Says, 'Yes, okay.'

'But,' Ronni continues, 'I am going to leave them behind to *come with you* to this party. I am not letting you do this alone.'

Evie searches for words. She's suddenly imagining a very different version of the birthday party scene in which Ronni is standing beside her, furiously analysing a woman who may or may not be Hamish's girlfriend and anyone in the room with bad hair.

'Even though Perth is thirty-six hours away,' Ronni says, 'I will do this for you.'

'It's five hours.'

'*Still.*'

'Still.'

Evie doesn't say yes but equally recognises there hadn't actually been a question to answer. Ronni is coming to the party – this now seems unequivocal. Letting the idea settle into the folds of her mounting anxiety about the event, Evie also notes the arrival of relief. Whatever complications Ronni's presence might add, it will also mean Evie won't be alone, and it's this, she realises, that she has

146

been fearing the most: the prospect of appearing to Hamish like the very thing she now is.

25

Evie had felt small on James's boat, happily reduced by all the elements. An uncharacteristic surrender of sorts. The willingness to accept whatever beauty or calamity lay beyond the bow, beneath the water.

She suspects the appeal was very different for him, that James feels much bigger on the water than he does on the shore. The wheelchair far behind him, a picture of abandonment on the dock, James had looked to Evie like a man with new claims on the horizon. Someone who had a particular right to be out there, conjuring speed out of air and mastering forces that were still his to master.

It made her wonder more carefully about what sailing was doing for Angus, what nerve it was tapping in her lost boy. He'd barely missed a Sunday since the season began, always returning home a picture of salty spent contentment, ready to sleep away the afternoon on the couch. She'd asked him if she could come along with him next time, just the once she promised, and Angus had minutely shrugged by way of agreement.

And it's not quite the same brand of day she'd experienced with James, when the sea and the sky had been ablaze together, but it's warm and alive and it feels a long way from melancholy. The water is a darker blue today, its insides a secret, and the sky seems unsure about whether to give in to the hovering clouds.

Having completed the club's learn-to-sail course and paid his full membership, Angus is now free to hire out their Laser boats at reduced rates whenever they're available. The Laser, he explains to his mother once she's ensconced in the seat beside him and trying not to look conspicuously adrift, is one of the most popular single-handed dinghies in the world. Barely anything about the Laser's design, Angus says, has changed in twenty-one years. 'Just like Sera,' he adds and the comment catches Evie by surprise.

'Very much like Sera,' she says, seizing upon the segue, ever the counsellor. She watches Angus's eyes scan the length of the boat's mast. 'I think she might be one of the few twenty-one-year-olds to have nothing to fear about the speeches at her party.'

Angus offers no reply to this. He is apparently, and somewhat deliberately now, concentrating hard on changing the boat's direction.

'Anyway, I've booked our flights,' Evie continues. 'It's a really early start in the morning but what can you do? Such a long flight. You forget how far away it is.' *And what a blessing that can be.*

Angus gestures at something in the water. Evie sees nothing but regardless makes a 'wow' face with her mouth and eyes. 'So,' she continues, trying hard not to yell above the insistent wind. 'How are you feeling about the party, anyway? About going back to Perth?'

'Perth's fine,' Angus says looking straight ahead, ears pinned hard against his wet hair.

'Okay. And how are you feeling about seeing your dad?'

Evie waits. She badly wants an answer to this, something to measure herself against. She looks on as Angus pulls on handles and ropes that may or may not have any real purpose in this moment. Her son looks over the side of the boat as though there might be something new of interest there, a shark or crocodile perhaps. Finally he says, 'I mean, you know, it is what it is.'

'God,' Evie says, 'I hate that saying.'

And now Angus looks at her hard and long, as though the boat can actually sail itself whenever the awkward situation requires it. 'Well,' he says almost incredulously, 'what do you *want* me to say?'

Evie bristles. 'I don't want you to say anything. I'd just like to know how you feel. Because I can tell you how *I* feel about it. I feel pretty fucking scared.'

And it's a classic mum move, Evie thinks with a measure of embarrassment. Swearing to get a teen's attention. *I can be relevant!*

Angus's response is literally mechanical. He begins to detail the specifications of the boat, as though it was this that Evie had asked of him. 'It's cat-rigged,' he says. 'Just a main sail, no head sail. Four metres top to bottom. Tough construction but very light. You can throw it on top of a car. Probably not *your* car.'

Evie smiles and nods. Her cramped little car is often the target of his jibes. Hamish had had the 'real' car, the one they could all fit into without contortionism. She wonders where that is now.

'And every boat has the same design,' he says. 'Same hull and structure. So any competition between Lasers is about the sailors not the boat. It's like a huge leveller. It makes things fair.'

'Right, wow,' Evie says, hoping it sounds like a summation of the boat rather than her son's recall of details. She's happy that Angus wants to show her this, this knowledge he's procured himself, even if it was simply a means to shift the conversation out of harm's way.

The water soon gets choppier and Angus appears busier. It's harder to maintain a conversation, even harder than in a suburban house full of too many closed doors, but Evie perseveres regardless. 'Have you thought about a costume for the party?' she asks him. 'Because I still don't have any ideas.'

'Surely we don't *have* to wear a costume?' Angus says. 'I wasn't even alive in 2000.'

Evie thinks carefully about her response here, not wanting to generate any sibling rivalry where traditionally there's been thankfully little. Whatever irritations her children have had with each other over the years and through various life stages have largely been absorbed by her son's quietude. He simply doesn't entertain conflict, though Evie knows these are the same people who can one day become human volcanoes of repressed enmity.

'I think Sera would really like us to,' Evie says. 'I can help you think about a few ideas.'

'What's Dad going as?'

She wasn't ready for this. For Angus to be the one doing the probing.

'I have no idea,' Evie says. 'I still haven't heard from your father since he left.'

151

The comment slips lightly to the water, where it's quickly lost. Evie rests her back against the side of the boat, allowing herself to settle into its motion. They're moving steadily at speed now, the wind shooting across every surface, whistling past Evie's ears and paring back her thoughts. She looks at her son anew: a picture of cool concentration. This activity is giving him dominion over his world, however brief and contained. It's as much a victory as an escape. And she envies him in this moment, his ability to fill a hole with something new and unknown.

Hamish might have thought his near-grown children had finished the arc of their adolescent interests. That the essence of their characters had already been revealed in the sum of chosen sports and activities, their friends, their favourite movies, the music they listened to. The bulk of the rapid evolution preceding adulthood was complete, or so Hamish must have thought. He could walk away from it all not as a shallow man leaving behind young and unformed children but as someone who'd already done the hard yards, who knew his children well and could even make claims on their successes.

But he couldn't have known *this*, Evie thinks, this side of Angus revealed by the act of sailing. Arguably it's a side that might never have been uncovered if not for Hamish leaving, but regardless Evie feels a sense of sadness that he's missing it, watching their son command a boat with ease. And she's angry too, increasingly angry, that Hamish must have so little sense of the many things he's left unfinished.

Angus expertly turns the boat around to head back to shore,

glancing at his mother as he does so. She quickly shows her best *Look at you go!* face. The wind is at their backs now, taking up less presence in the boat and Evie realises she's running out of this precious time on the water with her son.

'So,' she ventures gently, hoping her ambition isn't too obvious. 'Did you ever write that letter to your dad, the one I said would be good to write regardless of whether you sent it or not?'

Angus's gaze doesn't shift from the shoreline. 'No,' he says after a long pause.

'Oh, you didn't?'

He shakes his head. 'Nuh.'

And Evie's not sure what frightens her most in this moment – that her son is lying or that he is making it look so convincing. That he might be more like Hamish than she thinks.

There is no one else, Evie. I just need some time.

'Well, I still think it would be a good idea,' she says.

'Yeah,' Angus says, tugging his soggy cap down tightly over his eyes. 'Maybe.'

Evie wants to tell him one thing she knows for certain: that rejection can become its own punishment. The fact of his father's leaving will fade in comparison to the apparently bigger problem of Angus being unwilling to counter the possibility of forgiveness or understanding. Even parental abandonment has a statute of limitations. Angus will lose any kind of relationship with his father. A hollow victory.

Evie knows all this because it's her own story. Her mother, a permanently exasperated woman, had wielded ambivalence like a weapon, punishing those people in her life who meted disappointment by actively looking away from them for a time, as though they didn't exist. Adolescent Evie had clearly disappointed her mother in many ways and on many occasions, for she was wilfully ignored throughout most of her teens. Evie began to fashion rejection of the woman as a pre-emptive strike, but it had backfired spectacularly. By the time she left home, Evie looked like a young woman with an ironic chip on her shoulder, troubled unnecessarily, prone to overreaction and outbursts, not a girl deeply wounded by neglect.

Their relationship had never been repaired, not even when a degree in psychology taught Evie how to better understand her mother. Not even when she learnt, as everyone does at some point, that parents are just people too. And that family is a lottery. Evie wants to say all of this to Angus now but doesn't.

Instead she says, 'You know I love you. With every part of my being.'

'Yeah, Mum,' Angus says, 'I know.' He says something else that is stripped and lost in the bow waves.

'And you and your dad will be okay. You'll work this out.'

Angus sniffs the air. Closes one eye to line up his destination. 'I can teach you, you know,' he says after a time, and Evie doesn't understand at first.

'Teach me what?'

'To do this,' Angus says. 'To sail.'

'Oh,' Evie answers after too long a pause. 'I guess.'

'You guess?'

'I mean, I don't know that I could. Even with a good teacher.' *Oops.* 'Like you.'

Angus yanks hard on a rope and the effort steels his jaw. His bared teeth challenge the salty air and the sight startles Evie. 'Of course you can,' he says to his mother. 'If you want to.'

'Yes,' Evie manages to reply and hopes it doesn't sound like a question.

26

She'd wanted to find a way to thank James for the sailing. The conundrum wasn't so much what to buy – wine, a pot plant, just a card? – but rather how to give it to him. Evie has a keen sense now of James's desire to manage perceptions of his disability, to limit the reductive power of first impressions. She doesn't think he'd be likely to answer an impromptu knock on the front door, even by someone bearing gifts.

So she asked Cobie for her dad's phone number and then sent him a text message to invite him for a coffee at Le Cose Semplici (*To make up for the cold tragedy I served you last time*, she wrote). She first checked with Ronni's sister that the cafe was definitely wheelchair-friendly and also where inside would be the easiest table. Given that it was the same area in which all the prams tended to congregate, Evie also then checked which mornings were most likely to be mothers' group-free (and ideally cyclist-free too, just because) and then she tried to line up those days and times with James's workdays and her own workdays.

Many text messages were exchanged in order to make the event happen, but the playful tone James quickly established in this new mode of communication between them made the exercise feel less like organisation than an outing of its own.

And they are here now, a blustery Friday morning, unseasonably cold and grey in tone. Coffee weather. James has arrived before Evie (of course) and chosen, somewhat incredibly, Evie's favourite table, her poky hidey-hole in the corner that hardly looks like a very accessible option.

'This is my spot!' she exclaims and kisses James on the cheek. She totally hadn't planned that and it briefly startles her. 'This table knows all my secrets.'

'And yet here it is,' James says with a cheeky smile, 'still standing.'

Evie slides somewhat inelegantly into her seat, reminding herself that she's a little nervous. 'Well, it's a little rickety,' she says.

She's about to ask James what coffee he'd like when a girl in seriously torn overalls lands by their side. 'Table service today,' she says. Evie looks past her shoulder to the front counter, where Ronni's sister flicks a wink in her direction.

'James, what would you like?' Evie says. 'My shout.'

'Well, okay then,' James says, running his hands together with mock glee. 'I'll have a flat white, extra hot, and the lobster please.'

The girl in overalls looks crestfallen, as though her first real waitressing gig has just gone pear-shaped. 'Um, I'm so sorry, but we don't actually have lobster ... *today*,' she says. 'But we do have some pumpkin muffins.'

'So much better!' James says. 'A flat white, extra hot, and a pumpkin muffin, please.'

Evie smiles. She feels an out of body moment coming on – floating above herself, looking on at the scene below like taking an extra step back from a painting to see if it reveals itself differently. These moments are happening more often these days, always unsolicited and too often unrevealing. It's a consequence, she suspects, of the schism between her old life and whatever this is. Evie sees herself across from James now, two people occupying a small circle, drawn from different worlds, nervous eyes on the exit. A random composition after twenty years of certainty.

Who are the people to invest in now, she finds herself thinking, when you've gone big and lost? How do you preserve the leftover pieces of the heart? Is it best, at the very least, safest, to just keep every new friendship no deeper than a flat white?

Evie's mind returns to ground level in a rush. She feels discombobulated, like the plane passenger jolting awake and hoping they haven't been dribbling.

'Three-dollars-fifty for your thoughts,' James says, gently tossing a handful of coins on the table. 'It's all I have on me.'

Evie laughs. 'That's all they're probably worth. You might even get change.'

She glances at the front door of the cafe: no sign of Ronni. Evie doesn't know if she'll be in today – there's never a set day or time that Ronni arrives, though it always delivers Evie a sense of levity and relief when she does. Her very own Fremantle Doctor on the other side of the country.

On a nervous whim, she decides to tell James about Sera's party, about the various ways in which it's presently occupying her thoughts, invading her dreams. In no particular order: returning to Perth after all this time, making sure Sera has a great birthday, finding an outfit for the party, seeing her husband again, Angus seeing his father again, standing in a room full of people and wanting to evaporate.

James shifts in his chair as though adjusting his sense now of what type of conversation they'll be having today. 'Don't forget climate change,' he says. 'This is no time to stop worrying about that.'

And Evie knows enough about him now – not a lot but enough – to see that James is not being dismissive but quite the opposite. His empathy is always implicit, his humour a welcome balm. And if there was any doubt about this, James now places his hand on Evie's and leaves it there for a few seconds.

'Which part of all that should we attack first?' he says.

Evie retreats. 'No, no,' she says. 'I don't want this to become a counselling session. It'll be fine. It is what it is.'

'My least favourite saying.'

'Mine too!' she says, throwing her hands up in exaggerated consternation. 'I can't believe I actually said it.'

'Everyone says it these days,' James says. 'I've probably said it myself without thinking. But that's the thing, isn't it – it's such a throwaway comment. If any of us really thought about it, we'd see how reductive it is as a philosophy for living.'

And Evie leans in now, literally and figuratively, because these are her favourite sorts of discussions and they seldom materialise anymore. She can see why someone in James's position would particularly loathe platitudes about life's inevitability.

'I think,' she says, 'that human beings need to make sense of things, even though we're not particularly good at it. It's a coping mechanism of sorts. I think we just retrospectively ascribe meaning to all the shit things that happen to us so that we can simply live with them, and so that the chaos and randomness of it all doesn't overwhelm us at least once a day.'

James edges closer to Evie and smiles at her. She feels his gaze in that moment as a kind of potent force, displacing the arrangement of ions between them. The moment stretches itself to the limits of comfort. 'Philosophy,' he says at last, 'is very sexy in the right light.'

Evie's certain that a hot rash just bloomed on her neck.

Their coffees arrive – *thank God* – a steaming muffin shortly behind them. James cuts the muffin in two and offers half to Evie. She declines because she already feels like something that just came out of an oven.

'So what is mostly worrying you about going back to Perth?' James asks, applying butter to his muffin half. 'Party aside.'

Evie's been thinking about this, because she knows it's irrational to fear a place that mostly holds good memories. But that's the illogical thing: when good memories become too painful to look at, they're tainted somehow and so is where they happened.

'It's like,' she explains, 'and I know this will sound stupid, the old Evie is still there in Perth, like she never left. I mean, I literally picture her mopping my old kitchen. She feels very real. And I just don't want to see her again. Because she has no idea what's ahead.'

'What about your old friends?' James asks. 'Aren't you looking forward to seeing them again?'

'Well,' Evie says, 'that's just it. I'm terrified about seeing them too. Because I've neglected those friendships. I pushed them all away after Hamish left, even before then. I was running from something when we left Perth. We both were. And I didn't understand what it was and I still don't. But there was a sense of time running out, of something that was going to happen if we didn't get out.'

'But' James says, 'it happened anyway.'

'Yes.'

'It's like that magnet on your fridge, isn't it? *No matter where you go, there you are.*'

And Evie is momentarily taken aback by this, by the closeness of James's observation, not just of her fridge but of her.

'You know, when I had my accident,' James says, 'I never thought I'd be able to go back to my house. I spent a lot of my time in hospital looking up rental properties that could handle a wheelchair. Because I knew that to be back home would mean I would just keep running into the old James, the version of me who could walk out to the mailbox and stand on a chair to change a lightbulb and dance in the shower. And it would kill me. I'd want to punch myself in the head. Pop a dozen pills. Take out my own legs.'

'I can understand that,' Evie says softly.

'But you know what? I did go back there. Not happily, but I did. Because while I was in hospital, my wife and a bunch of our friends worked really hard on changing up the house, making it as accessible as possible, rearranging the rooms, the furniture. They even painted the whole thing new colours inside. And I thought … that's bloody good of them, you know? I have to at least give this a go.'

'The same house you're in now?'

James pops the last corner of his muffin in his mouth. 'It's the same house,' he says, 'but I have an entirely new relationship with it. It definitely took some time … too long probably … but I eventually learnt to let the old me and the new me live together in the same place.'

Evie wants so much now to ask about his wife, but something stops her. She has no idea what shape that question should take.

'Anyway, enough about me,' James says and waits a few beats. 'What do *you* think of me?'

Evie laughs loudly. Even though Hamish had often trotted out the same line from *Beaches*, James's delivery was much better.

'You're very funny,' she says.

'So's your son,' says James. 'Angus always makes me laugh when he's at our place. Very dry sense of humour. Master of deadpan.'

'*Really?*'

'Perfect comic timing too. He's a crack-up.'

Evie can't remember the last time she heard Angus laugh, let alone try to induce one. She doesn't know whether to be thrilled that there's still a spark within her son or devastated that he doesn't conjure it in her presence. She's clearly created a house of misery.

James must sense he's struck a nerve. 'They're always different around other people,' he says reassuringly. 'One of Cobie's teachers recently told me how polite she always is and I straightaway held up a photo on my phone and said "Is *this* the girl to whom you're referring?"'

And Evie now tells James about what Ms Keenan had said about Angus, about him seeming troubled and angry and confused, though not about the letter that had prompted the conversation. She explains that Hamish was a good father, albeit of the quality-over-quantity variety, and that this perhaps was the hardest truth for her to process – that Hamish has walked away from their shared idea of parenthood, not just from Evie.

'I mean, I try to imagine what Hamish tells himself,' Evie says, 'how he squares it all off. How he sleeps. I think, well, maybe he just sees this as another absence, a prolonged one. He always travelled a lot for work and maybe he sees this as no different. Maybe he thinks he can just parent via WhatsApp.'

'Bit of a stretch,' James says, looking down at his empty coffee mug.

'And then I think,' Evie continues, 'maybe he just believes that all the major parenting work is done now anyway. One child finished school, another one almost there. Close enough, right?'

'Not really.'

'Maybe he'd been holding on for a while, biding his time, waiting to walk away with minimal guilt and therefore no great need for explanation.'

James seems to think hard about this. 'Does that fit with his personality?'

'I don't know!' Evie exclaims, instantly realising that came out a little loud, even for a busy cafe with terrible acoustics. 'Sorry.'

'Don't be sorry.'

'I mean, you think you know someone, especially after so much time, but maybe that's the problem too,' Evie says. 'Maybe being with someone for twenty years makes you the least reliable witness of their character.'

'You might be on to something there,' James says. 'What do they say about staring closely at a screen for too long?'

Evie turns this analogy over in her mind like a glass marble. She thinks it's more likely that, in recent years at least, she wasn't looking at their marriage closely enough. It's possible she understood everyone else's relationships, the ones laid bare in her counselling room, far better than her own.

'Anyway,' she says now to James. 'I think I've failed Angus since Hamish left. I needed to step up as a parent but I haven't. I've been so afraid about making things worse.'

'Well, maybe you can't see it from where I stand ... or sit,' James says and flashes her a mischievous grin, 'but Angus is doing great. He leaves his bedroom, he has friends, he has a hobby. He's doing a lot better than most of the boys I teach. You think you should be doing more for him but that could easily backfire. Teenage boys are like landmines waiting to explode.'

'Maybe,' she says, still unconvinced. 'I don't know.'

'Well, here's what I know,' James says, 'and it's not much, so don't get excited. The fairytale is that we all get two decent parents in this life, but most people don't. Most of us get one if we're lucky and the good news is that's all you need. I was raised by a single mum. Cobie's being raised by a paraplegic dad. And it's enough. It absolutely is. As long as there's love, it doesn't matter how many people are managing its distribution.'

And Evie realises she needed to hear this today, even if it should never have come from someone she is ostensibly trying to thank, someone overcoming more challenges each day than Evie could ever comprehend. It's been a selfish indulgence to let the conversation go this way.

'Don't do that,' James says to her now.

'Do what?'

'Tear strips off yourself for opening up to me,' he says. 'I can see by the way you're wringing the life out of that serviette. Don't feel bad. You shouldn't. Because I'm enjoying this, I really am. Since Liz and I broke up, I haven't had a female friend to talk to about, you know, *life*. The stuff that actually matters. It's good for me, even though I'm terrible at it.'

A name. *Liz.*

Female friend.

Evie puts the butchered serviette to one side. *Don't ask him.* 'So, how long ago did you break up with Liz?'

And there you go.

James looks at the nearest grimy window. Says, 'About two years after the accident. That's how long it took to successfully push her away.'

'Oh,' Evie says and no other words come.

'But we're on good terms these days,' James says. 'It takes a while but it's possible. If there's no, you know, betrayal. She lives in Darwin now. Married a chef a couple of years ago. He had a couple of kids already and I think that's starting to put a strain on things. The kids' real mother makes life very difficult for Liz and it doesn't seem like the husband stands up to her. Liz sounds pretty wrung out on the phone these days.'

'I've often said the Brady Bunch have a lot to answer for,' Evie says.

'Exactly,' James laughs. 'Any family could thrive with an Alice!'

'And how is Cobie's relationship with her mum?'

'Well,' he says, 'it's as good as it can be given the distance. Cobie doesn't visit very often. I don't think the other kids make her feel very welcome. But it feels like she's okay with that.'

'She does seem very level-headed.'

'That she is,' James says. 'I'm so bloody lucky to have her, Evie. I tried to push her away too, you know? Both of them together. I just wanted them to *go*. I didn't want this to become their life. But Cobie wasn't having a bar of it. It wasn't even negotiable. And somehow she managed to stay with me without it ever looking like she'd picked a side. Even Liz could see Cobie wasn't making a choice. It was a compulsion.'

'Wow,' Evie says, looking anew on Angus's choice of friend. 'What an extraordinary young woman.'

'Yep, pretty sure there was a mix-up at the hospital,' James says, 'but I'm keeping it quiet.'

'Ciao, bella!'

Ronni launches upon their table like a rogue wave, kissing Evie on both cheeks and frantically rearranging her fringe as though Evie is about to take the stage.

'Ronni,' Evie says, 'this is my friend James. James, this is Ronni.'

And it's the quickest of glances, almost undetectable, that Ronni now directs at James's chair. Her eyes widen in recognition. 'Oh!' she says. 'James with ...'

Oh God.

'... the boat.'

James smiles broadly and holds out his hand to Ronni.

'No,' she says, 'I'm a wog. We kiss!' And Ronni leans into James's left side and brushes her cheek against his, making a kiss sound as she does. Evie watches him carefully throughout and is relieved to see how happily James receives the gesture. 'I've just brought in some fresh muffins. Let me bring you some.'

'That's okay,' Evie says, catching Ronni before she races off to the front counter, a fixer in flight. 'We already had a pumpkin muffin.'

'Che schifo!' Ronni says, tossing her head to the ceiling. 'Pumpkin in a muffin – *why?* Let me get you a proper muffin.' And she's off in a flourish of good intent and indignation, the words 'fucking pumpkin' flying over her shoulder.

James laughs. 'What a character. She's terrific.'

'She really is,' Evie says. 'I'd never met anyone like her before. Sometimes I think that if everything hadn't happened the way it did, I wouldn't have met Ronni, and I can't even imagine that now.'

James pulls a long curl behind his ear but there are so many that it looks like a pointless exercise. 'I want to say something about good things coming out of bad,' he says, 'but I'm afraid I'll sound like a dick.'

A plate of colourful muffins drops between them, sending

a spray of icing dust into the air. 'Cappuccino, mocha and berry,' Ronni announces like a performance chef. 'Enjoy!'

'Why don't you join us?' James says to her and wheels his chair back a little and sideways to make room.

But Ronni can't stay, she says. Her first hair appointment will be arriving at home shortly. 'But before I go, Evie,' she says. 'Your costume – I have an idea. Look up "J-Lo, Versace, 2000". If you like it, Francesca can make it for you. A few little changes to stop your boobs falling out. Okay, gotta go. Ciao, ciao, ciao!'

They watch her fly out of the shop like a spent balloon. James pulls out his phone and starts typing. 'Okay,' he says as he does, 'J-Lo … Versace … 2000.' Then he says, 'Oh wow.'

He holds the phone up to Evie and she instantly recognises the dress worn by Jennifer Lopez to a big awards night back in 2000. It's astonishing Wicked-Witch-of-the-West shades of green, all flowing chiffon and impossible angles, the neckline plunging to below J-Lo's navel where it meets the top of the split below. A dress designed for shock and awe.

'Oh my God,' Evie says. 'Is Ronni serious?'

James takes another look at the image on his phone, then rests it in his lap. 'I don't know,' he says. 'I reckon you could pull it off.'

27

Jess and Mick

When Evie met Jess, the image that first sprang to mind was of a designer lounge chair, beautiful and expensive, with a busted upholstery button at its centre, flung out of its mooring and dangling ignominiously. All you see is the button, the flaw spoiling the look.

Jess's button was a wild wing of lacquered hair on one side of her head, completely at odds with the rest of her carefully arranged appearance. Evie could see Jess was unaware of it, as large as it was. The wing had opened like a car door at some point during the day and Jess had neither felt it nor seen it. Clearly no one had told her (and Evie wasn't about to in this moment). It was a small but unmissable sign that Jess was a woman just holding on.

Beside her sat Mick, a practised salt-of-the-earth type, crumpled in the chair like an old drop sheet. The man looked exhausted. Glassy eyes, mottled cheeks. It looked like Jess had pulled him from the field of battle to be there.

Evie admired the couple even before she got to know them. They were that brave species who'd taken on each other's children to forge a relationship together. The blended family – a creation as hopeful and fraught as any parliament.

Jess had begun their first session with a summary worthy of a seminar presentation. She knew, she said, that the failure rate for blended families was significantly higher than for any other family type. She wasn't keen to become another statistic. She'd be receptive to all of Evie's good counsel.

'But, darl,' Mick had said when Jess finally finished. 'The issue isn't that we don't want this to work. It's all the other little bastards in the house who are the problem. No one wants this to work *except* us. And I don't know if I can keep fighting them. I'm stuffed.'

Evie could see that the very second Jess gave up this mission Mick would be out. Not because he didn't love her – he clearly did – but because that didn't seem to be enough in their circumstances. Jess's determination, though hollowed out like an old tree by their children (two from him, three from her and one of their own together), was the only thing keeping him in the game.

It was a determination carved out of experience. Jess was an accomplished senior HR manager for a mining company, adept at negotiating the thorniest of union disputes, managing workplace bullying complaints and untangling the debacle of every annual Christmas party. 'If I can handle a militant workforce of six thousand employees,' she'd said to Evie that first day, 'surely I can handle these six little shits.'

But hard up against this doggedness and patience was a Jenga tower of competing forces. For a start, there were a lot of children involved, and while parental love is (at least in theory) infinite, capable of endless cell division, time and resources are not. Though Jess had started the whole enterprise in bootcamp-efficient style, her enthusiasm for systems and rosters and fridge charts was not roundly shared – sometimes sparking all-out revolt – and even she had started to feel like someone screaming into the abyss.

Her methods, she reasoned with Evie, had stood a chance of gaining traction if Mick had remained a true believer, but instead he'd 'practically jumped' at the chance to accept a three-weeks-on-one-week-off FIFO position at a mine in the Pilbara the previous year. Jess said she'd actually begun to envy him, scorching red dust, death adders and all.

The children now ranged in age from two to seventeen, ensuring that at least two or three trying stages of childhood development were in full swing at any one time. That the melding of their worlds had changed up the birth order of their children hadn't helped matters, and everyone bar the two-year-old felt they'd got the rawest deal, even while Jess pointed out that wasn't technically possible.

The eldest, Mick's daughter Kaylee, was the centrifugal force of the household, literally (Jess had looked this up) an 'inertial force that appears to act on all objects'. Beautiful and brooding and belligerent, her moods were everyone's weather system. She was at her worst, Jess pointed out, when she returned from her mother's house, which could be at any moment of the day or night. Kaylee kept her own schedule.

'Let's not get into this,' Mick had said.

'Into what?' asked Evie.

'Into my ex-wife and all that,' he'd replied. 'At least we get a break from *my* kids. Yours are there twenty-four seven because your ex is too useless to look after them.'

Evie had sidestepped that issue for the moment, though she knew from her own friendship network that one of the few unspoken benefits of divorce was regular breaks from daily parenting. Jess and Mick were getting no reprieve.

Instead she focused on their chosen terminology: 'your kids', 'my kids'. Jess had quickly jumped over the top: 'We only talk that way when we fight,' she insisted. 'We never talk that way in front of the kids. They are all *our* kids.'

'And there's too many of them,' Mick had said, and laughed unconvincingly.

Coming back to Kaylee, Evie pointed out that stepchildren often feel powerless, forced into a situation not of their design. A step-parent is an all-too-present reminder that their parents are no longer together, a constant grief trigger.

'I don't think,' Jess said, 'that Kaylee is lacking any power – quite the opposite – and I don't think she's grieving. I think she's a manipulative you-know-what just like her mother.'

'And here we go,' Mick said, sliding down his chair so that his eyes had nowhere to look but the ceiling. 'This,' he said to Evie, 'is what I'm dealing with.'

In fact, it wasn't even the half of it, as Evie quickly learnt. There was also a hornet's nest of sibling rivalry underfoot, meddling grandparents, increasing financial pressures, and a ten-year-old wrestling with sexual identity questions.

'And the wifi,' Mick had added. 'There's never enough of that to go around.'

Evie had felt for this couple, especially as they weren't experiencing the benefits of time. Most blended families found things got easier eventually. Once early resentments and conflicts had finally settled – an endurance event lasting anywhere from two to five years – there arrived an equilibrium of sorts. But it was the opposite experience for Jess and Mick. They'd been worn down by too many elements, their union leaching away in spite of what had been a powerful love between them. The best indicator that their relationship still had life in it was the fact that they were even sitting in this room.

'There are,' Evie had said to them, 'dozens of relationships going on under your roof, but they all live or die on yours. The relationship between the two of you is the most important one of all. So that's where we're going to start.'

In time, Evie said, family therapy would be the next step. She said she could organise a budget-friendly rate through a partner counselling service when the time was right.

Jess had seemed grateful and relieved to have a way forward. 'So,' she'd asked Evie, 'family therapy would involve the *whole* family?'

'That's right,' Evie said.

'All in the same room at the same time?'

'For the most part.'

'Well,' Mick had said with a resigned grin, 'that's gunna be a ripper day out.'

28

'Ryan wants your number,' Ronni says, so out of breath that Evie doesn't properly hear her.

'Who wants what?' Evie asks.

Ronni stops dramatically, one hand on her chest, the other holding back the sky. It was her idea that they start walking together once a week, having dived into a Facebook forum about weight gain in a woman's forties and emerged punch-drunk and scared for her life. Ronni never intends to stray far from the likeness of Marisa Tomei.

'Not-Fat-Anymore Ryan,' she says at last, gulping air like it's vanishing. 'The date you blew. He texted me yesterday wanting your number.'

Evie throws her hands on her hips, equally dramatic. 'I didn't blow that date,' she says. 'The date was *fine*. I got a bit too counsellory. He didn't kiss me. I would've died if he had. I wasn't ready. I told you that.'

'Well.'

'Well.'

Ronni huffs, resumes walking at pace. Together they wind their way across several suburban blocks without speaking. But it's an easy silence, not the kind Evie would have dreaded when walking with a friend back in Perth. Back there, for reasons probably more to do with Evie's counselling sensibilities than anything else, she'd found her friendships to be a lot like keeping a garden – something natural that shouldn't require as much work as it does. Each friendship had been different, requiring and summoning a different version of Evie, but common to all was the way they made her feel sometimes: not enough to just be.

Perhaps, as Evie's often thought over the past year, she'd been so in need of an easier friendship after Hamish left that she'd literally summoned Ronni into being – at the very least moulded her into an idea. It seems less likely that she simply found exactly what she needed when she needed it most. Evie shudders at how selfish that all sounds.

'There it is!' Ronni says now, pointing upwards to an enormous conflation of concrete and glass at the top of a hill overlooking the ocean. 'The House of Sex.'

'What?'

'That house.' Ronni points again. 'It's where they have big swingers' parties.'

Evie doesn't have to ask how Ronni knows this. Whether it's via the cafe or the conga line of locals getting cheap but excellent haircuts on the stool in Ronni's back shed, neighbourhood gossip is her preferred Jeopardy category.

'There's a private Facebook group,' Ronni explains, 'that puts out the details of the next event but most of them are held in that big house. Can you even *imagine* the cleaning?'

Evie looks up at the innocuous structure, unsure if Ronni is referring to the size of the house in general or the after-party tidy-up.

'And some of the people who go along,' she continues. 'Evie, it *blows my mind*. They're like our age! With kids and flabby bits and everything. I just don't get it. I still back out of the bathroom so Vince doesn't see my fat barbone. Imagine waving it around a roomful of people you'll see at school drop-off on Monday.'

'Your bum isn't fat,' Evie says.

'I know,' Ronni says. 'That was a test.'

'Anyway,' Evie says, 'it's probably a good thing that people our age feel confident enough in their skin to, you know, put it out there like that.'

'But imagine what it *looks* like,' Ronni says, breathing sharply up the long hill. 'All those lumpy bodies bumping up against each other all slappity-slap. Imagine a pizza delivery guy walking in on *that*.'

Evie laughs but it almost hurts at the speed they're going. It's classic Ronni, she thinks, to first address the optics of a concept like swinging before considering its busy intersection with monogamy.

And she remembers now a couple who came to see her several years ago on the ambiguous premise of 'marriage difficulties'. It transpired they'd tried swinging to address those difficulties – the principal one being boredom – and that the experiment had produced a whole other suite of problems, some entirely new and some that'd been sitting in their peripheral vision for some time.

Evie had needed to read up on the practice. She'd learnt that while there's a wide variety of people who engage in swinging, they largely fall into two groups. The first are those singles and couples who already have open views about sexuality and relationships. These are the ones who can sustain swinging lifestyles for many years, viewing it as no more dangerous or weird than weekly yoga.

The second group are those who arrive at swinging to fix something, to scratch an itch or snatch the dying light. This was the story of the couple who'd come to see her.

It'd been the husband Toby's suggestion. Statistically, Evie had learnt, this was usually the case. He'd asked his wife many times before she'd agreed to give it a try. But having little idea of what they were actually signing up for, the couple had barely agreed on ground rules and expectations. 'It was like taking a mystery flight,' Toby's wife, Helena, had said to Evie, her voice leaden and sad.

Toby, as Evie uncovered over several sessions, had long had attachment issues. It wasn't just bedroom boredom that had led him to the idea of swinging; it was also another way for him to emotionally disconnect within his marriage. While those weren't his words, Evie could see Toby had basically wanted to have his cake and eat it too.

For Helena, the sight of her husband with another woman had been almost too much to bear at times. No matter how Toby framed it, Helena had seen not just the physical act of sex occurring in front of her but a connection she'd long hungered for. She even suspected that Toby took pleasure in her jealousy, which would broil away under her skin and sear her eyelids even as she drove the kids to school. As much as Toby had believed his wife secretly wanted to 'explore her bisexuality', Helena quickly learnt she actually didn't.

Evie bristles at the memory of this couple, the way they'd both looked to her as though handing over a smashed vase. And she imagines now, though she wishes she wouldn't, the last time she'd had sex with Hamish, just four days before he left. What had he been thinking? Had he known it might be their last time?

Ronni cuts through Evie's thought. 'It's the party bit I don't get,' she says to Evie. 'I mean, do you put your clothes back on for the dancing?'

Evie muses at Ronni's idiosyncratic pathway through logic. 'Maybe there's no dancing.'

'Then what,' Ronni says, throwing her arms at the dark clouds above them, 'is even *the point*?'

Together they reach the coast and turn back inland. Evie's right calf is starting to pinch, taking some welcome attention away from her knee.

'So,' Ronni says after a time, 'can I give Ryan your number?'

Evie thinks about this only briefly. 'No.'

'But I already did.'

'Ronni!'

'It's *fine*. I'm sure he just wants to say hello.'

'Why would he want to say hello after weeks of not saying anything?'

Ronni shrugs. 'Maybe he's been busy?'

'Well, so am I,' Evie says. 'Really busy.'

And she thinks now about just how genuinely busy she is. It's only a month until Sera's party and there's still so much to arrange. Angus's exams start in a week's time and Evie wants to cushion his load as much as she can. Her own marking piles are out of control and she has two new first-year units to write for next semester. She *should* be tearing her hair out right now, but oddly she's feeling more on top of things than she has in a long time, as though circulation is finally returning to a body that'd forgotten how to move.

'Or,' Ronni says, looking cheekily across at Evie, 'maybe he just wants sex? Can you maybe squeeze that in?'

Evie punches Ronni's arm by way of response.

'Because,' Ronni says, 'it might be time to just rip off that bandaid.'

29

The stasis wrought by Hamish's departure, the lost hours of staring at hard surfaces, of watching TV with no sound, has begun to shift. It can only be credited to time, Evie knows, that gormless ghost, and the black magic of distraction. In the past few weeks she's busied herself with the party arrangements (the most pressing of which was convincing her daughter not to cancel the event altogether as Sera had suddenly become haunted by visions of empty rooms and sad balloons drifting to the floor), as well as marking assignments, keeping Angus fed and watered during his exams, and walking three times a week with Ronni.

Far from triumphantly pushing the heavy foot off her own neck, Evie's simply felt less conscious of it being there. She feels compelled to move again, though not in any certain direction. She watches Polo running mad-eyed loops in the lounge room most evenings and politely looks away.

Two memories have returned to her lately, neither with warning nor context. The first is having had Restless Legs Syndrome during her pregnancies, an utterly bizarre and purposeless condition that causes the legs to pull and burn and itch until only shaking them can make the sensations subside, and only then for a few minutes at a time. It had driven Evie mad, and Hamish too, though for different reasons. 'What use,' he would say, 'is an unexplainable condition? There's no purpose without *purpose*.' It made her wonder anew what purpose was driving him now.

The other memory had been from the same camping trip on which Evie had first been on a catamaran. She remembers sitting with her friend on the sharp edge of a waterfall. It was maybe twenty metres high, pouring itself into a small pool the colour of oil. Evie and her friend had watched the running water changing its course around them and wondered aloud how deep the pool was, if it would be safe to jump. Either, they'd reasoned, the water would simply be too shallow and they'd die of broken necks or it would suck them into a vortex leading to the centre of the earth. Only these two possibilities. And then a rush of water from behind had removed all choice in the matter, lifting Evie and her friend off the edge and shooting them into the pool. It had been so cold, so endlessly deep, that she remembers finally coming to the surface, propelled by the twin engines of joy and terror, and seeing the sky as if for the very first time and as if it had been waiting for her all along.

She has no idea why this memory, so vivid now yet unretrieved for decades, has come to her again now, what it's meant to be telling her – that it's time to make a leap again or that even the notion is fraught with danger.

Tonight a complicating factor may be the few glasses of wine

Evie has had to steel herself for the task at hand: making a photobook for Sera's twenty-first. It's a Friday night, Angus is at Cobie's, and so it's just her, two decades of visual triggers and The Whitlams on high rotation.

In a decade's time, this will be a much easier exercise for parents, Evie thinks: a night or two of scrolling through a smartphone on the couch. But because Sera's life span neatly straddles the analogue and digital eras, it means Evie's knee-deep in old boxes, cracking the chalky spines of photo albums she hasn't looked at in years.

Evie's intention had always been to defiantly continue this practice – the printing out of photos, the compilation of albums, the familial rhythm of it all, evidence of devotion – even as the sheer volume of photos on her own phone rendered the intention hopeless. Time and all its tricks had scuppered the exercise, as had the kids' increasing reluctance to throw Evie a genuine smile beyond the age of about twelve. Regardless, she still worries that at least a generation of Western society's memories will exist on social media pages only, curated to meet the conventions of a crude online aesthetic.

I can do this.

They're just photos.

Evie is sat messily on the rug in her lounge room, boxes on every side like a makeshift fort. She hadn't bothered to remove her afternoon walking clothes, bar a cap and sneakers that now sit in a pile beside her like a vaporised person. She suspects she's starting to smell.

Chronology forms as a plan so Evie begins with Sera's baby

photos. And immediately whatever hope she had of not falling into a deep chasm of nostalgic emotion vanishes like new year's resolve. Here she is holding Sera for the first time in hospital, a moment captured by Hamish. Evie looks closely at herself in the photo, utterly exhausted and enraptured at the same time, gazing down at Sera's downy head as though recalibrating life itself. The baby had taken all of Hamish's strongest features, the darkly framed eyes, the mouth already arranged as a smile, and infused them with fresh innocence and a giggle that made strangers in the supermarket turn around and laugh along with her. So determinedly herself even as a new arrival on this earth, she was also unmistakeably *him*.

This is going to be hard.

Evie gets herself another glass of wine from the kitchen, swaps out The Whitlams playlist for The Cure, and takes a long, deliberate breath.

Hamish had adored the baby years, for both children. Evie works her way through dozens and dozens of pictures of baby Sera in her father's arms, where she was always most likely to be. Besides being the one always behind the camera, capturing every expression and every milestone as though time might suddenly stop, Evie was the panicked doer of the pair, running after the tasks of parenthood as though on a constant timer. 'You're missing all the good bits,' Hamish would sometimes say to her in that smug way of people who've worked out life (and naturally assume the responsibility for it all is shared), and she knew he was right but she also couldn't stop.

There's a photo here of Evie and Hamish with Sera at her first birthday party. They're standing on either side of a high-chair, a piece of chocolate cake in front of the baby that Evie recalls making in the middle of the night. Sera looks delighted, about to demolish the gooey concoction, while Evie and Hamish are smiling at whoever's telling them to. Evie pulls the picture out of the album to get a closer look. She can see Hamish is immensely proud in this moment, at ease with his place in the world, the boxes he's ticking, the beauty of his daughter. Then Evie looks at herself, squints fiercely and tries to see what she was at pains to hide on that day and every day of the baby years – the fear of all that responsibility, the endless struggle to get it right.

She recalls now the words of Margaret, a client so often at the forefront of her memories. *It hollowed me out,* she'd said of motherhood. *The weight of all that love. The work of it all. The worries, every day, every night, eating through your skin.* Evie remembers those worries, the immense weight on the heart, like it was yesterday. It *was* yesterday! It's been every day for almost twenty-one years now. And the wheels might just as easily have come off for Evie as they had for Margaret had Hamish not changed their course.

All too soon the pictures are of a toddler and a new baby. Angus's arrival rattled Sera, though most of the photos Evie chose to keep show a proud sister leaning over Angus in his baby bath or holding up a spoon to him at dinner. In fact, Sera vacillated between intense jealousy and tearful joy about her brother, often within the space of minutes.

Hamish was sporting a moustache around this time, a phase Evie had all but forgotten until now, while she's clearly carrying two dress sizes of extra weight. At least. Evie cringes at these images, less out of vanity than sympathy. She remembers how that Evie felt, conspicuous and invisible all at once, stuck in a loop of mindless morning teas at neighbourhood centres, pushing swings until her arms ached. 'Just wait,' she'd wanted to say to Hamish, to the whole world in fact, 'I'll be back eventually. I just have to get through this.'

A family holiday. Somewhere beachy. Hamish's idea, to help Evie find her smile. He'd been travelling a lot, each conference a more exotic location than the last (in Evie's mind at least – Hamish insisted they were all amorphously dull). The photos here are vivid and sunlit, almost glowing at the edges. Sera is five and Angus three. She's dragging him on a boogie board down a sand dune. They're playing with a small dog they encountered on the beach. They're devouring ice creams, Sera with an empty cone and eyeing off Angus's. Pages and pages of these pictures, an amount disproportionate to the length of the holiday as Evie recalls, but Hamish had wanted it to be wonderful and it had been.

On the last night of the holiday, although there isn't a photo of this, Hamish hired a babysitter for the children, the first they'd ever had. He took Evie to dinner at an expensive seafood restaurant where every dish had tasted like the sea and every minute seemed bigger than time. 'Thank you for everything you do for our family,' Hamish said to her, holding up his glass up to touch hers. And Evie hadn't known till then just how much she needed to hear it.

We have been happy.

Whole-family photos start to peter out from this point, not in an alarming sense but in the way that most families eventually get used to the miracle of their existence. From primary school

onwards, the photos are mostly of Sera and Angus individually –
dressed up in costume for a school assembly, accepting a ribbon at
Little Athletics, catching a fish for the first time, holding up a plaster
cast after a bingle on a bike. Children growing into who they are,
their parents shrinking into the eaves, hopeful, proud, vanishing.

There are no photos, Evie notes, nor would anyone expect
them, of the gaps between the moments. Long gaps. Seasons of
disconnection. Hamish's travel absences. Sera's terrifying dalliance
with an eating disorder. The summer Angus simply didn't speak.
Evie's lengthy postgraduate study, for which they'd all suffered.

Boxes exhausted, Evie takes her near-empty glass of wine and
moves to the home computer. She's heard there are now apps that
can create order out of any amount of photo chaos but she doubts
they'd be equipped for this particular digital wasteland. There are
about six years of photos on here in one single document file. How
had she let this go? Where to even begin?

Evie fetches a refill of wine. Realises she should have eaten
something.

And soon there are tears. So many tears. Hot and wet. Evie
wipes them off the keyboard as quickly as they land. A wall has
collapsed. There are too many memories here. There is *so much*.

The big family holiday: America, west coast to east coast.
Hamish driving them all in a rented Pontiac across the utterly mad
and beautiful country. He was terse the entire way, frustrated by
driving in a foreign country, exasperated by the proximity forced
on the four of them, but you'd never know it from the photos. Big
smiles, big adventures. Theme parks. Happy days.

Christmases with his family: loud, rude, funny. Faces fighting for space in the frame. An uncle who liked to signal peak inebriation by removing all his clothes. Will she ever see them again? *Do I want to?*

Christmas with her family: quiet, long, sullen. A photo of Evie, Sera, Angus and her parents two years ago. Forced grins. A clock in the background that may well have stopped working years ago. Hamish must have taken this one. How he hated those Christmases.

Evie moves to the couch and commences phone scrolling. Her fingers rapid-fire across the screen – thousands of pics across the last four years, some her own and many texted to her from Hamish and the kids. Time and more time.

The whiz of it all, the very blur of it, becomes the message: *There's a lot to this thing.* Choosing a person, making children, keeping it all aloft when it's not sinking. Holding on to the parts of yourself that haven't been taken by others. Coming back to each other over and over. *Who actually gets away with it, really?*

There are fewer photos from the past year. Evie hasn't felt much impulse in her shutter finger, hasn't hounded the kids to share their phone galleries. A few nice pics of Angus sailing. A sunset down by the water. Ronni's family in full flight during a Friday-night dinner. Polo looking pensive and cute.

She scrolls back. To the last photo she can find of the four of them. In front of their house in Perth, a *SOLD* sticker on an oversized real estate sign beside them. Hamish had asked the agent to take it, an auspicious symbol of the big adventure ahead. They're all squeezed into Hamish's embrace, laughing at something or nothing.

Aliens would advise the mother ship of a confirmed 'happy family' sighting.

Do old photos, Evie wondered, make the present look like a lie, or is it the other way around?

No more wine.

A text message suddenly lands on her screen, obscuring the photo she's looking at. Evie adjusts her vision to make out the words.

It's from James. *What are you up to?*

Evie pauses. She leans back on the couch. Tries to think of something clever to say, but it's too late and winey for that. *Getting drunk on my couch*, she writes. *You?*

He sends back a laughing emoji. Then: *Want to come here for dinner tomorrow night?*

Evie's watches her fingers move faster than her thoughts. *Sounds good*, she replies.

Does it?

He suggests a time and Evie manages a thumbs up, relieved the conversation is stopping short of banter, something she'd likely read back in the morning with deep shame.

That night she dreams of the ocean. Of being on a boat so far out that she can't see the shore. Nothing wakes her until well after the sun comes up.

30

Angus is clearly amused at this unfamiliar sight of his mother shadow-boxing a hangover. Moving through his third heaped bowl of cereal at the kitchen bench, he watches Evie standing in front of their open fridge, waiting for it to reveal itself. She's frozen, it would seem, mesmerised by the white light and grateful for the fridge door's unwavering support.

'There's nothing in here to eat,' she finally declares, a voice scraped from the dry sides of her throat.

'I keep telling you that,' Angus says with a laugh.

'I mean, *nothing*.'

'Right?'

Evie shuts the fridge in mock disgust and heads back to her bedroom as though struck by a pressing thought.

The day is painfully slow, but more bearable once Evie decides to lean into her compromised condition instead of denying it. Angus suggests that what she needs is a generous serving of fried chicken (and of course he'd love some too), and to this Evie fails to find a counter-argument. They head for the nearest KFC, Evie driving like someone who should probably be wearing a large hat for a day of lawn bowls.

She orders everything on the overhead menu boards that looks appealing, prompting the young man who is serving her to helpfully suggest she simply order a mega family dinosaur beast bucket extravaganza super-size gates of hell deal. Something like that.

Evie winces, then shakes her head defiantly. 'No thanks,' she says and waves her arm across the menu like an evangelist. 'I'll just have *all of the things*.'

Angus looks on in hysterics.

The grease and salt and secret spices work their magic and at last Evie declares herself restored. 'God rest his soul,' she says to Angus, nudging her head at a picture of the Colonel.

'What were you doing anyway?' He smiles, still enjoying the show. 'Getting drunk on your own?'

'I didn't mean to,' Evie insists, abruptly mindful of the many terrible examples she's setting for her son today. 'I just forgot to eat and I was getting a bit emotional and then … It doesn't take much for me to get a little under the weather.'

'Why were you emotional?'

Evie recognises this as an unusual question for Angus, who normally spends his time evading sensitive conversations rather than initiating them.

'I was looking at old photos,' she says. 'For that photobook for Sera's birthday. I had to go right back through all the old albums, all the baby photos, all of it.'

'Oh,' Angus says, his expression suggesting this wasn't where he thought the discussion was going to go. He eyes the store's exit.

'It's just ... you forget, you know,' Evie says, pushing another fistful of chips into her mouth. 'How much we've all been through together. All those years. You *forget*. And then you stop for a minute and actually look at it all again and it doesn't seem possible that all that time has passed. You were just babies. And I had no idea what I was doing. And somehow you get through it all and just when you think it might be time to breathe out again, it's over. Because someone says it's over. Only they don't really say it, they just ... oh God ...'

Evie looks down from the ceiling at herself, crying at KFC. Possibly still drunk.

'It's okay, Mum,' Angus says and hands her a tiny moist towelette that she can't for the life of her unfold.

~

'Full disclosure,' Evie says. 'I might be a little hungover.'

James is moving swiftly about his kitchen, replacing one tray with another in the oven and checking something in a saucepan on the stove. He's a picture of industry and apparent contentment, a foil to Evie's current states of lethargy and regret.

'Angus did mention that,' James says, looking over at her seated at his kitchen table and offering a reassuring wink. 'The wonders of KFC are sadly short-lived.'

'I just can't handle a big night at my age anymore,' Evie says. 'It's brutal.'

'At your age?' James laughs. 'I think it's great they still allow alcohol at the nursing home.'

He moves around to the table and hands Evie a glass of something orange-coloured. 'A watered-down Aperol Spritz, purely restorative,' James says. 'Hair of the dog and all that.'

'Thank you,' Evie says, holding the glass in both hands as if to assess the weight of its potential damage. 'You're very good to have me when I'm like this. And whatever you're cooking smells incredible.'

Evie's reminded now of Ronni's house, the pungent aromas of garlic and basil and family, the warmth, the implicit welcome. She doesn't deserve this today, to bear witness to the thrum and alchemy of someone's home cooking.

'This is all pretty much ready if you are,' James says, pouring pasta into a sieve over the sink. 'I asked Angus if you were a vegetarian or allergic to anything and he said he didn't *think* so.'

Evie laughs. 'Classic observant teenager.'

James begins to bring steaming dishes across to the table one by one, his chair making dozens of tiny and smooth movements across the space, incremental adjustments for benches and edges that seem pre-programmed. He politely declines Evie's offers of help and so she simply watches him, feeling as superfluous as she probably looks.

The table had already been set, elaborately so, right down to a small bowl of butter curls (*butter curls!*) for the crusty bread and a huge array of condiments. James most likely, Evie reasons, did most of this earlier in the day, ensuring she only saw him at his capable best. The ninja maintaining appearances. Evie hopes he might start to loosen this ability narrative around her, for she barely notices the wheelchair now compared to when they first met.

'This is sensational,' Evie says, sampling one of the two pasta dishes James has prepared. There are also two salads, a potato bake, a tray of zucchini fritters and two giant stuffed mushrooms. 'You must have been cooking all day. There's so much food!'

'I may have gone a tad overboard,' James says, surveying the spread now as though through Evie's eyes. 'But I'm also a huge fan of leftovers. The gift that keeps on giving.'

'Cheers,' Evie says, lifting her glass up to invite James's.

'Cheers,' he says in return. 'Thanks so much for coming.'

And it's not just the food that makes Evie sigh and smile in turns for the next hour or two. It's James, the ease of his company, the warmth of his intent. The way he makes her feel enough, in any state. More than enough.

He shares more of himself tonight, perhaps sensing that Evie's closer to listening than talking mode this evening. He tells her about his time in the hospital, about some of the people he met there who he often thinks about but will likely never see again.

'You can't imagine a worse setting for strangers to be thrown together,' James recounts. 'It just reeks of catastrophe. Everyone's trying to process something they never thought they'd have to. You're looking for the case that's worse than you, the case that's better than you. You're trying to place your own despair on the spectrum somewhere.'

And Evie can't help herself at hearing this. She puts a hand on James's hand, hoping it's okay to do so. Hoping it doesn't seem patronising, that it isn't too much.

'The young men are the worst,' he continues. 'Their anger. It's the meanest kind of rage because you can't just punch a wall or kick a door. A lot of them have put themselves there of course. Driving drunk, speeding, diving into shallow rivers. And they're so mad, so furious, at pretty much everyone but themselves. Eventually they hate themselves too, but first the world.'

James looks up at Evie now and she's careful to reflect an expression that wills him to go on.

'Don't get me wrong,' he says. 'I was angry too. Anger gives you something to grab onto when you think you've lost everything. But the thing that someone needs to tell you, and someone did, thank God, a very kind and patient therapist who saw me almost every day, is that you *have* to feel anger in order to let go of it. It comes back again and again, and you just get better at staring it down.'

Evie looks at her empty plate now, its unfamiliar shape in this unfamiliar house. She thinks of all the people who've looked to her for help in the past, clients with their extramarital affairs and sex addictions and seven-year itches, the endless parade of problems with boredom at their core. And she feels selfish now for indulging any of it when there is so much worse and unthinkable, so irrevocable, that can happen to a person in an instant.

'You never seem angry to me,' she says at last. 'You always seem so positive.'

James gives the smallest of shrugs and she's careful now about how to proceed.

'But maybe,' Evie goes on, 'I've just seen you when you're happy to be seen, when you're feeling good about everything. I'm sure there are dark days, hard days.'

'Not as many as there used to be,' James says, lifting Evie's eyes with his own. 'You know what they say about time. It heals all wounds once it's finished actually *being* the wound. Can you believe I made butter curls?'

Evie splutters a laugh and eyes the butter curls on their little plate, an untouched ornament of effort. She sips the last of her Spritz, which has gone down much easier than she'd expected. 'What do you mean by that?' she says to him now. 'About time being the wound.'

James spears a tomato in his salad, then seems to change his mind about it. 'Well,' he says, 'for quite a while, especially when I first got home and the reality kicked in, that this is my life now, time just stretched into this horrible thing. Interminable. I hated time. Literally *hated* it. I'd started to think of it as something real, not a passive thing that just happens, but like a bully that I woke up to every day. I mean, obviously that started to change and here I am, I'm doing okay, but for ages I thought time was just the worst kind of arsehole.'

Evie laughs at this description. 'I completely agree with you,' she says. 'And I was thinking about this last night, actually, when I was, you know, slowly getting smashed on my own in my loungeroom—'

'When all light and wisdom descends,' James says with a smile.

'Exactly. I was thinking we all give time too much credit. Everyone's always saying give it time, everything gets better with

195

time, but time itself is often the problem. I think time probably wore down my marriage. I think after enough time people can just get sick of each other, sick of themselves.'

'Maybe,' James says. 'Or maybe you just married a sprinter instead of a stayer.'

'Maybe,' Evie says, and instantly regrets bringing this back to her own story. *Selfish, stupid, hungover.*

She insists on helping James clean up the dishes and he lets her. Evie used to loathe the feeling of other people being in her kitchen when she was cooking or cleaning up, but James doesn't seem to mind, moving easily around her and continuing the conversation as though they're still sitting opposite each other.

'I wonder if they're getting much study done over there,' Evie says, referring to Angus and Cobie, who are allegedly ensconced at her house for maths revision.

James shuts the dishwasher and lobs a tea-towel in the sink. 'Well, I think they got a fair bit done here last night,' he says. 'I mean, that's all two teenagers do in a bedroom together, right? Just study?'

Evie audibly gulps. 'Do you ever worry,' she says, 'about them taking … you know …'

'Liberties with each other? I kind of assume it.'

'No, about taking drugs. I found a bong in Angus's room.'

'Oh,' James says. 'Well, I'm not really surprised, to be honest. And I'm not too worried about it either.'

'Really?' Evie hears the slight shock in her tone.

'Look, firstly, they're both good kids,' James says, 'so I'm not worried about them being at the crossroads of bad decisions or spiralling into dangerous territory or anything like that. A little experimentation at this age is pretty normal. Probably not a bad thing actually.'

'Oh,' Evie says. And then unconvincingly, 'Okay.'

'I've worried you here, haven't I? Don't be worried, Evie. I'm not reckless about this stuff. I keep a close eye on Cobie, almost as close an eye as she keeps on me. But when it comes to the occasional use of recreational drugs, I take a much more liberal view than I used to.'

Evie steps back into a corner of James's kitchen cabinets, painfully denting her backside with a drawer handle. 'Why more liberal?'

'Small-l liberal, let me be clear on that,' James says. He turns now to look at Evie. It's the first time tonight she's felt him looking directly up at her, as opposed to across from her or just milling about each other in the kitchen, and Evie doesn't like it. Not because of how it makes her feel, but because of how she presumes it might make James feel. Her face must be conveying this, or perhaps it's the pain in her bum relaying discomfort, but James seems to pick up on it. Something between them shifts.

'Shall we finish this chat out on the deck?' James says, turning towards the side bench to flick the kettle on. 'I want to make you a special coffee.'

~

A constellation of fairy lights rings the entire back garden of James's home. Woven through thick bushes and hanging plants with leaves spilling to the ground, the lights cast a Disney glow onto an old cubby house, a vintage bike and various other decorative items that each might look kitsch on their own but somehow work together here. It reminds Evie of a garden restaurant in the hills of Ubud, verdant and sultry and intoxicating.

'This is such a gorgeous space,' she says to James as he brings out two cups of coffee on a small tray. He puts them on the table in front of the two-seater wooden bench Evie's sat on, then directs his chair to face the bench diagonally. James makes a couple of quick adjustments to his position and Evie sees what he's about to do.

'Make room!' James says. He lifts each of his knees with his hands to place his feet on the ground, shuffles forwards on the chair, then takes his weight in both arms, one on the bench and one on his chair, to pivot his body alongside Evie's. It's quick and methodical and Evie isn't sure what to say except, stupidly, 'Welcome.'

'Warm enough?' James asks her, 'because I can get you a jacket inside.' Then he laughs and adds, 'Actually, I'll probably just tell you where to find one.'

Evie assures him she's fine. The air is cool but it's pleasant and her body is still warm from the meal. The combination of these things makes Evie almost sleepy and she stretches out her legs in the manner of a happy retiree, feeling instantly self-conscious for doing so.

'Did you do all this?' she says, gesturing across the backyard. 'It's like an oasis.'

'It's something I've been working on for the past couple of years,' James says. 'Cobie's been a big help too. It's a bit of a father–daughter project. She brings the decorative ideas, like that old bike over there. And that's actually Cobie's old cubby house from when she was little.'

'It's all really lovely,' Evie says with an unexpected yawn she's too slow to stifle. 'If I had a garden like this, I would be out here all the time.' *Hiding. I'd be out here hiding.*

'A yawn,' James says, smiling at Evie. 'It's definitely time for a coffee.'

'I'm so sorry,' Evie says.

'Don't be silly. But let me explain this coffee to you first, Evie, if you'll indulge me. You asked me why I'd become more liberal about certain things. And to answer that I need to go back to what we were saying about time.'

'Okay,' Evie says uncertainly.

'When I came home from hospital and started to hate time as though it were an actual person, an old school friend of mine came around to visit me. That's what happens at the beginning – everyone comes out of the woodwork to call in and see you, to see the wheelchair really, to see you living their worst nightmare. To make sure it's you and not them. They all come around and say they heard about what happened, how sorry they are, how they're going to call by each week, take me to a movie, how they're sure I'm the kind of person who will turn this setback into something meaningful. Anyway, they all stop coming after a while. Which is fine. I get it. But this one old school friend of mine brought me something no one else had thought of, not even me. He brought me some weed. And Evie, it was the only thing, the *only thing*, that sometimes made time itself bearable. I didn't have it very often and

I still don't, but it helped me escape a little when I really needed to. So yeah, when I'm not wearing my teacher's hat, I'm a bit Switzerland about marijuana.'

'Well,' Evie says, rolling her hands over themselves in the folds of her skirt, 'that makes sense. I can completely understand why you'd feel that way about it.'

'Are you sure?'

'Of course. I'm just a little embarrassed now that I came across as such a wowser.'

'You didn't, not at all,' James says reassuringly. 'You're a good mum. Angus is lucky to have you. I guess I just wanted to be totally upfront with you, not just because the kids spend so much time together but because I care about what you think of me.'

Evie barely hears this last comment, so concerned is she now about appearing puritanical.

'I've done marijuana before,' she says now and hears the weird jump in her voice. 'Plenty of times when I was young. But it just doesn't have any effect on me. I guess it doesn't work for everyone.'

At this James laughs (a little too hard, Evie thinks). 'Well,' he says, 'would you like to test that theory tonight?'

'What do you mean?'

James points to the two cups on the table, no longer steaming. 'That coffee I made contains a little mull butter,' he says. 'Not much, just enough. It's so much nicer than smoking. But it's completely up to you. I won't have it if you don't. I don't need it. I just like it every now and then.'

'Oh,' Evie says. 'Right.'

Mull butter.

How did I get here?

Evie's concern about marijuana, now that she actually thinks about it, is less about the drug itself than her son's use of it and what it might signal. That he could be unhappier than she knew, that he might be hiding much more. He's too young and, right now, too vulnerable. And there is of course the simple fact that it's illegal. A criminal record wouldn't be a great way to begin life after school. Aside from all that, Evie doesn't hold any strong views about weed because she simply hasn't thought about it for a very long time. Hasn't needed to.

Post-Hamish life seems to bring her these moments of strange newness in which she feels watched, as though her life has become a performance, a completely unrehearsed one, raw and improvised, for a crowd (small, bemused, Saturday-matinee amateur theatre-goers) that she can't see. 'What will she do next?' she imagines the crowd whispering. *What will I do next?*

Sometimes she pictures Hamish in the crowd and has to blink her way through the moment until he's gone. He definitely wouldn't approve of Evie trying mull butter, she thinks now, and that helps her make the decision.

'I'd love to try some,' she says to James, even though she suspects she'd probably get a stronger hit out of straight coffee.

And it's an odd taste, Evie quickly discovers, though not disagreeable. Bitter and creamy, still just warm. As smooth as an oyster across the arc of her tongue. Evie can just sense the shape of the melting butter knob itself. She wonders if James had curled that too and the thought makes her smile.

James is looking anxiously at Evie's face. 'Well?' he asks.

'It's nice,' Evie says, taking another sip. 'Weird but nice.'

They sit and sip, steadily sinking into the silence. The air is warmer now, the sea breeze retired. Evie shuffles down into the bench seat to make it as comfortable as a bench seat can ever aspire to be. After a time she starts to point out various plants in James's garden, asking what their names are and if they'd grow from cuttings. 'Are you interested in gardening?' James asks her after they've worked through most of the backyard.

'God no, I hate it,' Evie says, and this makes him laugh for a good few minutes.

The coffee's odd taste starts to sit more easily with Evie until she finds that she's savouring each sip and wouldn't say no to another. After a time James puts on some music, using a playlist on his phone connected to an outdoor speaker. The sound seeps into the stillness, teasing the fairy lights to find the rhythm. The songs are playful and languid and shouty in turns, nothing Evie recognises.

'I don't know any new music,' she says with a dejected shrug. 'It's like I can't enjoy anything I don't already know the words to, so I keep going back to the old stuff. Every now and then I try to shock myself into coolness by putting on Triple J, but I feel like I've walked into the wrong party and everyone's staring at me.'

'I'm picturing you now,' James says, smiling at her, 'cruising down the Sunshine Motorway, belting out every single word of "We Didn't Start the Fire", slamming the steering wheel when he sings *I Can't Take It Anymore!*'

'You've seen me, haven't you?'

'Can't unsee it.'

'And why, James, *why* do I remember every single word to that song, yet I can't remember to defrost meat most days?'

He laughs. 'That's the magic of Billy Joel.'

'And here's another thing,' Evie says, recognising now that she's possibly talking a lot, quicker than usual. 'I read an article about Billy Joel just yesterday and then you go and mention him today. Don't you find that happens all the time, like there's always one *very specific* reference linking every book or movie or conversation to the next one? Like there's this constant daisy chain going on? It's a thing, right? There should be a name for it.'

'Stream of coincidence?' offers James.

Evie ponders this for a moment. 'That's very good,' she says. 'Am I talking too much?'

'Not at all, Evie.'

'I *really* like this coffee.'

The sky cracks open like a fault above them and Evie shoots upwards and then sidewards into James. 'Please tell me you heard that,' she says, panting. 'I'm not hallucinating?'

James laughs, says, 'The coffee isn't that strong. I think it might be fireworks.'

Evie cranes her neck skywards, waiting for the show, but there's only more sound, no colourful lights.

'They must be too far away,' James says.

Evie doesn't shift back to her original position on the bench. Instead she feels the heat of James's arm next to hers, the hairs touching her own, the crackle of proximity.

This? What is this?

The feeling takes a moment to announce itself, an unfamiliar visitor: attraction. And something else. Desire. *And these things feel good*, Evie thinks in her now slightly hazy state, *but misplaced*. She's opened the wrong door at the wrong time, needs to go back to the beginning. To reassess.

She turns to say something to James now, something about fireworks on TV being the saddest thing a person can watch, when he lifts his hand to Evie's cheek and pulls her face gently towards his and kisses her.

Evie's breath draws itself in, as though she's about to dive.

I'm being kissed.

This is happening.

Now.

And now.

It is still happening.

James kisses Evie for a long time, pausing to open his eyes and find hers, to ask if it's okay, if this is okay, and Evie nods because speaking might make this stop and she doesn't want it to.

They kiss until the air is empty again, the last firework expired.

31

Margaret

Dear Evie,

I hope this letter finds you.

I went back to see you again after blowing up my life. The counselling centre said you'd moved across the country, that you were teaching at a university. I did some Googling and found this address.

I wanted to thank you for your advice, all of which I ignored. I was a runaway train. You couldn't have stopped me. I wanted to tell you what I have learnt about myself in the past two years. Maybe you can use my story in your future counselling or teaching. Maybe not.

Evie, you may remember how lost I was. How I was struggling to pin down exactly which emotion was at the core of my pain – fear, exhaustion, sadness, regret, anger. They were all hitting up against each other. I couldn't see which thread to pull to start the unravelling (though unravel I did).

What I see now, very clearly and far too late, is that all of it is grief. All of it.

You can mourn time just like you mourn a person. It's no less devastating, no less final. In many ways, I was mourning both: the time I had lost and the person I used to be, the mother who was needed, the wife who was seen. It's not a midlife crisis, Evie – it's grief. And it can make you crazy.

No one tells you: that's the problem. No one says, 'This car isn't just going to stop one day, Margaret, it's going to crash.'

No one tells you and therefore you're completely unprepared. You have no idea what is happening to you, no words to pin to the board, nothing to grab on to. Except grief.

Evie, I left Stephen. I fell out of love with him as easily as deciding I could no longer stomach bread. It wasn't his fault, not entirely. He was pulling at all the wrong threads, but so was I. He thought I was something that had to be fixed, and fast, not someone who had changed.

Grief pulls you under.

I felt a desperate need to free myself, to get to the surface. I'd become trapped, stuck inside a photo frame on a wall, frozen in time and fading.

I had no plan. Grief has no plan.

And I made a terrible fool of myself, Evie. You can probably guess what I did next. I fell in love with a man I worked with. I say 'fell', but there was nothing accidental about it. Is there ever? It's a silly phrase. I chose him, I must have, as the target for this thing I needed to feel. To fill. Like kicking dirt into a grave.

I pressed him into shape. Pushed and patted and kneaded him into an idea I could love.

Projection, they call it.

I didn't know I could feel the way I did in his presence. The anticipation of proximity. The language of stolen glances. Words under my skin. The imprint of grief.

And here's the thing, Evie. You can manufacture almost everything in this life except the truth. I imagined it all, every last sign. Every coded message. Every widened eye. Every secret smile. Every innocent question. Love, reciprocated. You can build it out of air.

What a fool I was.

What a fool I am.

I had to leave my job. I couldn't bear to continue, to marinate in my mistake. Surely my crush had been visible to all, a running joke, the stuff of private message boards.

I went on a trip. The clichéd kind: India. And no, I didn't find myself. That would have been unbearable. I got a tattoo – 'Poenitet'. Latin for regret. Of course I did.

The logistics of misplaced grief: one family home sold, two small units purchased, furniture reassigned and reassembled.

Lawyers. Settlements. Shouting matches in all caps. Tears. Blame. Shame. The I-told-you-sos of in-laws, the division of friends.

My children.

Maybe you think it's telling that I'm only now mentioning them in this email, as if they were an afterthought in this whole debacle. Evie, they were. I put myself first in all of this – a frontline responder to my own grief.

And that is what my children will remember. Of course it is. Not the past seventeen years of care and devotion. Just the past seventeen months. When their mother fell apart and left them staring at freezer meals and a father sat on the couch with empty eyes.

I can't fix it, Evie. Grief burnt for too long, razed it all. And I can't say sorry now. God, no. It's not enough. To be sorry would be the worst thing of all at this point.

Stephen is dating someone. The kids told me. I said to them, 'That's nice for him' and then I went to bed for three days and wept and howled into dirty sheets.

I have a new job. And I have breast cancer. Fresh purpose. Together these things might stop me from jumping off again. From looking too hard at anything. From letting more grief seep under the door like gas.

Distraction as framework – that's how I'm staying upright these days, Evie. The rebuilding process is under way.

I do hope you are well.

Best,

Margaret

32

Evie's remembering kisses.

The first, when she was just six. The boy next door, literally. They'd spent a whole day finding the right location, somewhere dark and secret. That'd been the fun part. They'd finally settled on the banana trees at the back of his father's shed. Straggly old leaves shielding them like a plastic strip door.

Cameron. Somehow she remembers his name. He'd instructed Evie on how to hold her head. Slight angle to the right. *Now be very, very still. Eyes closed. Wait. Get ready to twist your head from side to side. You ready?* Cameron had finally landed on her mouth like a fly hitting a window. Evie twisted her head as told and Cameron did the same. A lot of mutual, frantic twisting. Sometimes the seal between them broke and Evie would quickly open her eyes to see where she should be aiming.

When it was over, they ran in to their respective homes and never once spoke of it.

Another: her first teenage kiss. A school disco. A basketball stadium pretending to be something else. Phillip. The fastest boy in Evie's year. She hadn't known he'd liked her until he leant into her ear during 'Run to Paradise' and yelled 'You're so *unique.*' Then he'd proceeded to vigorously pash her and Evie had worried she might fall over.

Pash. Evie hasn't thought of that word for years.

The best kisser, technically speaking: Scott. Tortured poet from a bad movie script. They'd been two-sixths of a share house during Evie's university years. He'd made her his project one summer, a vessel of his devotion. When Scott had kissed Evie, her whole body responded, blood simmering under flesh. He was a master at work, committed to excellence, spinning perfect webs out of Evie's abandon. His were the kisses you remember almost thirty years later.

Hamish then. Ticklish bristles and coffee. The smell of home. Of safety. Kisses that evolved over the years from opening statements to closing arguments. Kisses like full stops. Like reminders.

Enough.

Evie lies back in her bed now. She hasn't slept in this late for years. Rain comes down hard on her roof, making the room feel like a bunker. She thinks about last night, about James's kiss. It had been unexpected. Not the act, not entirely, but Evie's reaction to it. She had leant into it, wanted it. The smell of him, the shape of his jaw, the taste of his tongue. The foreignness of it all. To be pulled in and wanted.

God.

Of course James's special coffee might have played a part in

210

events. Softened Evie's resolve. It had already been a night in which she'd felt a step outside herself, maybe even ahead of herself, as though a new part of Evie was grafting itself onto her life.

What am I doing?

Evie remembers things feeling a little rushed after the kiss. She was home before she knew it. Neither of them seemed to know the shape of the conversation that should follow such a moment.

Moments.

And so what is this now? Evie thinks. Just an impulsive act, now extinguished, snatched from blurred thoughts and rogue fireworks? Something else? How does this work?

I hate this.

It was wonderful.

Evie feels her body responding to the memory of James's mouth. She decides to text him, to say thank you for the evening, but mainly to elicit a response she can decipher. To make sense of this.

And just as she's moving the words around in her mind, a message lands on her phone screen and Evie blinks hard to see it carefully. She reads it several times, willing it to change.

James: *I'm so sorry, Evie. I should never have done that last night. I hope we can still be friends.*

Oh.

Oh.

Evie rolls her head into her pillow, smothers every thought from her mind.

33

'One week to go,' Sera says, followed by something that sounds like 'Squee!'

Evie does her best to echo the energy in her daughter's voice and feels guilty it has to be such a conscious effort. She *wants* to enjoy this milestone, for it to be memorable for Sera for all the right reasons. But as each day passes now, the fact of the party being where and when she might see Hamish again feels increasingly fraught. Somehow she should have undone this before now.

Her dreams have been of nothing else. A messy collage of reunion scenes, wounded glances, angry words and abrupt departures. Awful silences. Sometimes Hamish is standing beside a woman, a person Evie is able to scrutinise forensically behind the veil of dreaming, and sometimes he's alone. Sometimes he's crying. Sometimes he's smiling stupidly. Last night Evie dreamt she'd arrived at the party with no clothes on. That she'd looked down at her body and seen right through her skin to pulsing organs.

Shit. Costume.

'Have you got your costume sorted?' Sera asks. 'No pressure if you don't want to wear one, Mum. It's fine.'

'I definitely do plan to wear one,' Evie says, 'but I haven't landed on anything yet. The most interesting thing about the year 2000 was you.'

'Aw, Mum.'

'I mean, I thought about going as a Mad Cow, but the point is to dress up, isn't it?'

'Comedy gold.'

Evie looks out at the ocean. She's seated on a wooden bench atop a lookout over a quiet beach. She'd found this spot recently, on yet another long drive to outrun her thoughts. 'What are you going as?'

'Peak Britney Spears. The schoolgirl outfit from "Hit Me Baby One More Time". I know, technically 1998 but *anyway*. And yes, a lame choice for feminism but I'm doing it in a kind of ironic way.'

'Irony is great.'

'Plus I will look hot.'

Evie smiles. 'Of course.'

'What's Angus going as?'

'He was talking about that film, *Castaway*. Either going as Tom Hanks in the lap-lap thing and a long beard or as Wilson with a basketball over his head.'

Sera laughs. 'Nice.'

'We can't wait to get there, Sera. I'm really sorry it's been so long.' And Evie hears the inadequacy of each word as it leaves her mouth.

'All G, Mum.'

Evie gives Sera the details of the Airbnb she's booked for Ronni, Angus and herself. She knows it will be strange to be in Perth as a visitor, aware that her old house is just a few suburbs away, the last place everything made sense or at the very least felt normal. For a long time after Hamish left, Evie had wanted to turn back time, put them all back in that house and force everyone to take a deep, deep breath before proceeding with new jobs and hasty plans. It's less an urge now than a question mark.

'Mum,' Sera says now, 'Dad arrived here yesterday. He's staying in a hotel.'

And this news makes contact, striking Evie right in the chest. The thought of him occupying physical space again, as though he hadn't yesterday but does now.

It's okay, it's okay, it's okay.

She pictures Hamish walking quickly through an airport, a single bag trailing, a plan marinating in his mind about how best to tackle this, which conversations to have and in what order, the politics of it all. Always the politics.

Evie wants to think that this must be, *should be*, so much harder for him than for her. But that would be certain if she really knew Hamish, and clearly she hadn't or at least no longer did. That would be certain if she knew any of the details – the hows and whys and wheres and who – but she didn't and she doesn't. Because they weren't made available and she hadn't wanted to ask. Evie had been too afraid to know any piece of information until she thought it might not dismantle her.

'Oh okay,' Evie says to Sera. 'That's good. And is he alone or will he be, you know, bringing someone along to the party?'

Sera pauses for an aeon.

'He's alone,' she says finally. 'He actually asked me if *you* were coming alone and I said you were bringing a friend called Ronni. He kind of freaked out a bit until I explained that Ronni was a woman.'

'Right.'

'Mum, are you going to be okay with this?'

'Of course, darling,' Evie says. 'I'm going to be fine.'

Fine, fine, fine.

34

She's hardly slept. Her coffee should taste better than it does, more therapeutic. She's here at the shop at Ronni's invitation, which is unusual. Most of their catch-ups are unscheduled. But Ronni had insisted she be here at nine am, a request she's clearly forgotten as it's now nine-thirty and Evie is two coffees in.

So that she doesn't now think about Hamish, about this weekend and everything she's hopelessly unprepared for, Evie thinks about James. He'd sent her a message yesterday to invite her sailing this weekend, as though his last message had never happened or perhaps to soften it. A cloud of confusion had temporarily settled upon her until Evie simply explained she was off to Perth, that she hoped the weather would be kind for him. James had wished her all the best, signing off with an X. After much staring into space, she'd done the same. Evie had subsequently re-read the messages maybe eight or forty-eight times to arrive at the most reliable interpretation of intent and emotion.

James is trying to reset their friendship, she figures. Pre-kiss.

And Evie's happy to do the same, or at least try to, except that she can't forget the kiss and all it revived in her. She also can't ignore the fact that she's attracted to James, charmed and fascinated by him in a way one doesn't expect to feel after twenty years of marriage, and that his kiss had only confirmed for her that old unmistakeable feeling that is desire.

'*I should never have done that last night*'. Evie has gone over James's words many times, trying to establish the transgression he thinks he's made. Or the transgression he's possibly inventing to get past the fact Evie's a bad and hopelessly out-of-practice kisser.

Less likely is that James is apologising for what he himself can't do, physically. Evie knows it's possible James doesn't have normal sexual function, some paraplegics don't, and that he might be protecting her from that, putting an early handbrake on the situation. If that's the case, Evie has thought, she would've liked a say in matters. Sex is not where her head is at these days.

'A penny for them.' The voice comes from above her and to the left, muffled by the mid-morning rush. Evie turns to see Ryan.

Blind date Ryan. Didn't-care-to-kiss-me Ryan.

'Oh hi,' Evie says, willing Ronni to materialise *now*. 'I'm just waiting for Ronni actually. I think she might have stood me up.'

'Mind if I sit here for a bit?'

Yes.

'No, of course not.' Evie redundantly points to the only seat opposite her.

It takes just minutes to realise this meeting is no coincidence, that Ronni's had her hand in it. And she's irritated by this fact, yet equally unwilling to imagine anything bar good intent on her friend's part. Ronni's forgiveness-over-permission approach to life is hardwired.

Ryan's nervous. He looks at Evie now as though she's someone he's greatly wounded and deserves an explanation. His words tumble out without pause, at times sounding rehearsed though not insincere, while in other moments he seems to surprise himself with a realisation. Much like she did at the Mexican restaurant when Ryan had revealed his weight battle, Evie feels her counsellor status is assumed here, that she should be saying something reassuring or helpful. Instead, she forces herself to simply listen.

'I'm sorry,' Ryan says. For not contacting her after their date. For not thanking her for being so kind to him that night. For not kissing her when he'd badly wanted to. For leaving Evie to think there was something deficient about herself.

This is all too much and unnecessary, Evie thinks, but she lets him continue, too tired to interject. She nods and smiles in the right places, hoping her face is saying *It's okay, it really is.*

'I wasn't ready to date,' Ryan continues, 'but everyone wants you back on the horse, don't they? My ex was practically throwing me in the ring, anything to make her feel better about what she'd done. But it's so hard, it's *too* hard, to work out which picture of yourself to present to someone new, because you've just been rejected, right? You've been tossed aside. You're not enough. And now you've got to cobble something together with that. Something that will appeal to someone else who you know nothing about. It's brutal and I wasn't ready for it. And halfway through our date I realised that. I remembered that someone I loved more than anything had left me, hadn't even looked back, and that I was still that person. I *am* that person. The fat guy, minus the fat.'

Ryan takes a deep breath and Evie can't help but place her hand on his forearm at this point, leaving it there just long enough to convey empathy, nothing more confusing. She sees this exchange is about so much more than their date, that Ryan has set up his own watershed moment of sorts.

Evie's phone shudders. A text message from Ronni: *Running late. Kids!*

'I really wanted to kiss you that night,' Ryan says now and looks hard at Evie's sleepless eyes. 'And somehow I couldn't, and it took me a little while to work out why. Because you looked so beautiful, Evie, and you do now too.'

'God,' Evie says, not expecting this at all and not for a second believing it. 'I must look hideous.'

'Not at all,' he says, and Evie twirls her hand weirdly in the air as if to say *Move on*.

He does. 'Evie, I realised afterwards that I hadn't wanted to kiss you that night because it would signal to myself that I'd moved on, that I was starting a new chapter and letting go of the old one. I hadn't kissed anyone but my wife for fifteen years – I still haven't. And somehow that became a big thing for me, bigger than it needed to be, I suppose. It's one thing to have a nice dinner with someone new, but a kiss is so … something else.'

And Evie sees James now, his eyes centimetres from hers and shut tight, their kiss playing on the wall above Ryan's head from a rear projector.

He is right about this, she thinks: the weight of a kiss. She misses them far more than sex.

'Anyway,' Ryan says, pressing his hands on to the table now as though ready to summarise his case, 'you dodged a bullet that night, Evie. I had so much going on up here. You were the collateral damage of all that, and I'm really sorry.'

Evie wants to say that any damage she sustained was very minor and fleeting, but also doesn't want to hurt Ryan or change the narrative he's developed through introspection. And actually, now she thinks about it, the evening *had* landed her in a strange coffee shop late at night, stalking her husband's possible new partner and finding a woman's face she can't now blink away.

This, she thinks, is the problem at the core of middle-aged dating – the near impossibility of sitting opposite someone without years of memories and hurt and questions and issues to project upon you. Someone hoping to recreate themselves on the canvas of another life. To be loved better. To love better. Quid pro quo. *Impossible.*

'Ryan,' Evie says and it comes out sounding like the first time she's actually spoken his name. 'There's no need to apologise. Honestly.'

'Well,' he says, 'I wanted to. And I also wanted to ask if you'll let me make it up to you?'

Evie looks at him blankly.

'Let's not call it a date,' he says, 'but let's call it dinner, maybe a movie. This weekend.'

Evie explains why she can't this weekend.

'Tomorrow night, then?'

And Evie thinks about last night, and the night before, the long hours of not being able to lie still, let alone sleep. The dark tunnel and all its slippery fear.

In spite of herself, in spite of everything, she nods to Ryan: *Okay.* She tries to make her face present something other than acquiescence borne of tiredness. Her right eye starts to twitch.

Perhaps anticipating a change of heart, Ryan thanks Evie and says he has to go now. Barely a minute later, Ronni sweeps into the seat just vacated. *She might as well be holding a relay baton,* Evie thinks but manages a smile.

'So what'd I miss?' Ronni says with a wink.

35

Kyle and Juanita

Couples of fifty years or more often boast (somewhat smugly, Evie's long thought) that their union has proved impervious to change. 'She's still the same woman I married all those years ago,' the proud patriarch will say, as though his sound early judgement had snapped up a car for all ages. As though evolution of either personality was never a desirable goal.

A generation later, Evie usually heard a far different refrain in her counselling room: *They've changed.*

Many of the couples who came to her – one party striding first into the room as though holding aloft a pair of shoes that bore no resemblance to the ones they'd ordered online – wanted Evie to exhume the person they once knew. The one they'd pledged their life to, had children with, sacrificed careers and dreams and waistlines for, endured a painful extended family for. Where has *that* person gone?

It's what had brought Juanita to her door several years ago, though not with the confidence of someone leading the charge. She'd seemed weary and brittle sitting before Evie that first day, wrung out by self-doubt. It wasn't so much a solution that Juanita was seeking as confirmation. Evidence she wasn't going mad. A witness to her wit's end.

Her husband, Kyle, on the other hand, had quickly surveyed the room, and Evie, as terrain to be mapped. He'd taken up one of Evie's chairs as though testing it out in a furniture store, positioning himself for maximum comfort. Counselling might not have been his idea, but he was clearly ready to steer the ship.

Kyle, Juanita had explained when prompted by Evie to start the conversation, had been her proverbial knight fifteen years earlier. He'd lured her from small-town life in Western Australia's goldfields and brought her to the city. It wasn't, Juanita said, that she'd needed rescuing, just that she hadn't ever considered leaving behind her family, friends and secure banking job until she met Kyle.

Sharp-cornered and thirsty for everything, Kyle had waged an all-out campaign for Juanita's devotion. He'd peeled away her cautious shell, travelled to every corner of her being and all but devoured her with his desire. He was the first person to make Juanita feel arresting, sexy, interesting, all of it. She brought out the best in him, he would tell her over and over, and Juanita believed the same of him. It was less a relationship than a mutual transformation, much more than the sum of its parts.

Kyle had wooed not just Juanita but everyone in her circle. The 'golden couple' people had called them (Juanita winced at that recollection). Even her indomitable father had weakened to Kyle's charm – it's hard not to like the guy who brings his wife's family on the second half of a Hawaii honeymoon. 'He was just that guy,' Juanita explained to Evie, 'that everyone liked. And he'd picked me.'

Kyle, Evie had noticed, seemed to be enjoying this version of events very much, even if it did sound like the premise of a movie with an uncomfortable twist.

'And then,' Juanita said, 'he became someone I don't even know anymore.'

It began with a comment two years back, months after their third and unexpected child had been born. Kyle had told Juanita he was no longer attracted to her body and that she should try harder to lose weight. 'I'm just being honest,' he'd said at the time. 'You're lucky I'm not one of those guys who would cheat on his wife.'

Juanita said it was the first time Kyle had been blatantly cruel, though veiled digs about her weight had begun after the first baby arrived.

Kyle had quickly countered this story, telling Evie he was trying to be helpful, to spur Juanita into action so she could feel good about herself again. Juanita told Evie the opposite was true. Starting to cry, she said it was clear Kyle no longer wanted her to feel good about herself, that he seemed happiest when she was low and weepy and paranoid. Perversely, Juanita had started better serving his moods by denying herself all the things that used to make her happy.

Kyle shook his head at all of this, unperturbed by the shuddering of his wife's shoulders.

Juanita continued. When Kyle had lost his job last year (a casualty, he'd said, of 'overpaid egos and idiots'), he'd added Juanita to the list of offenders, saying she hadn't been supportive enough since the kids had come along. In fact it had been the fourth job he'd lost in as many years. A chain of fools had apparently undermined him out of jealousy.

'It's true,' Kyle had said to Evie. 'I've been surrounded by imbeciles.'

He spent most of his spare time now at the gym, Juanita said, working on a body he'd said 'is probably wasted around here now'.

And even Kyle had heard how that sounded out loud to a stranger. 'Evie,' he'd said, slowly raising his hand like a defence lawyer with ample time left to sway the jury. 'I'm being misrepresented here. This is unfair. I've devoted my life to Juanita. She is the love of my life, always has been, always will be. That's why I'm here today. This is as much my idea as hers.'

Juanita shook her head: 'That's just not true.'

'But I won't be blamed for her depression. I want to be part of the solution. I am *not* the cause.'

'*Depression*,' Juanita had said, glaring at her husband. 'That's your word, not mine.'

Evie was finding it hard to keep this one on the rails.

'Paranoia then,' Kyle had said to Evie, his palms raised now to the ceiling in exasperation. 'That's the real reason we're here. Juanita thinks I'm having an affair with every woman I meet, and I meet a *lot* of women. Her trust issues are killing us. And they're all in her head.'

In subsequent sessions with the couple, Evie had tried to prise open these 'trust issues', finding that as inextricably linked as they were to the way Juanita had come to feel about herself, they were not preposterous, not unreasonable. Kyle was openly flirtatious – 'always have been' he'd cheerfully offered – but he spent far less time at home than he used to and no longer felt any need to explain his absences.

'Why should I,' he'd put to Evie, 'when I'm not doing anything wrong?'

'Because you know it makes your wife upset,' Evie had responded, gently, carefully.

'Well,' Kyle said, nodding at the pile of sodden tissues on Juanita's lap. 'She's always upset. It doesn't matter what I do or say or how much I spend on her.'

At this point Evie glanced down at her notes and underlined the last word she'd written: *Narcissist?*

The term had become overused, frequently misused, but Evie suspected Kyle would qualify for a diagnosis. The arrogance, self-prioritisation, lack of empathy, tick, tick, tick. She also suspected that Juanita might be wrong, that Kyle hadn't fundamentally changed at all, that perhaps he'd always been this way. Narcissistic traits tended to become more pronounced after marriage, after the deal was sealed. The interdependence of commitment is kryptonite to the narcissist, the arrival of children a disaster of dilution.

Evie didn't use the term in her sessions with Juanita and Kyle. She knew it could prove reductive, possibly disastrous. Instead she'd suggested they each start coming to her separately for a period, her best chance of short-circuiting the dynamic.

In her sessions with Juanita, Evie had focused on what could be realistically expected from Kyle, how to reset Juanita's personal boundaries and ways to mend her own self-esteem. Evie had known she was likely preparing Juanita for life after Kyle.

In Evie's only session with Juanita's husband (throughout which he'd worn steel-rimmed sunglasses and rested his hands on either side of his crotch as if to assist with size calculations), Kyle had asked if she was allowed to date clients.

36

She looks up at the ceiling, its unfamiliar shape. A bed cover heavier than her own.

The wrong side. She's on the wrong side of this bed.

Evie moves slightly: she is naked. She never sleeps without clothes on. And she has slept – actually *slept*. The almost foreign feeling of deep rest.

And she has had sex.

Oh God.

I had sex.

The word summons every ion of awareness to Evie's physical body. Separate from her now, peculiar and dangerous.

The man beside her, Ryan, is snoring heavily, his bare back rising and falling. It's a back she's never before seen, not even last night, and which belongs to the man she had sex with.

No, no, no.

It's too much. Evie looks around her for the untethered bedsheet promised by every post-coital movie scene. But there's nothing here to wrap herself in and she can see her clothes in a pile near the bedroom door.

Now. I need to leave now.

Guided by the rhythm of Ryan's contented heaving, Evie wends her way slowly from the bed and across the room to her clothes and shoes, an almost comic little pile that reminds her in an instant of lost nights at university, a time before she became a happily married woman and someone who thinks about creasing consequences.

She dresses quickly and clumsily. Glances back over to the occupied bed and wilfully shuts her eyes on the story. She finds her way out of the small and sparse unit and into the blinding truth of the day.

In her car, Evie tries to remember how to drive and in which direction. She allows herself four suburban blocks of forced brain silence before thinking about the events of last night.

There had been, she recalls now, a sense of inevitability to it all, at least from about eight o'clock when Ryan had slipped his hand into hers while in their cinema seats. When she hadn't moved, hadn't politely retrieved her hand, Ryan began gently stroking the inside of her palm with his finger, maybe a knuckle. They'd continue to stare at the screen like teenagers quietly on fire. She would never remember the movie.

This needs to happen, Evie had thought in those moments. For both of them. It simply did.

She stops now behind a school bus at a set of lights. Remembers her text message to Angus – *Having a few drinks with a friend. Might sleep in her spare room if it gets too late. Love you!* – and wonders what he'd made of that.

Ryan had been nervous but in the confident way of someone who acknowledges his nerves (in stark contrast to Evie, who literally shook in silence when he reached around to remove her bra). His voice was a constant presence, talking them through foreplay like a tour guide through an earpiece at the Louvre.

It felt nothing like she remembered, being entered. It didn't, at least not immediately, conjure any flashbacks or inconvenient visions – Ryan's head switched out for her husband's. It felt entirely new.

He'd moved with her. A rhythm was quickly established and still he'd talked throughout. *Are you okay? Is this all right? You feel incredible.*

And Evie had ever so briefly lost herself in this ancient act. The visceral joy of it, of being removed from everything else, couldn't be denied. It could only be embraced. *This feels good,* she'd thought, opening her eyes to glance past Ryan's shoulder. *It does. It does.*

So good!

But then.

Evie's thoughts had flown back into her. Up at her, like bats in the dark. Everything was wrong. This was not her husband. Not her room. Not her life. Surely not her life. Rapture left her body like an ocean receding, like the rogue tide that had so terrified her client Sanaya.

'You're the first person,' Ryan had said, breathing hard and loudly on his back when they'd finished, 'I've been with since my wife.'

And Evie had said, 'Me too.' But she could see they were feeling the significance of this in very different ways. Because there was both jubilance and relief in Ryan's voice, in his breathless recovery, his sighs to the ceiling, but all Evie had wanted to do was cry. And she wished she didn't.

Now in the car, Evie looks up at the rear-vision mirror, not knowing what she'll see, who'll look back at her. Her eyes are dark and smudged like fire pits. She had waited for Ryan to go to sleep and then wept as quietly as she could, the tears propelled from deep within, finding their way out like old secrets.

There'll be mascara on those sheets. Evie almost laughs at herself for the thought.

How many years had she counselled couples (albeit hesitantly, like a dismantler of explosives) about their sex lives, about whether they were *good* or *bad*? Such reductive words, she thinks now. As though the act itself is something you can get fundamentally wrong. It's not. The act is simple assembly. It's everything *around* sex that can be good or bad and in that sense she'd liked what she and Hamish had once shared. Their sex life had been something beyond good, or so she'd thought.

Of course there's a sameness that sets in after five or ten or fifteen years together, of course there is, but Evie had found this oddly comforting rather than devastating. It didn't panic her. The shape she'd worn into Hamish's left shoulder and chest, her head burrowed into his side directly after they'd made love, resting there, serene and sated, until one of them had to move – it was a shape worn from time and everything that goes with it. That shape, now she's allowing herself to think about it, is what Evie misses most.

The truly memorable sex with Hamish was never about trying

out a new position or a boozy foray into dirty talk or an unusually long go of it. They were, for Evie at least, generally attached to a place. In the pool at a villa in Bali at midnight. A noisy cheap hotel room in Brighton-Le-Sands – their first childless getaway. And, just six months before they'd left Perth for oblivion, a weekend at a dreamy doll-like cottage in Margaret River, when Hamish had said to her, seconds before he came, 'It just keeps getting better, doesn't it?'

Well. *Not enough evidently.*

But yes, it had got better, in the sense that it had never got worse, as it might have. There had been gaps. Long gaps. Silent gaps. But they were like treeless plains on a long drive.

Evie had simply never imagined being with anyone but Hamish, not even after he'd left. So this. Last night. Sex with someone else. It had, finally perhaps, pushed her marriage up against a hard border, one she hadn't been willing to see until now. Rendered it finished, unfixable. *Over.*

That's why, Evie sees now, she cried last night. Silent and unstoppable, her tears had washed away the last of her doubts.

Simple Minds comes on the radio. 'Don't You Forget About Me.'

Don't. Don't. Don't. Don't.

She switches it off and pulls into her garage.

~

Angus is sitting on a stool in the kitchen, about three hours before he would normally turn his face to the sun. He's phone-deep in apparent concentration but Evie knows he must have been waiting for her.

'Hi!' she says with purposeful zest.

Angus works hard to convey impassivity, but a twitch in his jaw betrays him. 'Hi,' he says eventually. 'Big night?'

'Not really,' Evie says, putting her keys beside the fruit bowl and carefully inspecting a banana. She has definitely not thought this through, didn't expect Angus to be awake, let alone curious and possibly angry with her. *Shit.*

'It wasn't big,' Evie says, 'but it just got a little late. I thought I'd better not drive home tired. I haven't been sleeping lately.'

Angus looks at her. 'Me neither.'

'Oh. I'm sorry, Ang. You should have told me. I've got some herbal sleeping tablets I could have given you.'

'Do they work?'

'Nope, useless.'

Angus refuses to laugh. Says, 'Whose house were you at?'

'A friend of Ronni's.'

'A male friend?'

Evie commences peeling the banana in her hand, then looks at it differently and throws it back in the bowl.

'Yes,' she says gently. 'Is that okay?'

Angus shrugs. Says nothing for a long time, then, 'Dunno.'

Evie feels the dampness between her legs now. The tawdriness of it all. The sadness and desperation. Ryan's ceiling. Her endless tears.

'I don't know either, Angus,' she says. 'I wish I did.'

'It's all pretty fucked,' he says.

'Well, it's certainly partially fucked.'

'I would never hurt someone the way Dad's hurt you.'

'I know you wouldn't. And you won't.'

And Evie hopes this will be true, even if Hamish's actions as a failed role model will prove unhelpful. She wishes she didn't know the statistics.

'But I'm okay, Angus,' Evie says. 'I really am. And you will be too. We all will.'

We will.

He stands and puts his phone in his pocket. 'Okay.'

'And this weekend is going to be great. I promise. We're going to have fun.'

Angus leaves this comment untouched. He walks towards the front door, Polo nipping at his hairy ankles. Says, 'I'm going to Cobie's.'

37

It transpires that Ronni hasn't been on a plane since 1985. She was thirteen when her parents took their family of six on an epic journey back to the mother country, the expense of which they've never let any of the children forget. Ronni's memories of the flight are that her parents chain-smoked from start to finish and that she got her first ever period in the air.

'Why haven't you flown anywhere since then?' Angus asks her now as they wait for their flight to be called.

Ronni shrugs uncomfortably. 'Too busy,' she says. 'Can't sit still for very long.'

Evie sees her friend is eyeing the departures board as though it might explode in front of her. That everyone is wearing masks, an end-of-world-ish sight that unluckier parts of the country have reluctantly grown accustomed to, is not helping Ronni's demeanour. She is frightened, an airport terror stare holding her face rigid, and Evie can't imagine what she did to earn this sort of sacrifice from someone she has known for such a short time. How will she ever repay Ronni?

She has booked them exit-row seats for extra leg-room, she and Ronni on one side of the aisle and Angus on the other. When they're finally able to take their seats after several unexplained delays, Ronni's nerves are on full display. She stabs at the touch screen in front of her, its poor sensitivity signalling something much bigger to her about the integrity of the plane. Evie watches her buckle and unbuckle her seat belt several times to openly query its robustness. When a cabin attendant begins explaining to them the special responsibilities of these seats, Ronni asks her to please pause so she can retrieve a notebook and pen from her bag. To the question of whether she would be willing to take action in an emergency, Ronni answers in a grave and serious tone, speaking extra loudly as though the mask she's wearing is a heavy hand: 'I am prepared to save us all.' Evie sees Angus pull his shirt up to his eyes to hide laughter.

Take-off is assisted by thirty or more vigorous signs of the cross issued by Ronni (her relationship with God is predicated on threat more than faith). Evie talks her through it – ten deep breaths to get them off the tarmac and then another twenty minutes or so of distraction to see them above the clouds. She shows Ronni how to navigate the in-flight entertainment menu but quickly sees that her friend is simply too wired to sit and watch a movie. And that five hours might not be enough time for Ronni to get through everything that's currently on her mind. For she's not just here for moral support, as Evie's quickly come to understand. This is not just a short reprieve from her literally grounded life to pat a friend's hand. She is mission-bound, steadfastly attached to the goal of no harm befalling Evie this weekend. Fred's Barney.

Maverick's Goose. Thelma and Louise pre-canyon.

Ronni wants to roleplay *all* the possible scenarios that might go down when Evie sees Hamish again. She has seemingly thought of every possibility: if Hamish approaches Evie first, if he's with someone, if he ignores her, if Evie feels confident about approaching him first, if he's attached to a drip stand, if any limbs are missing. Many more. Ronni makes Evie briefly remove her mask and perfect at least ten variations of a look that says 'happy indifference'.

'And I can't,' Ronni says when she's finally satisfied with Evie's facial interpretation of ambivalence, 'promise you I won't say anything to any puttana your husband brings to this party. It could happen. I don't know. I have no control over this.' By 'this', Ronni indicates she means her whole head and everything it contains and displays.

'Okay,' Evie says.

'Okay.'

In defence of this position, Ronni offers a story Evie could not have expected. She tells her that about three years ago, she intercepted a flirty text message from the receptionist at the large car service workshop where Vince is employed. It read: *Where are you? You've been hiding from me.* Wink emoji.

For a whole day, Ronni had let the words move about in her head (Evie in fact pictures a washing machine on the highest setting), trying to arrive at their most likely context. She'd doubted, though not blindly, that Vince had initiated the exchange but that more likely the receptionist ('Let's call her Tina,' Ronni says, 'because that's her stupid name') was starting something. The first division of cancerous cells.

'That's how these things *begin*, Evie,' Ronni says at a volume to educate at least three rows of passengers. 'With a little look or a laugh or a *wink emoji*. It's all nothing and innocent until it's not. And then it's all "Oh I didn't *mean* for anything to happen. It just *happened*."'

'But I don't,' Evie says, 'think that Vince is really the type.'

'Who knows!' Ronni says, throwing her arms up so wildly that her knuckles hit the bulkhead above them. 'Jennifer didn't think Brad was the type. Maybe some people just *become* the type because fucking Angelina Jolie says "Where are you? You've been hiding from me. Here's a wink emoji to jerk off to."'

Evie can hear the woman behind them chuckling. Thank goodness Angus is already ensconced in a movie.

'So I was lucky, Evie,' she continues at pace. 'I caught it. Nipped it right in the germoglio. I replied to the text myself and said *Hi Tina. No he's not hiding from you. And you can't hide from me.*'

'You didn't!'

'Of course I did. And then I deleted it. Vince still has no idea.'

'Well,' Evie says, 'maybe he does.'

Ronni appears to think about this. 'Maybe,' she says. 'But even if I was wrong about *Tina* –' (she says her name as though it's dripping in entrails) '– it doesn't matter. This is about *all* of the predators. We have to look out for each other.'

Evie sees the words like the title of a book: *The price of marriage is eternal vigilance.* And instantly wants to dismiss the idea. She had not been vigilant with Hamish. She hadn't been a phone-checker. She had trusted trust itself. Time served. But maybe Ronni is right.

'Can you still wee on a plane?' she asks, and Evie points her to the toilets at the back.

When she returns, Ronni walks right past their seats and continues to the very front of the aircraft, where she pivots and starts walking slowly back again, eyes shifting left and right to canvas every passenger on each side. Finally she resettles next to Evie, buckles her seatbelt and practises the crash position. 'Not one famous person,' she says when upright again. 'You'd think there'd be one on a plane this big.'

Ronni's clearly disappointed and it makes Evie smile. Her friend's fascination with celebrity has been a source of fond amusement since they met. It's not the standard obsession: the want to stand beside a shiny thing, to plug into a false power source. It's something else – a base desire to remove the artifice of fame and rescue the person beneath. She'd once told Evie she could see the *real* Kylie Minogue trapped within the girl-woman who put her trust in flighty men. She said what Kylie really needed was a best friend like Ronni who would sit on the couch with her on a Friday night and eat caramel popcorn and dissect John Hughes films and laugh until one of them had to pee. That she'd sent Kylie a letter inviting her to meet up and hadn't got a reply. That Kylie may have misunderstood.

'Maybe she thought it sounded a bit stalkery,' Evie had said, and Ronni had shaken her head emphatically and said, *No, Evie*, the letter had clearly opened with *Kylie, I don't wish to harm you in any way.*

And Evie still laughs about this whenever the memory surfaces.

In many ways Ronni's proprietorial interest in Evie is similar though in reverse: she sees something special beneath the ordinary, something of broader interest, something worth excavating.

Their meal arrives and Ronni is aghast at its meagre proportions. It offends her cultural sensibilities. The jigsaw-puzzle assembly, the evidence of factory forethought – the very same things Evie always appreciates about plane food – these dismay Ronni. And the coffee, she whispers to Evie, is *a crime*.

Displeasing as it all is, the food finds its way to Ronni's corners and she starts to settle, no longer thrusting her head into the aisle every few minutes as if to say *I see you* to the cockpit and all its secrecy. Evie helps her pick a movie and is at last able to sit back and think, or not think, whichever presents itself. She closes her eyes and the space behind them immediately becomes Ryan's bedroom. A picture that keeps returning, like shame itself. The collision of desire and disbelief. Evie hasn't told Ronni what happened two nights ago. She won't. Ronni would talk it into something it isn't, something with a future. *No.*

Sex with Ryan was, Evie has decided, if she can't simply erase the thought and must instead find a space for it, an event that served a purpose, possibly two. Firstly it had drawn a hard line under her marriage, a line she'd been too slow to draw herself, a line that could now be linked to a date and time, to verifiable events, not simply to a provisional expectation that it was time to move on. And it had shown Evie that sex itself, the simple act of it, was indeed not what she missed. It wasn't part of the ache. That was something else.

She looks at her phone now, at the text message James sent her late yesterday. *Hope you've recovered from your big night. Just wanted to wish you all the best for Perth. It'll be better than you (over)think. See you when you get back. x*

Big night. They must have been Angus's words. Evie had winced, and then she'd found herself smiling, just as she always did when she saw James's name light up her phone, or when she let herself think about their kiss, the kiss he'd summarily squared away, or when she saw a sailboat on the horizon.

That was what she missed. *That* was the ache and the emptiness. The flare of connection, of being thought about when you weren't standing right in front of someone, of being understood and seen even when you felt like a void.

When she hadn't been able to sleep last night, Evie had found herself looking up James's condition. *Incomplete lumbar spinal cord injury* – that was the term Cobie had recently used. *L3 vertebrae.* She'd found this ...

The spinal cord does not stretch through all the vertebrae. L3 is the first place it does not reach and the symptoms of an injury are, therefore, less severe. These include loss of sensation, muscle weakness and reduced flexibility in movement.

Loss of voluntary bladder/bowel control can be managed effectively with the appropriate support and assistive technology.

And after spotting this ...

Although spinal cord injury often causes sexual dysfunction, many people are able to have satisfying sex lives and fulfilling relationships.

... Evie had spent an hour or more seeking out real-life accounts of people who've had to reshape a life, to grudgingly and bravely accept life itself, after a traumatic spinal injury. She'd found dozens of them, stories well hidden from view, wedged in the cracks of a world humans are meant to walk through. Invisible tragedies, triumphs big and small, played out in quiet corners and endless days. Evie was dwarfed by each of them, the size of the struggles, the enormity of the questions she wanted to ask. How much a heartbeat can demand of a person.

The sheer logistics. One man with paraplegia shared, with requisite humour, the amount of money it costs him just to pee each year: six catheter bags a day at $1.74 a pop. *And they say humans need to drink more water*, he'd written. *I say show me the money!*

The invisibility. *No one sees me anymore*, one young man had shared. *They only see the chair. I could be anyone sitting on this thing.*

But then there are others who desperately *want* people to see the chair, to recognise its importance. *My disability is part of who I am.*

And love. So many stories of relationships rebuilt, replaced and altered forever after catastrophe.

When she'd finally found sleep, Evie was completely hollowed out, humbled by her own tiny problems. She'd dreamt of James.

She wishes she could sleep now, here on the plane. But she's never been a member of that small group. Hasn't napped since the children were born. Instead she looks out the little window and stares at the parched landscape far below: dirty-white roads snaking between giant properties, dustbowl dams and indomitable bush.

There's no putting it off any longer. No more shuffling dirt on the fire. This plane is going to land and she is going to see her husband again.

38

Evie's mother had once told her, apropos of nothing, that there comes a moment for every parent when they first see their child as separate from themselves, as their own person. She'd told Evie this had happened for her when Evie was just six years old, her first year of school. That she'd watched her walk into the little classroom and thought, I've done as much as I can do for her now. She's her own person.

In Evie's mind, the sentence was immediately followed by a dramatic wiping of her mother's hands in the air and a heel-clicking walk to the car.

This had never happened for Evie, though she'd long been on alert for it, until today. Walking out through the boarding gates at Perth Airport, she sees Sera before Sera sees her. Her daughter's neck is craned upwards at the arrivals board, a purple woven bag swinging by her side, shiny Doc Martens rooting her to the tiles. It's just a few seconds of unnoticed observation but Evie sees it so clearly and it catches her in the chest: her daughter is part of the world now, no longer a creation of hers or of Hamish – a creation of her very own. When had this happened?

When you weren't looking closely enough, Evie. When you hid from the world.

Evie knows Sera will by now have shaped a version of events, her parents' break-up, as a story that is both palatable to herself and relatable to others. It's the smart thing to do. Hamish will have given her his own account of what happened, something heavy on ideology and light on detail, and Sera will have polished this into something a little better, more usable. It's a skill the two of them have, one conducive to success in life, that Evie and Angus sadly lack. She and her son need something more, something closer to the truth, if there is such a thing on its own.

Evie hugs Sera far too fiercely, doesn't want to pull away. Imagines climbing into her ear and whispering *sorry sorry sorry* until Sera forgives her for taking so long to return here, for not facing things sooner, for being just a voice on the phone asking questions, never the one providing answers. She'd actively dissuaded her daughter from visiting, insisting she focus on her studies but really not wanting to see herself in Sera's eyes, a picture of stalled indecision, a long way from the strong mother figures cited by her daughter's political heroes. It's possible, Evie thinks, that you can devote the best part of a life to raising children in a way that bears no resemblance to your own experience, only to fail them in entirely different ways.

She watches Sera hug Angus, who does his best not to look like a tall tree leaning into the wind. And then she introduces Ronni, who overcomes a microsecond of apparent shyness to loudly fawn over every aspect of Sera's appearance – outfit, accessories, make-up, skin tone, all of it. 'Now *that's* how you style hair, Evie,' she says, and quickly fixes the back of Evie's head where it had rested on the aeroplane seat.

Perth Airport was clearly built before airports were viewed through a marketing lens, before the city had anything of interest to say about itself. Drab and functional, it's a first impression that does nothing to reward the time it takes to get here from anywhere. Evie's quick to point this out to first-time visitor Ronni, assuring her the airport is the least impressive part of the city. It all gets better after this, she says. Once they're in Sera's car and on the Great Eastern Highway, flanked by shelled-out buildings and noisy roadworks, Evie says, 'Actually, Ronni, just close your eyes until we get to Scarborough.'

Ronni sits up front and quickly wins Sera over with her rapid-fire questions and random observations. (The stadium: 'A Colosseum rip-off if ever I saw one.' The inner-city tunnel: 'It's like they *started* building a tunnel and then got too scared and came up.') Evie looks on happily, at this seemingly effortless bringing together of two people who each mean so much to her for very different reasons. And it's more than just that: she sees within this car in this moment the fusion of her own two lives, the old and the new. The old and the *now*. And it doesn't feel as scary as it had on the other side of the country.

Sera asks Ronni what she's wearing to the party and Ronni quite fairly tosses the blame for their lack of costumes over into the back

246

seat. 'Your mother is harder to pin down than an All Black,' she says.

'Sorry, Sera,' Evie says. 'I've had lots of ideas. I just couldn't settle on anything. Dress-ups are a nightmare at my age.'

'I'm sorted,' Angus says, not looking up from his phone. Then, 'Actually, I think I might have left it at home.'

The word causes Evie to bristle. *Home*. She's always been careful not to use the term with Sera when talking about the Sunshine Coast.

'At *your* age,' Sera scoffs to Evie. 'Mum, you still look amazing. Why don't we call into that cool costume shop on Scarborough Beach Road and see if we can find something for all of you.'

Evie remembers the shop well. It was their go-to for costumes when couples in hers and Hamish's friendship circle hosted theme parties, an inclination of middle age as apparently common as sharing every tedious detail of one's marathon training program. The couple who run the shop appear to remember Evie, even though it's been at least two years since she's been in here. This is both impressive and alarming, a too-quick slingshot back into her old life.

But Sera's suggestion is a masterstroke. The four of them share a loud and funny hour or more in the shop, flinging open dressing-room curtains to wild applause and laughter. A party before the party, worthy of any movie montage. Ronni's at the epicentre of it all, in turns transforming into Madonna, Pink, Britney Spears and hilariously Big Bird, who Angus reliably informs them was declared a Living Legend by the United States Library of Congress in 2000. But, as if there was ever any doubt, Ronni settles on Kylie Minogue, the popstar's gold hotpants moment circa 2000, which she will no doubt pull off on the strength of attitude alone.

Angus elects to go as Charlie Brown, 2000 being the year Charles Schulz published his last Peanuts comic. Evie hadn't even known Angus was a fan. The woman who owns the shop pulls together the costume from bits and pieces all over the store, nailing the final look with a bald cap. Angus delivers an impersonation that puts them all in hysterics. Evie can't remember the last time her son was so unguarded, so unashamedly happy.

This is going to be okay.

Evie is hardest to dress, each costume picking up on her trepidation. She can't help but see every outfit as Hamish might, doesn't know what impression she wants to portray. She's sure Sera and Angus see it now, the fear on her skin, the slowness of her resolve.

'Ex-husband,' Ronni says to the shop owner with a wink that Evie catches.

'Aha,' the woman says. 'I've just the costume for you.' She briefly disappears to the back of the store, returning with a Roman tunic that she holds aloft on a hanger, all leather straps, come-hither ropes, gold embellishments and a cape. In her other hand is a pair of knee-high boots with gold strapping to snake around the calves.

'Gladiator came out in 2000, didn't it?' the woman says.

Angus confirms via a quick round of tapping on his phone that it did.

In the dressing room Evie arranges herself into the outfit, which fits as though made for her. There's no mirror in here so she steps cautiously out through the curtain and is immediately greeted with a round of faux gasping and wild clapping, the loudest coming from Ronni.

'It's perfect,' she says to Evie and takes a picture on her phone. 'You look hot, hot, hot!'

'Thanks,' Evie says, still unconvinced but also mindful of how long they've spent here and what still needs to be done before tonight. As she turns back to the dressing room Evie notices a foreign inscription on the belt of the tunic. 'What do you think this means?' she asks of the group.

Ronni bends down to Evie's waistline to carefully read the tiny writing. After a moment she smiles with certainty, stepping back as though to behold the word of God on a postage stamp. 'It says,' she declares, '*Don't fuck with Italians.*'

Angus and Sera are still laughing when they all climb back into the car.

39

Some calm before the storm. *Must there always be a storm?* Evie thinks, reclining on a deckchair on the balcony of their Airbnb in Scarborough. The Indian Ocean is splayed out before her like a ball dress. Its scent is familiar, different from the Pacific over east, more dangerous, more pungent. It rises up to her from the cream sand and over the busy carpark.

She loves this ocean and its vastness. The spectre of it, the magic trick: how the clearest of waters can hide so much. The way it nurtures the city, nipping at its toes every day, hugging its isolation. She and Hamish had loved swimming in these waters, joking about sharks but with the requisite amount of reverence, always keeping at least one (large-ish) person between themselves and the horizon.

Through the sliding screen door she can hear Ronni snoring softly. Evie had tried to nap, was desperate to, but as usual couldn't manage it. The walls are too thin, the air too hot, her thoughts too loud. She can hear the tinny old air-conditioner struggling and knows its pain.

A memory now, so clear. She and Hamish on a short break at a resort in central Queensland, most likely where Sera was conceived. It's unbearably hot, the only thing people are talking about. The sort of humidity that renders make-up redundant. They are holed up happily in their room, the air-con running like a jet engine.

The engine stops abruptly. The lights go off, as does the TV. The light on the bedside clock has vanished. A power outage too unwelcome to sit out. Hamish and Evie retreat to the pool.

The outage lasts for almost a day. The pool becomes the epicentre of the resort, a replacement for dark hot rooms. The vibe is apocalyptic, if the end of the world involves getting drunk in the sun and forging instant friendships with strangers.

Hamish was the happiest Evie had ever seen him, untethered from plans, from control of his environment. He'd surrendered to the situation: she could see that. He chatted with everyone. No, Evie thinks now. He'd *talked* with everyone. Big talk, no small talk. Hamish had wanted their back story, their views on the state of the world, their unrealised dreams. People gravitated to him throughout the day, keen to have their turn with the man who seemed so interested, who *was* interested. Hamish's curiosity was real and alive, the essence of him. Evie saw it as if for the first time, cast in this different light. And she'd felt so grateful, so lucky to have met someone who would always be interested in her, who would want to know what she was thinking. When all of these people had gone back to their lives, Hamish would still be hers, his generous curiosity perusing her soul. She had never felt so close to him, never so in love.

How do the best memories become the ones we must forget?

Evie looks now at her phone for a distraction. *Anything, please.* She looks at the last message from James and on a whim that she doesn't stop to interrogate sends him Ronni's picture of her in the gladiator costume. Writes: *Landed safely. Finally found a costume. Now having a lie-down to prepare for battle.*

James's response is immediate: *God help him. Think I need a nap now too.*

Evie swallows, looks hard at the ocean. The wind has just come in.

What is this thing?

40

Evie hadn't expected a combat costume to manufacture any confidence about tonight, but equally she didn't think it would have the opposite effect. Now, standing in the carpark of the party venue as Ronni rearranges what exists of her gold hotpants, Evie feels unnervingly timid and exposed. The gladiator garb is nothing but an exoskeleton, essential rather than optional. She takes several deep breaths and looks up to a sky streaked with orange.

'You look amazing,' Ronni says, turning her attention to Evie with approval dipped in pride. She'd expertly straightened Evie's hair then gently curled the parts around her face as though revealing a flower. She'd done her make-up 'like a Roman newsreader', all serious smudge around the eyes and bronzed cheekbones Evie hadn't even known she possessed.

'I don't feel it.'

'Doesn't matter,' Ronni says, shifting the wavy locks of her Kylie wig to the front of her shoulders. 'As I say to my kids all the time, it's what's on the outside that counts.'

The venue's a sprawling bar and restaurant occupying an old Federation house right on the river in Fremantle. Evie can see Sera standing at the entrance now, ostensibly waiting for all her guests, yet Evie knows she's mainly waiting for her, leaving nothing to chance and bad timing. She and Ronni are deliberately early but Evie has no idea whether Hamish might have taken the same approach.

Looking disarmingly like Britney Spears, Sera grabs both Evie and Ronni in a tight hug and then guides them towards the kitchen at the rear of the large party room. Evie catches a glimpse of the decorations along the way, a riot of colour and light and a giant *2000* sign made of lightbulbs. It looks dazzling and party-worthy, everything Sera had wanted.

'He's not here yet,' Sera says softly to her mother.

Evie nods and swallows. *Here I am*, she realises. *This is happening.*

A woman called Sue greets them in the kitchen, shiny-faced and quick to enforce affectionate hugs. Evie remembers now that this is the person she's spoken to on the phone a few times about the catering. She seems so pleased to see Evie, so keen to make her feel welcome and at ease, as if they're old friends. Evie reads her instantly as one of those rare people who carries kindness in her bones.

'Now, Evie,' Sue says earnestly, placing both her hands on Evie's arms as if preparing her to walk on stage in front of thousands or jump out of a plane, 'if you need anything at all tonight, *anything*, even just a place to hide out for a bit, you come in here, okay?' Sera's clearly painted a current familial picture for Sue.

'That's really nice of you,' Evie says. 'Thank you.'

'Because we girls need to stick together, right!' Sue says, hugging Evie once again. 'Plus,' she adds with a comical wink, 'this is where we keep the *good* gin.'

Evie laughs gratefully and they leave Sue to the busyness of her noisy kitchen. 'Her ex-husband,' Sera whispers as they find their way back to the main room, 'started sleeping with her best friend every Monday afternoon when Sue was at chemo last year.'

Overhearing them, Ronni says something in heated Italian and makes a wild scissoring gesture with her hand as though cutting off something large.

Evie goes over to inspect the birthday cake, which she'd ordered online and is pleased to see looks even more impressive than the photos: a tall silo of sponge decorated in that now fashionable way, as though the icing has been scraped off rather than applied, as though the humble sponge is finally having its day in the sun, its moment to shine, no make-up required. The top of the cake is piled high with ornate greenery and frangipanis oozing their sweet peachy scent. Cutting it will be impossible, Evie thinks, but eating is probably beside the point.

U2's 'Beautiful Day' is playing through the speakers and Evie thinks it can't possibly be two decades since that song came out. She thinks about Hamish arriving any minute, about racing back to the kitchen now to hear Sue's entire life story. She imagines being somewhere else altogether, on a boat perhaps, headed straight out to sea. She realises she's been staring at the cake for too long now, hiding in a moment.

Angus appears by her side just as a swarm of young people make their way through the entrance like they're caught in a rip. There's much squealing and gawping about each other's costumes and Evie can see now why this was a smart idea on Sera's part, that an off-the-wall theme can breathe life into a party when it's most important, at the fragile start, when none of the other ingredients have had time to kick in. She can see a Cathy Freeman in her full body suit, a green-painted Grinch, a young man holding a golf club and wearing a polo shirt with *How 'bout it?* printed on the front (*Tiger Woods?*) and a very convincing Hillary Clinton. Sera's quickly swept up in a tumble of embraces and group selfies, her face alight with joy.

'Look how happy your big girl is,' Ronni says, hugging Evie from behind now and nodding towards the group swirling around Sera. 'You did good, Evie.'

And Evie isn't so sure about that, about any part she's played in Sera's current happiness, but she feels a rush of pride nonetheless and something else that might well be relief.

When Sera dropped Angus back to the Airbnb late this afternoon, Evie took the opportunity to give her daughter the photobook she'd made: *Twenty-One Years of You.* They'd sat together and leafed through every page, laughing and sighing in turn, recalling episodes of the past through their own exhibitions, as subject and curator, daughter and mother: times they'd each forgotten, things they hadn't known. History captured for endless reinvention. Evie had never spent so much time on a single project, never spilled so many Friday-night tears.

'I'm glad you didn't Photoshop him out,' Sera said, referring to the many pictures of her and Hamish together, of the family as one.

'Too much hassle.' Evie laughed. 'You know how I am with technology.'

And because you're so much your father's daughter, she had thought. *I can't erase him without erasing you.*

The party room quickly fills with Sera's friends, only a handful of whom Evie recognises from before. These are the ones who spot her now and give her rapturous hugs by the cake, as if there'd once been a relationship beyond Evie giving them lifts home from parties and pretending they weren't drunk. She's grateful now for their fresh enthusiasm, for not seeing straight beyond her, and hugs them back with genuine affection, her eyes darting to the entrance of the room between each encounter. She sees that Angus has found a small group he seems to know and this makes her throat catch with relief. Only she can see how nervous he is about tonight, how tightly he's gripping the sides of his trouser legs. *My boy.*

The air starts to feel thicker, the music louder, and Ronni takes Evie to a large balcony adjacent to the party room. It's much cooler out here, the breeze off the river sneaking up through the timber boards beneath them. Ronni's blonde wig is iridescent in the moonlight.

'What are those?' she asks Evie, pointing to the giraffe-like cranes lining Fremantle Port, their long necks puncturing the sky with orange light.

'Dinosaurs,' says a voice behind them and Evie spins around.

It is Hamish.

'That's what Sera used to call them,' he says to the two women as though he were part of their conversation. As though he wasn't a foreign missile fired at them just now from a ship in the port. 'Remember, Evie?'

He's standing there right in front of her now, a constellation of his parts willing her to bring them into focus. His jaw, his eyes, clothes she doesn't recognise, a beard. *A beard.*

It's him.

And here we are.

'Ronni, this is Hamish,' Evie says, pointing at her husband as if he wasn't the only other person on the balcony, as if he wasn't as much a practical stranger to her now as to Ronni. 'Hamish, this is my friend Ronni.'

Hamish steps forwards and Evie can clearly see the grey flecks in his beard. All new: the beard, the grey. 'Pleased to meet you, Ronni,' he says and offers his hand to her.

In this moment Evie imagines all the things that could happen right now simply because this is Ronni and not any other person in the world. She pictures her slapping Hamish's hand away, slapping his face, delivering a prepared speech about fidelity and honesty and wink emojis and puttanas. She pictures Ronni tracing a target with her finger on Hamish's forehead.

A boat horn cracks the air like a sonic boom and Evie jumps. Ronni moves her hand protectively to Evie's arm, but she's clearly rattled too. 'It's okay,' she says to her, looking accusingly at the dinosaured horizon. 'It's just a stupid loud thing. Should I get us some drinks or would you like me to stay right here?' Her delivery of *right here* has a Liam Neeson quality about it, Evie thinks with a measure of amusement.

She smiles at Ronni, says yes, she'd love a drink. Hamish says the same once it's clear (though it really isn't, at least not to Evie who can see that Ronni's lips are pursed, her jaw tight) that the offer extends to him too. Ronni guides her hotpants back inside, looking back over her shoulder as she does.

'A friend from over east?' Hamish asks. He has his hands in his pockets now and Evie realises she'd forgotten to look at his hands. She still has her wedding ring on.

'Yes,' she answers.

'So,' he says, but it's a sentence in itself rather than the start of one. Evie momentarily hates him for this. A place-saving word: a word that simply makes people wait longer for the things you should be saying. She does nothing to fill the long seconds of silence that follow.

Another boat horn. A long wail into the night.

'You look,' Hamish says at last, 'like you're ready for battle.'

'You look costume-less,' she replies. Of course he hadn't worn a costume, she thinks now. The idea lacked sufficient purpose; it reeked of herd mentality. *Not even for his daughter.*

'Yes, I know, I had meant to organise something, but I've been moving into a new place and—'

'Where?' Evie jumps in and immediately wishes she hadn't. She senses she needs to slow things down, lest a single piece of information engulf her. 'In Perth?'

'Yes, in Perth. I—'

'Okay, stop,' Evie says.

Stop, stop, stop.

'But I'm not starting anything, Evie.'

'I know,' she says and wills her mind to slow *right down* now, to hold the moment and inspect it before it makes room for the next one. 'I know that. But let's not do any of this tonight. It can't happen here. Tonight is about Sera.'

'Yes,' Hamish answers. 'Of course it is.' He starts furiously rubbing his earlobe, the nervous gesture Evie knows too well.

'And Angus too,' she says, and their son's name seizes up in her neck, as though held back by a dam wall for pain. 'God, Hamish, do you have *any* idea how much you have hurt that boy? Any at all?'

Stop.

'I know, Evie,' Hamish says, stepping closer to her and then quickly back again, chastened. 'I know I have a lot to explain to him. And to you.'

Evie swallows hard. 'But not tonight.'

'When, Evie? Tomorrow?'

But she leaves this question adrift in the night air and walks quickly past him now, the sleeve of her tunic lightly grazing his shirt, her whole body about to catch fire. She re-enters the main room. Wait staff are moving about with trays of little things. A makeshift dancefloor has formed itself under the feet of early starters. Evie can see Ronni's back at the bar, while over in a corner Sera and Angus are standing close together and looking right at her. Evie gives them her middle-aged salute: two thumbs up. *It's okay!* Sera looks back at her mother, a half-smile of relief. Angus shifts his gaze to his feet.

Soon after Evie sees Hamish approach their son at the bar. She can see Angus's eyes over his father's shoulder and for a moment they catch hers. Evie wants to hold his gaze now, lock it in and keep him steady. She will run over there if she has to, she thinks, if she sees Angus falter, if Hamish says anything that breaks him. But it's all over in a minute, punctuated by a hug that is all Hamish's work. Angus's arms wobble at his sides, confused by muscle memory, by love.

She watches Hamish then move across the room to Sera. His all-arms embrace of her is warmly returned but it's clearly a goodbye and Evie can see in Sera's posture what no one else would be able to: the disappointment. He leaves via the entrance, just as other people are arriving, hands still in his pockets. His stride is one Evie could immediately identify on the busiest day in Times Square. The long steps, the sway of his shoulders. It hits her squarely and it hurts.

For it's not, Evie thinks now as she tries to regather, tries to breathe, the learning to unlove someone that hurts so much. It's trying to un*know* them. Familiarity feels a lot like love, might even be stronger than it, more resistant to fading. How does she even begin to separate the two?

She'd have to ask Hamish how he'd done it.

Tomorrow.

41

Text message from an unknown number:

Evie, can we meet up today? I'd really like to talk to you. This is my new number. Hamish.

She'd deleted his old number some months ago, if only to save herself from (or at least stall) wine-fuelled rants and middle-of-the-night questions she hadn't wanted answers to. She hadn't wanted 'Find My Phone' to find anything. Now it transpires she might not have reached Hamish anyway, that he'd likely changed his number to prevent the very same things.

She and Ronni have already been for a swim this morning, a saltwater reply to their long night of dancing and too much champagne. Sera's party had been a success, as declared by the birthday girl herself when they'd all tipped messily into a cab in the very early morning. Ronni hadn't once left the dancefloor, requesting Kylie Minogue's 'Spinning Around' at least a dozen times. 'Even my eyelashes are sore,' she'd said when they woke.

Evie responds to Hamish's message that she can meet him at

the Teahouse at Cottesloe at three. Just like that. A quick decision made oddly easier by tiredness. Though it's an iconic Perth venue, the Teahouse has no special significance for either of them. As benign as it is beautiful. After so much time apart, the canyon-like vacuum of the space between them, the shapeless questions, the Spanish Inquisition of her mind, Evie finds the ordinariness of this appointment – an afternoon coffee by the water in broad daylight – strangely reassuring. As though she might finally be ready.

But the afternoon creeps forwards like rust, like a life slipping away. By one o'clock, Evie wishes she'd arranged an earlier time, wishes she'd drunk less champagne. She wants this to be over now, wants it not to start. All the suspicions she's carried inside her, the theories and doubts crammed into corners and caught under rocks, now they seem like something she could simply keep living with. A manageable condition. Better than knowing anything irrefutable, having no choice but to throw a match over your shoulder and start again.

Answers. The currency of her life's work. People wanting to know what went wrong, how to make it right, when to call time. A trained set of eyes to spot the fault lines. Answers, she should have told them all, every last Gideon and Lelia, every Mick and Jess, can be false idols. Traps. Move-on notices. You can't know what you're asking for. Don't ask until you're ready.

~

She sees Hamish almost immediately. Even though she's half an hour early, he's here already, seated at a table in the far corner, a window vista of the ocean on every side. The place is a polished mob of polo shirts and crushed linen, diners toe to toe and seat to seat, but Hamish spots her quickly too. She walks over in his direction and he stands to greet her. Evie quickly gestures that he should just sit lest there be any moment when two people meeting for coffee might first exchange a polite kiss.

Evie takes the seat opposite her ex-husband and feels the moment slowly turn upon itself. She has pictured this so many times, in different settings, different cities. She has directed this scene a hundred different ways. Always she's been arrested by the initial sight of Hamish after so much time but having already seen him last night removes the shock of this. Always she's been clipped and non-committal, a quick flight to anger. Always ready to take off at a moment's notice. But now, finally on the precipice of answers, Evie finds that she feels strangely calm, that a welcome and unexpected stillness is taking over her, as though room has been made for the right words.

Thank God.

'Evie,' Hamish says. 'You look … sorry.'

'I look sorry?'

'No, I'm sorry,' he says. 'I was going to say you look lovely, but I guess that wouldn't be appropriate. Or maybe welcome.'

'Or relevant,' Evie says. 'Are we ordering coffee?'

It takes a long time to fall within a staff member's gaze and somehow it doesn't feel like anything can begin until there's something before them to hold on to. Hamish fills the gnawing pause with observations about the beach activity below: all the nonhuman activity, Evie notes. Erosion, rock weathering, the direction of the wind. Patterns of nature, no one's fault. Public lecture as safe ground. She lets him do it, this little dance around importance, just as she always has.

'Did you hear,' Evie asks, playing the game too, 'that Twiggy Forrest is knocking this place down and putting up some big shiny thing with a pool?'

'What?' Hamish says, seemingly incredulous. 'How can he just tear down something that's been standing for years? Everyone loves this place.'

'I don't know,' Evie replies as their coffees arrive, 'but everything's a metaphor, isn't it?'

Hamish's chin drops like a weight. 'Evie,' he says and looks hard at the china cup that's been placed in front of him.

'Hamish, would this be easier if I went first? Why don't I tell you what *I* think has happened to us, to you specifically, and you can let me know where I'm wrong?'

This had long been Evie's preferred plan for this moment but she'd always suspected Hamish wouldn't agree. To her surprise he nods the smallest of assents.

And Evie begins. Tiptoes. The gentlest of steps, back towards the start. Sticking to the path. Don't disturb the trail. Find the source.

'You didn't,' she says to her husband, 'mean for this to happen. Not many people do. I know that part,' Evie says, 'and I accept it. It does matter, the absence of intent, but only a little.'

You weren't unhappy, she tells him, but you were restless. 'Restless deep in your cells. Restless in that invisible way that other people can see better than we can. Midlife restless,' Evie says. 'What am I doing? What have I done? What's *left*? Only so many beats of the heart.' And she thinks now about the couple, Toby and Helena, who'd come to her when a foray into swinging had brought them undone. At least Toby had brought his boredom to the table in the hopes of a joint solution.

'I saw it,' Evie says to Hamish, 'the restlessness. The urge to move in any direction. To move across the country. I didn't say anything. Not enough. I *should* have. I knew at some point it would probably happen to me too. When the kids stopped needing me as much. When my work felt old and pointless. When I became unseeable, bored, quiet.' *When I became Margaret.* 'But,' she says now, 'it happened to you first.'

'*No*,' Hamish replies. His words are quick and hot, charging the air between them. He pushes his cup hard away from his body towards Evie, who looks at it askance. But he says nothing else, no further correction, and after a minute she goes on.

'You hadn't stopped loving me,' she says, 'but you'd probably stopped *seeing* me. And I don't blame you for that. There's an inevitability to it, maybe even something evolutionary. We look at our kids growing up and we see hope and promise, reminders of our youth, but when we look at our partners in middle age – I mean all couples, Hamish, not just us – we see *age*. We see the past, lots and lots of it. Nothing new to see.'

And if you weren't seeing *me*, Evie says even as Hamish slowly shakes his head *no*, then you weren't seeing any reflection of yourself either. He'd lost sight of himself.

'That's what most affairs are, Hamish. Not a play for someone else, not really. They're a search for ourselves, for a fresh version of ourselves.'

And the word sits in the air above them now, spoken out loud, beyond allusion. Evie pictures Ali, her old client felled by a receipt for flowers, destroyed by a piece of paper.

'Can I continue?' Evie asks him.

Tell me I'm wrong about the affair.

'You might as well,' Hamish says. 'Clearly you've got it all worked out.'

Evie reaches for her coffee. The cup is cold. 'And here's the part,' she says, 'that you really hadn't expected: that you could fall in love. That you could feel it again, feel it like the first time. The force of it. The madness. Devouring all the oxygen. The way it makes you forget, makes you pretend, makes everything else disappear. All the words are inadequate, so there aren't any. None. Not to me, not to the kids, not to anyone else. You couldn't believe it was happening, that it felt the way it did, the way it does. You couldn't explain any of it to me without crushing me, so you didn't. You couldn't give it a name, because what *was* it? You couldn't turn around or it might disappear. You had to keep going, clean it up later. You couldn't let those worlds collide. And none of this, none of it, is what you might have imagined you could ever do to me, or to the kids, such is the power of it.'

Hamish pulls hard on his beard now as if to tear it off. Evie can feel his fury and knows the exact shape of it: predictability. Of all the lapses attached to infidelity, this was the one she knew

Hamish would want to reject. He's a clever man and clichés aren't so clever. He had once said of a colleague, a man who'd left his family for a student half his age: 'God, it's just so *embarrassing* for him. He's like a midweek movie on legs.' Evie wonders now if her husband remembers this, if he sees his own situation as somehow less prosaic.

'Evie,' Hamish says after a long silence that she lets sit between them untouched. 'Life is not one of your psychology textbooks.'

She feels a laugh escape her, a small and bitter fruit. 'No, it certainly isn't.'

'And I'm not one of your patients,' he says, 'so you can spare me the professional analysis. Please.'

The 'please' sounds like the quick correction that it is, a word to temper his indignation. Because they're not good at this, open combat. They've never done it, have no idea what the rules are and how far things can be pushed.

'Spare *you*?' Evie says, forcing herself to whisper now, resisting an unfamiliar urge to scream. 'This isn't for you, Hamish. I've had to work all this out for *me*. I've had to try to make sense of it all, try to work out what would make you leave, where things went wrong. What *I* did wrong.'

'You didn't—'

'I *know*, Hamish. And that's the one thing I've learnt from all of this, from us, more than from anyone else's marriage. Something doesn't have to be *wrong* for this to happen. Someone just has to make a decision, to go with an impulse or not.'

'I hardly think it's that simple, Evie.'

'Falling in love is easy, Hamish. It's literally the thing anyone can do.'

Are you in love, Hamish? Tell me. Don't tell me.

'Are you guys, um, thinking of eating?' A waitress beside them stands uneasily, rubbing at the screen of an iPad like it's a magic lamp. A few short years ago she would have been scribbling an inky hole into a notebook, Evie thinks. She hadn't even noticed the young woman was there.

'Maybe in a little while,' Hamish says to her.

What? Evie thinks. 'Hamish, we're not eating anything,' she says, watching the waitress now walk away at pace. 'We're just about done here.'

'No we're *not*, Evie,' he says. 'We're nowhere near done.'

And she knows he means the conversation but quickly steals his intent. 'Of course we're done, Hamish. Did you really think we weren't? Did you think I was waiting for you to come back all this time? How pathetic would that make me?'

Evie feels her cheek start to twitch, tugging at the corner of her eye. She hears the word too loudly. *Pathetic.*

'What were you thinking all this time?' she goes on, and now it's her left knee starting to shake. 'And how would I know? How was I supposed to know? All this *time.*'

Hamish stares down at his hands upturned on the table as though they don't belong to him. 'I know it was too long, Evie,' he says. 'I know that. I got stuck ... I got—'

'You know I used to think nothing ended unless it ended badly, Hamish. You've heard me say that before. But it's not true. Some things just end quietly and slowly and barely anyone notices. And it still hurts but the pain is spread out and stretched and maybe it's better that way, I don't know. Because you realise one day that the hard part is already done. You got through it. It's done.'

And as the words tumble out of her like little stones, Evie finds that she believes them, that somehow in taking so long to force Hamish's hand, she'd made a space for pre-emptive recovery, for healing before the bandages came off. 'Now,' she says almost triumphantly, 'the rest can be worked out in a few legal letters. It's not like we have to sort out custody or anything.'

'I'm not talking about money here, Evie,' Hamish says. 'I'm talking about us. There's still an us, Evie. I want there to be. I don't accept that we're done.'

A hand, Hamish's, lifts slightly off the table and moves clumsily toward hers as though remote-controlled by someone elsewhere in the room. A salt shaker tumbles over to mock the effort. Evie yanks both her hands under the table, pushes her knees hard to the floor. The promise of violence in her shaking shoulders shocks them both.

And he tells her then, in a pained staccato voice, that he's no longer with 'the woman'. He struggles with the phrasing like it's a second language, baulking at words just as he reaches them, checking Evie's face for recognition, finding nothing that gives him confidence.

Evie cuts him short. 'You mean Jo, don't you? Is that her name, Hamish? You can just use her name if that's what it is. She's a real person, with a name.'

Tell me I'm wrong, Hamish. Tell me I'm wrong.

Hamish sits rigid in his chair. 'It's over, Evie,' he says. 'It's completely over. I ended it. Some time ago.'

Evie looks down into her lap, at her hands rolling over each other. She says, 'That must have been hard. Ending two relationships in such a short space of time.'

And even she's surprised at the tone of this, its acrid aftertaste. Sarcasm has never been part of their lexicon.

'I get that you hate me, Evie,' Hamish says. 'I don't blame you. I hated myself for all of this too.'

Hated. Past tense.

Evie realises now, and wishes she didn't, that she's been looking at Hamish's beard almost this entire time, at six or seven or eight flecks of greyness on either side of his mouth. Her eyes won't lift to meet his. The beard is safe, if unknown to her. He's never worn one. For all the tools of cosmetic tinkering available to women, she thinks, there are few things more physically transformative than a man's facial hair. In every sense she's looking at a different person from the one she remembers.

'So just to be clear,' Evie says, diverting her attention now to the window, to the water and beyond. Away from his beard, his mouth. 'No terminal illness? Stage four brain cancer? Because that's the other theory I was running with.'

It wasn't, of course, the only other theory, but Evie wasn't about to let Hamish glimpse the dark swamp she'd been slowly wading through. Once she'd finally allowed herself to form actual hypotheses, when paralysis had worn off like the glorious anaesthetic it was, Evie had even imagined Hamish might have been gay, late to own it. She'd counselled couples at the same crossroads, a latent reckoning with sexuality after years of marriage, after children, even after grandchildren. The later in life it occurred, the more pressing the need to leave no stones unturned. But realising he was gay, or at least belatedly admitting it, didn't seem like something Hamish would hide from her or from the kids. Having a death notice, on the other hand, might have triggered his instincts to flee and protect.

Incredibly Hamish actually smiles at Evie's cancer diagnosis and the response catches her completely off guard. *That smile.* She knows it better than she knows her own, everything stored within it, looking back at her now, years and years of in-jokes and shared observations, all the good times crowding out the bad. A generation of memories stored in the folds of Hamish's mouth.

'Would you have preferred that?' he asks at last. 'That I was dying? Maybe even dead?'

Despite herself, Evie smiles back at him. Checks that she still can in his presence. Says, 'Can I get back to you on that?'

Hamish whisks his fingers across his chin. Back and forth. Evie wills herself not to look at it again. The handbag at her feet conveniently vibrates and she reaches down to retrieve her phone. It's a text message from Ronni: *Everything okay?*

Half a second later, another text. It's a picture of James, taken of himself, hair askew in the wind, saltwater sprayed behind him, clearly aboard *Sans Serif* on a perfect day. It reads, *Wish you were here.*

'Do you need to respond?' Hamish says. 'It's fine if you do.'

'No,' Evie says. 'Not yet.'

And then he starts talking at her like a man being timed, as though he's about to run out of charge. He tells Evie she was right about some things but also wrong about others. 'I didn't fall in love,' he says. 'That's not what it was. I don't know what it was, but it wasn't love, Evie. It was something else, some stupid thing. And you're right – I *was* restless. Restless but also empty somehow. I didn't know what was happening inside of me. I even wondered if it was depression. I would find myself staring out the window during important meetings at work, wondering what it would take to feel something again. But Evie, I didn't go looking for it. It felt like this thing happened *to* me and that I was too lost and scared and empty to stop it.'

'Like you got hit by a truck full of infidelity,' Evie says. Impossibly, she hears the sound of Ronni's applause.

Hamish flinches as though wounded but then quickly continues, becoming more animated now, as though he's just getting to the best part of the story. 'I lived in Scotland for some time,' he says. 'I don't know if Sera told you that. She came back to Australia but I stayed there.'

'You mean Jo?' Evie interjects. 'Can we just get that name on the record, you know, officially?'

Hamish looks at her with eyes that threaten to glare but don't.

'Okay, good,' Evie says.

'I wasn't going home until I worked out what was going on, what was happening to me, why I'd done all of this. I couldn't get home anyway – it took me months to get an exemption. So I stayed there and I worked on myself. I even traced my whole ancestry while I was over there, Evie, because I wanted to know who I *am*. And I know how that sounds coming from me of all people. Believe me, I know. But I've changed, Evie. I think I'm a better man now than I was before. Someone who can be a better husband and a better father. I want the chance to prove that to you, to all of you, even if I don't deserve it. I will spend the rest of my life making this up to you.'

Evie feels tears now, warm and utterly unwelcome, pool in her eyes. She wills them not to drop, not one. *Don't, don't, don't.*

She remembers now something her father said to her on her wedding day, during their painful-to-watch dance together in front of the assembled guests. 'You've just,' he'd said, beery breath in her ear, 'attached yourself to the one person in the world most likely to break your heart or kill you.'

The memory makes her dizzy. She looks at the entrance of the restaurant, couples lined up waiting for people like her to move on. She wants to run. Just like that day in the supermarket, a lifetime ago or yesterday, destroyed by cauliflower, Evie feels an urgent need to disappear.

'Did you know?' she says to Hamish now, pressing her feet so hard into her shoes that she can feel the shape of the timber floor beneath, 'that while you were working out who you *are*' – she fills the word with all the judgement one might reserve for a person taking a selfie at a crash site – 'that your son was going through so much pain inside that a teacher at his school asked to speak to me about suicide? That for months I was afraid to open the door of his bedroom because I didn't know what I might see? That I spent so many nights worrying about him that I don't even know how to sleep anymore.'

Hamish's eyes lock on Evie's now and she registers his look of fright, of disbelief. His shoulders roll forward and his head drops slightly. He says something small that she can't hear. He looks like someone she knew a long time ago.

She could tell him good things too, of course, happy things. Angus's sailing, his friendship with Cobie, the fact he'd put on a little weight, had not resumed tearing out his hair. His adoration of little Polo. She could tell him these things, but she doesn't, not now. These are hers.

Hamish finds his voice again and starts to speak, but Evie cuts him off. 'Did you even *once* think to contact me while you were over there finding yourself, Hamish?'

'Evie,' he replies after an age. 'I couldn't.'

She looks out the bright window to the ocean, sees the breeze has arrived to mottle the water. It won't look perfect again until tomorrow.

'Sera told me you were doing well,' Hamish says, willing her gaze back inside. 'She kept saying you seemed happy over there.'

And Evie wonders if this is true, if Sera really thought she was happy or at least happily coping. Evie had never said she wasn't, not to her daughter and not in fact to anyone. *I'm fine.* There'd never been a question posed to her that might have required a higher bar of honesty or introspection. It's like the 'R U OK?' campaign, she thinks now, recalling a robust conversation with a group of her students some weeks ago. It's an inadequate question eliciting inadequate answers.

'I just had no idea about Angus,' Hamish continues. 'Why didn't you tell me, Evie? Why didn't you try to contact *me* about that? I'm so sorry. I'm so fucking sorry.'

She sees a shiny streak on his cheek now and looks down at her empty coffee cup.

'Did you *try* to contact me, Evie? Because if you did, I didn't ...'

'No.'

'Why?'

He asks again. 'Why, Evie? Why not?'

And she thinks about his question as if for the first time, not the thousandth. As if there could ever be just one answer. As if it matters now anyway.

Evie pushes back the heavy wooden chair and reaches for her bag. She looks directly into Hamish's eyes, into everything they used to see.

'I was tired,' she says, and looks toward the exit.

Weary down to my bones.

42

In case Evie should even briefly forget, Ronni reminds her constantly how much she's loved their trip to Perth. She stops just short of calling it life-changing, a deliverance of fresh perspectives she hadn't known she needed. It's not just the fact of having travelled far enough to need a plane, of visiting a new place; it's been her removal, however brief, from the needs of a husband and children, from her work and her sister's cafe, from the small and frenzied orbit of Ronni's everyday life. Like the sun-drunk tourist peering through real estate office windows and doing the math, Ronni wants the holiday to continue, for it to transform her normal existence. She wants to take dancing classes, hire a cleaner, eat meals she didn't have to cook. She wants to plan at least one trip somewhere new each year. Incredibly, Ronni sees herself as the friend who should be grateful.

'And if you move back to Perth,' she says to Evie now as their flight back to Queensland reaches altitude, 'I will come and visit you every year and we'll go out dancing until our eyelashes are sore.'

Angus had spent their final day in Perth with Hamish. Evie had insisted. 'Tell him all about your sailing,' she'd said to her son when it seemed he had no intention of leaving the bed. 'About how you're going to teach *me* to sail because you're so good at it.' And he'd remained reluctant at first, as Evie had expected, but in a way that was so passive and non-combative, so very Angus, that he hadn't a hope against Hamish's ambition. They'd spent most of the day at the beach, Angus returning to Evie with a tomato shade of sunburn and two updates – that 'Dad is acting like a different person' and '*He* says we might be moving back to Perth.'

Like Angus, Evie had never asked for a different person.

She looks across the aisle of the plane at him now, thumbs working his phone like pincers, and wonders how effective Hamish's pitch to Angus had been. Her son was giving nothing away. But she knew Hamish would be determined and that as much as he'd been the cause of Angus's hurt, he might also be the remedy. He would certainly try. She also knew Angus would be waiting on Evie's cue, watching her every move from beneath those downcast eyelids, looking for direction.

Hamish's appeal to Evie had the early makings of a political campaign. *Always politics.* Since the Teahouse, he'd sent her a stream of messages, recollections of years gone by, pictures of them together, promises and more promises. He would get his old job back, buy a house near the beach, love her harder, love her better, build the future they deserved together. A hundred different ways to say sorry, to win her vote. It was all so certain, as questionless as the day he'd said to her, 'There is no one else. I just *need some time.*'

Please come home, read the first message Hamish had sent her this morning when Evie was packing for the airport. And she thought, *Where is that?*

As if reading her mind, Ronni puts her hand on Evie's arm now and says, 'I don't want you to go back there. I really don't. But if you do still love him ...'

Evie watches the wing of the plane slice through clouds, scissors through silk. 'Love was never the issue,' she says.

43

Summer is impatient, arriving early and with ferocious intent. Heat clings to bodies, turns lawn into glass. Bushfire threats steal the headlines from snap lockdowns and bickering state premiers.

It's been three weeks since Evie returned from Perth and she's spent them like a visitor on holiday, swimming in the ocean every morning, reading slow books of an afternoon, having her evening glass of wine well before evening. Sometimes it's felt as though she's intuitively gobbling up the last of this beautiful area that she might soon leave, but at others it's felt like she's finally getting to know a place she'd been treating like emergency accommodation.

Hamish's political campaign has only slightly slowed and only because Evie insisted she needed some clear air to think. She doesn't tell him that it's actually too hot to think, that when she does, new questions push through the edging of her reason and common sense like noxious weeds. *But why did you really end it with her? Where is she now? What did it feel like to kiss her? Why, Hamish, why?*

Angus spends most of his time with Cobie who, after taking

care of Polo when they'd gone to Perth, now describes the two of them as the dog's 'co-parents'. Together they take the smitten pup to the dog beach of a morning and walk him late in the evening when it's cooler. To Evie, Angus seems lighter on his feet, quietly contented, relieved no doubt that the current holding pattern between his parents has delayed any talk of what he'll do next year, of where he'll be.

More weeks slip gently by and the possibility of Christmas in Perth, heavily promoted by Hamish, quietly dissolves. Sera says she'll spend it on Rottnest Island with one of her friends whose father has a boat. Hamish says he'll fly to his parents 'if it comes to that'. Evie winces at these announcements, wondering how she somehow became the person now splintering a family.

She and Angus spend Christmas Day at Ronni's house, bumping about in the zoo of her extended family like tourists. It's riotous and wonderful, endless laughter escaping from mouths and bellies filling with food. Bittersweet too, for Evie and Angus both know this is borrowed joy. Another family's rituals and rhythms. Their own lay elsewhere, suspended.

New Year's Eve. James has invited Evie to an easy dinner on his back deck. It's the first time she's seen him in person since Perth, though they've settled into regular, almost daily contact via phone messages, the perfect medium for a pair of over-thinkers, they both agree. Sometimes they message about the logistics of their children's movements but more often it's about books they've just finished, shows to watch on Netflix, pithy observations about people they've encountered over the day. When James sends her a picture of

281

something impressive he's just cooked for dinner, Evie can usually return a genuine photo of whatever inspiration-free atrocity she's just half-heartedly pulled together from the innards of her fridge. It's less the content of their exchanges that Evie so enjoys (although James's messages have made her laugh loudly in public places more than once) but the very fact of it, the steady swing of it.

He cooks a rogan josh curry for them tonight and it tastes nothing like the jar variety Evie has previously tried to pass off to Angus as gourmet. It's spicy and lush and Evie had quite forgotten how James's little backyard sanctuary simply makes everything look and taste better.

They drink red wine and Evie tells James about Sera's party, about Ronni's wholesale takeover of the dancefloor in her gold hotpants. When she tells him about Ronni's reactions to modern plane travel (*Who are the sad people playing Solitaire? What is the pilot hiding?*), James howls in amusement. And playing it back like this, the Perth trip minus Hamish, makes Evie enjoy it in a way she hadn't allowed herself to until now.

At one point James excuses himself to go inside and when he comes back out it's as though he's been thinking about what to say, fortifying his approach. 'Evie,' he says, swiftly moving out of the wheelchair and back onto the seat they're sharing. 'You know you can ask me.'

Evie thinks she might have missed something. 'Ask you what?'

'About ... *this*,' James says, nodding towards his legs. 'About what I can and can't do.'

Evie takes a deep breath before she can stop herself. She doesn't want it to look like she's ever thought about this, like it matters at all. At the same she doesn't want to sound dismissive, as though James's disability isn't a very real thing. She places a hand on his knee and waits for the words to form. Finally she says, 'I know what you can do, James. Pretty much everything you've ever set your mind to.'

'Evie, you know what I mean,' James says, and of course she does.

At midnight the black sky above them fills with light and colour. They can't see the fireworks but they can hear them. And just as Evie hoped he might, James pulls her body close to his and kisses her until the sky is dark again and for much longer too.

We'll work it out.

~

Moving forward, Evie writes to James when she's back home in her bed that night, *it seems I can only kiss you when there are fireworks. That okay?*

She can still feel his mouth on hers, floating across her cheek, down to her neck, back again and again.

May there always be fireworks, James replies. *Night, Evie. x*

44

Next summer

The couple locks eyes on Evie, their best hope of not looking at each other. Both appear frayed and spent, still unsure about the decision that led them here. Evie welcomes them back, praises them for the effort it took to get here today with three kids at home. She reminds them this isn't only a safe place but a positive one, that she's here for them.

'And at the very least,' Evie adds with a warm smile, 'it's a good solid hour in the air-conditioning.'

The space between the man and woman in front of her is filled with disappointment and regret – a failed business in Melbourne into which they'd pushed and squeezed every big dream, every promise, every cent. They were beaten by it, by their smallness against forces outside their control, the speed of a potent virus, the slowness of fortune to turn. And even though they'd pledged to get through it all together, to emerge stronger if poorer, the opposite had occurred. It divided them mercilessly, exposing their shortcomings and giving life to blame.

They'd chosen to see Evie, the husband had admitted at their first appointment, because she was the only counsellor who offered a discounted payment scheme for clients experiencing financial difficulty. It was one of the first decisions Evie had made when setting up the new business, that and letting Ronni choose the name: *Let's Talk*.

'Well,' Ronni had said, 'you can't just name it after yourself. Evie Shine sounds like a window cleaner.'

After a few months of searching, she'd found an ideal lease space – a large room within a renovated beach cottage a block from the ocean. Gap-year Angus, permanently tanned and smelling of sea salt, had helped her knock out a wall, pull up the worn carpet and polish the oak floorboards. A friend of Ronni's husband put in a skylight and installed shutters for ventilation. Evie had wanted to create a space where deep breaths and pained sighs could quietly disappear.

A cheery garden fronted the old cottage, entirely planted by Evie from cuttings – straggly little things given to her by a kind neighbour, now all thriving, apparently grateful for the fresh start.

Evie didn't dare quit the safety of teaching at the start, but within a couple of months of advertising in the local newspaper, her counselling diary was full. Very quickly she'd been reminded how much she missed her real work: this important and delicate opportunity to make a meaningful difference in people's lives, to help them find their way back to each other, to see what's left in their hearts. To at least try.

And she's good at this, better now than before. Better for all it took to bring her here.

Evie's hopeful about the couple in her room today. For all the pain and loss they've suffered, for all the angry words hurled at the back of doors, there is still a mutual fondness to be excavated, stories to be reshaped. And they'd moved quickly to ask for help. Leaving anything untended for too long can kill it. Evie knows this.

Most days she takes her final clients at three o'clock so she's out the door just after four. And if the wind is right and the sun's still high, Evie goes sailing, sometimes with Angus, sometimes with James and often just by herself.

Acknowledgements

While this book has been simmering away in my mind for a few years now, the decision to finally start writing it was a (poorly disguised) way to parachute myself out of a job that had become all-consuming. In hindsight, feigning a serious illness might have been easier.

Book writing is *hard*. Not in a lofty or labour sense, not completely, but in a lonely sense. It's a tough space to put yourself in for a year or two or more, a fact conveniently forgotten between each baby. If not for the support and encouragement and wisdom and expertise of other people, you'd never get through it. At least, that's my experience.

So thank you, *no, really thank you*, to these wonderful people. To my agent Lyn Tranter, formidable and steadfast, for finding the perfect home for this book in Affirm Press. To the effervescent Kelly Doust, for believing in the story and in me even when I'd try to talk you out of both. To Kate O'Donnell for your masterful copyediting, which made me re-examine every character and conversation with fresh consideration and care. What terrific hands I was in throughout this process.

Several people were instrumental in helping me research this story. Counsellor and university lecturer Karen Anderson armed me with helpful textbooks and sage advice, as well as the early assurance that it was far from preposterous that a marriage counsellor might herself be blindsided. Paraplegic sailor Mike Rowney, a truly extraordinary human (look him up!), shared with me his personal experience of acquired disability and introduced me to the beautiful folkboat *Gypsy Rose*, which he modified himself for solo ocean sailing. Sexologist Chantelle Otten generously answered my questions about the physical and emotional dimensions of a relationship after disability, and her superstar boyfriend Dylan Alcott's podcast *ListenABLE* has been extremely insightful.

Ronni is based loose-ishly on a real person, my dear funny friend Maria P. of Concord, who kindly and bravely let me appropriate the magic of her personality. Thank you, Maria, for enabling me to get 'Fuck me drunk, Vince' into a book, and for much else besides. I'm glad you didn't have the school principal bumped off.

When I first made it known around the traps that I was writing a book about middle-aged marriage, the stories landed at my feet like a festival of offerings. 'Here's another one for your book!' Painful, poignant, funny and fierce, these stories helped me fill a canvas and I'm forever grateful for the trust people placed in me.

To my beta readers Nikki, Mignon, Monique, Angela, Jodi and Luke – what a terrible first draft you waded through. I'm sorry, but also thank you.

Sue, thanks so much for letting me write a great deal of this at FlowSpace – my 'bra days' as I came to think of them.

To Coxy, who didn't baulk at the idea of his wife exploring such a potentially dangerous topic and who insisted I keep writing even when life threw us another curveball, thank you for your consistent encouragement and love.

To the family of the late Luka Davor Viskovic, thank you for letting me lift the title of this book from the eulogy at his funeral. A more beautiful description of a simple life well lived and well loved I may never hear.

And finally, to the readers, my very favourite kind of people: thank you.

Reading Group Questions

1. How much do you think Evie's role as a marriage counsellor influenced her own response to Hamish's leaving? Is understanding the complexity of marriage an asset or a roadblock?

2. Why didn't Evie simply return to Perth soon after Hamish left? Why do you think she got 'stuck'?

3. What is the effect of interspersing the chapters about Evie's counselling cases throughout the main narrative? How do they affect your reading of Evie's story?

4. Which of Evie's counselling case studies made the biggest impact on you, and why?

5. Evie says, 'Sera is of Hamish, and Angus is of Evie. Some families are painfully obvious.' How might a different family dynamic have shaped the story?

6. What did you make of Evie and Ronni's friendship, and how can a new friendship support someone better than a long-established one when everything familiar falls apart?

7. Ronni says one has to be vigilant about 'predators' around a marriage, whereas Evie chose to trust trust itself? Which position is safer?

8. Hamish's elderly father said that the secret to an enduring marriage was 'You pick one person and you make it work'. Has the pace and disposability of modern life made this advice redundant?

9. In having an affair, Hamish became the sort of man he once roundly criticised. Do you think there is a 'type' of person who has an affair or that anyone might be tempted given certain circumstances and conditions?

10. Evie's experience with Ryan shows her that what she wants from a relationship now is emotional connection more than physical. Do you think that's a product of where she's at in life or a response to having been betrayed?

11. The book hints at a future relationship between Evie and James. Do you think that relationship will work? Why or why not?

12. What is the meaning of the title? Does your interpretation of it change over the course of the novel?